The Gansett Island Series

Gansett Island Extras

More new books are always in the works. For the most up-to-date list of what's available from the Gansett Island Series as well as series extras, go to *marieforce.com/gansett*

View the McCarthy Family Tree *marieforce.com/gansett/familytree/*

View the list of Who's Who on Gansett Island here
marieforce.com/whoswhogansett/

View a map of Gansett Island *marieforce.com/mapofgansett/*

CHAPTER 1

*G*ansett Island residents counted down to Labor Day for weeks, during the frenetic last rush of tourists before the island shut down for the long winter. Jace Carson had loved being there during the season, had enjoyed his bartending job at the Beachcomber and was concerned about making enough money to survive the off-season.

His first order of business, after his daily AA meeting, would be to start looking for a place to live, since the Beachcomber housing was available only to summer employees. He was more than ready to get out of there, after enduring weeks of the crazy partying that went on with the summer employees, many of whom had already headed back to college. The only good thing about the housing was that it had been free.

He'd been counting down to today for another reason. A few weeks ago, he'd told Nina, the AA facilitator, that he'd have something to say by Labor Day. As she glanced his way now, he knew it was time for him to step up for the group the way they had for him since he first joined them in July.

Jace had gotten to know several of the regulars, including Dr. Quinn James and his new wife Mallory James, as well as the fire chief, Mason Johns, and Jeff Lawry, through the stories they'd told about their addiction struggles and how they'd overcome them to lead a sober life. He appreciated everyone in the group who'd talked through challenges and supported one another throughout the busy season.

Now it was his turn. Telling his story would never come easily to him, but he'd been in the program long enough now to know that sharing the tough stuff was critical to maintaining his recovery and supporting the others.

"I, ah, want to thank you all for welcoming me into your group this summer and for all the wisdom you've shared," Jace said. "It's made a difference for me as I became part of a new community."

"We've enjoyed having you, Jace," Nina said with the same warm smile she'd extended to him since his first meeting.

"Well, thank you again. I came here to Gansett because my boys live here. Some of you may know them, Jackson and Kyle. They're being raised by Seamus and Carolina O'Grady."

Mallory gasped.

"Don't worry," Jace said. "Seamus and Carolina know I'm here and have been generous about allowing me to spend time with the boys, although the boys don't know I'm their biological father. Not yet anyway. We thought it best to hold that back for now, until they're a little older and able to understand things that are too big for them after losing their mom so recently."

"She was a lovely person," Mallory said.

"Yes, she was, and she deserved way better than what she got from me." Overwhelmed by memories of the only woman he'd ever loved, Jace took a moment to get his thoughts together. "I can't remember when exactly it was that I started messing around with heroin and meth. I think it was probably middle school. My older brother ran with a crowd that was into everything we were told to avoid, and I thought I was so lucky that he would take me with him. Our parents encouraged it. They thought it was great that we were growing up as close brothers, but we were drug addicts and criminals.

"You couldn't tell us that, though. In our minds, we were just having fun, doing what kids do. Except, over time, we needed much more than we could afford. That's when we started stealing from our parents, grandparents, friends, strangers. We did whatever we had to do to support our habit.

"I met Lisa when I was eighteen and already a full-blown junkie. But she didn't know that. I'd gotten very good at hiding it from everyone. Even our parents had no clue what we were really doing. We got married young, had the boys one right after the other, and my struggle intensified when I had three people depending on me."

Jace's heart beat so fast he worried it might burst. The anxiety was familiar to him, though, as it happened whenever he revisited things he'd much rather forget. "My brother got the big idea to rob a convenience store. He promised me it would be just once, and then we'd have what we needed to get by for a year. I tried to talk him out of it, but he was determined. 'One big score,' he said, 'and then we'll be golden.' He was going to do it with or without me, so I decided to go with him to try to keep him out of trouble."

Jace ran his hand through his hair repeatedly, until he realized he was doing it and stopped, folding his shaky hands between his knees. "The owner of the store figured us out before Jess had the chance to use the gun that I didn't even know he had. The owner pulled one on us. Told us to get the fuck out of there before someone got hurt. But Jess… He was desperate for the money and the score. When I saw he had a gun, I was stunned, but I still tried to stop him. He tossed me aside and aimed the gun at the guy. The store owner shot him in the chest."

Jace took a shaky deep breath and released it slowly, clinging to his composure. "I'll never forget the sound he made when the bullet hit him or how hard he landed on the floor. I think he probably died instantly, but I was so shocked that I stayed with him, screaming at him not to die, not to leave me. I was still there when the cops came. They called the coroner for him and took me to jail. I was convicted of armed robbery, sentenced to ten years and released on probation after six. By then, my wife and kids were long gone, and no one knew where they were. I heard from Lisa once—when I was served with divorce and custody papers. I worked hard on myself in prison. I attended Narcotics Anonymous meetings, took college classes, learned a trade. If you ever need a plumber, give me a call."

A ripple of laughter went through the group.

"When I got out six months ago and finally found my family, it was too late. Lisa had died of lung cancer, and the boys were happily settled with people who truly love them. I lost everything to my addiction—the woman I loved, the sons I adored, my reputation. I'll always be a convicted felon and have to live with the memories of the day my brother was killed right in front of me. I'm focused now on rebuilding my life. I wanted so badly to see my kids, but it was important to me not to disrupt their lives any more than I already had, even if they don't remember the really bad stuff."

The emotional wallop that came with recalling everything he'd lost was familiar by now. His throat tightened around a lump that brought tears to his eyes. "They're such great little guys, so cute and funny and smart. Lisa did an amazing job with them. Seamus and Carolina have been so good to them, and I'm grateful that they have a nice, normal life. They deserve that. I hate that Lisa died before I could tell her… Before I could say how sorry I was for putting her through hell and forcing her to make a new life for herself and the boys without me. I hate that she suffered with her illness and that I wasn't there to take care of her and our kids. I should've been there."

He wiped tears from his face. "I'll never forgive myself for what I put her through. And that she died without knowing how much I loved her…" Jace shook his head. "I'll never forgive myself for that either." After a pause, he said, "I've learned in the program that we can't change the past. We can only focus on today and tomorrow and trying to do the best we can with the time we have left, to make amends to the people we hurt. I hope that wherever Lisa is now, she knows how sorry I am for what I did.

"I've tried to repair my relationships with my parents and sister, but they're reluctant to let me back into their lives, which I certainly understand. They lost both their sons and brothers in one dreadful night. I don't blame them for being cautious toward me. We talk on the phone occasionally, but they haven't been willing to see me. Not yet anyway. I hope maybe someday they will. In the meantime, I plan to stick around here so I can at least be close to my kids and see them once in a while. My next challenge is to find a year-round place to live on the island, so if you hear of anything, let me know. Other than that, one day at a time, right?"

"Thank you for sharing your story, Jace," Nina said. "You're doing all the right things to tend to your sobriety and make amends. We all make mistakes we regret, often terrible, awful mistakes. I hope you'll also find the grace to forgive yourself at some point."

Jace didn't see that happening any time soon, but he nodded in acknowledgment.

After the meeting, the regulars came up to hug him and thank him for sharing.

Mallory and Quinn invited him out for coffee, but he asked for a rain check.

After telling his story, he needed to move. If he sat still, the emotional storm might drag him so low, he wouldn't resurface for days. He didn't have that luxury. He needed to work.

Mallory handed him her card. "If you need to talk later, call me. Day or night."

"Thank you," Jace said, appreciative of her kindness.

He left the meeting and returned to his room at the Beachcomber to change into running clothes. Two laps around the island's perimeter road was just over six miles, which he ran at a punishing pace. Exercise had been his salvation in prison, where he'd run on the treadmill and lifted weights every chance he got. The freedom to run outdoors... That was something he'd never again take for granted.

As always, the physical exertion helped to center him. He found it ironic that he'd never been in better shape in his life than he'd been in prison. It took having his whole life taken from him to figure out what mattered and to regain his health. He'd lost things he could never get back, though... His wife and sons, his only brother, his parents, sister, niece and nephew.

Nina had encouraged him to forgive himself, but some things... Some things were simply unforgivable.

Cindy Lawry was up early printing flyers to hang at the salon, the diner, the ferry landing and grocery store, all the places people on the island were most likely to see her appeal for a new roommate. Her sister Julia was officially moving out at the end of the month, not that she'd ever really lived in the tiny house they'd shared. She was madly in love with Deacon Taylor and was basically living with him at his place while still paying her half of the rent to Cindy.

It was foolish, Cindy had told her sister, to waste her money paying for a place she didn't use, so she'd officially "kicked Julia out" as of October first. With the season ending and business at the Curl Up and Dye salon slowing, Cindy needed a roommate ASAP.

Before work, she hung as many flyers as she could, thanking the shop owners for letting her post them and asking them to talk up the year-round room for rent. They were hard to come by on the island, so she was confident it would go quickly. However, she wasn't going to settle for just anyone. It had to be a good fit. After growing up in a house with an abusive father, Cindy was all about peace and tranquility in her adult life.

Cindy had been hired to cut hair at Chloe Dennis's salon after Chloe was asked to spearhead the new spa at the McCarthys' hotel in North Harbor. Chloe suffered from rheumatoid arthritis that impacted her hands, so she had said the job at the salon was Cindy's for as long as she wanted it. With a thousand year-round residents on the island and no other haircut joint in town, Chloe had assured her she'd make enough to get through the winter after the tourists left.

She put the last flyer on the door to the salon and then flipped the sign from Closed to Open. Her first appointment of the day was a cut and color for Mallory James, the nurse practitioner who'd married Dr. Quinn James in August. They were the medical directors at the Marion Martinez Senior Care Facility.

Mallory came in bearing coffee and a corn muffin for Cindy.

"You're too sweet. Thank you. I'll enjoy that during my break."

"Rebecca's corn muffins are the best." Mallory put her coffee on the counter and backtracked to take a photo of Cindy's flyer on the door. "I have a friend who's looking. Are you accepting men?"

"As long as they aren't creepy, I'm fine."

"He's a good guy. I think he'd be a nice roommate."

"Thanks for passing it along. I hope I can find someone soon. Julia has already moved out, but she's hoping someone will move in right away and reimburse her for this month's rent, which she insisted on paying so I wouldn't be caught short. She wants to buy a car."

"I'll see him in the morning and will give him the info. Is it okay for him to text you to set up a time to see it?"

"Sure. That works."

They got down to business with color to cover the few gray hairs Mallory had noticed, followed by a cut and blow-dry of her dark hair.

"So how was the honeymoon?" Cindy asked as she cut two inches off the length and added some layers to the front.

"It was amazing. Neither of us had ever been to Ireland, and we loved every minute of it."

"That's on my bucket list, along with a hundred other places." The Lawry family had moved frequently when her dad was on active duty, but none of the places they'd lived had been particularly interesting.

"I hope you get to go. It's magical."

"And your brother's wife going into labor during the wedding. You McCarthys don't do anything the easy way."

"I know, right?" Mallory said with a laugh. "I wasn't expecting the Life Flight helicopter to come to my wedding or for Maddie to have the babies *on* the chopper, but thankfully, the girls and Maddie are doing great, and Mac is adjusting to being a father of five."

"Five kids," Cindy said. "That's a lot."

"I know."

"My mom had seven with a husband who deployed. How'd she do that?" Not that her father had been much help to anyone when he was home. They'd all preferred the deployments that had gotten less frequent as he'd risen through the ranks.

"Mothers are superheroes. Maddie sure is. She handles everything with good humor and sarcasm that makes me laugh. They're blessed to have a wonderful nanny helping during Mac's busy season, which makes such a big difference."

"Will the nanny stay on in the off-season?"

"She promised Maddie she'd stay until the twins' first birthday, which also my birthday, Quinn's birthday and our anniversary. How cool is that?"

"Very cool. How's Abby doing?" Abby was married to Mallory's brother Adam McCarthy.

"As well as can be expected with four babies on board."

"*Four.* How does that even work, anyway?"

Mallory laughed. "You wouldn't think it was possible, but it is. I expect her to be seriously uncomfortable in the last trimester."

"I can't imagine that. They had to be so shocked to get that news."

"They were, especially because she was told she had almost no chance of conceiving."

"I had a friend in Texas with PCOS like Abby has, and it was miserable. She's still hoping to get pregnant." Polycystic ovary syndrome had caused fertility challenges for Abby.

"That's so rough. Abby is trying to count her blessings while coping with the shock of it all. Considering her struggles, it's hard to see this pregnancy as anything other than a miracle."

"If you're us, that is. For her, not so miraculous right now."

"No," Mallory said, smiling. "But it will be after the babies arrive."

"Is everyone asking you when you're going to have one since the wedding?"

"We're old!" Mallory said with a snort, her dark eyes dancing with laughter. "I think that ship has sailed for us."

"You're not old!"

"We're both forty-one."

"Forty is the new thirty."

"Tell that to my moldy old eggs as you're coloring my gray hairs."

Cindy laughed. "Stop that. You're not old."

"I guess we'll see what happens. We're not doing anything to stop it, so if it's meant to be, it'll be."

"That's very exciting. I'm so happy for you that everything worked out so well for you guys."

"Thank you. We both had a lot of hard times before we got to the good stuff, but I guess all that makes what we have now that much sweeter."

"I'm sure it does."

"What about you? Have you met anyone on Gansett who interests you?"

Cindy thought immediately of the sexy bartender at the Beachcomber who'd become a good friend, as she sat night after night at his bar. "There's this one guy…"

"Do tell!"

"He's very nice, sexy as all hell and funny, too."

"Sounds like the perfect man."

Cindy shrugged. "Maybe."

"What's the hang-up?"

"I'm not sure. We see each other just about every day." Mostly because she couldn't seem to work up the willpower to stay away from his bar. What did it say about her that she was sad to know she wouldn't see him on his nights off? "Lots of subtle flirting and stuff like that, and I'm pretty sure he likes me, too, but it never goes beyond that."

"Hmm. You could invite him to do something."

"I could, but I guess I was sort of hoping he might be the one to ask."

"We're women of the new millennium, Cindy. It's okay for us to do the asking."

Cindy was aware that her outdated expectations came straight from her asshole father, who'd told his daughters never to be "forward" with men lest they be branded sluts. And yes, he'd used that word. She shook off that unpleasant memory to keep her focus on Mallory as she inspected her dry hair for uneven edges. Satisfied, she grabbed her hand mirror to show Mallory the back. "Everything look okay?"

"It looks great, as always. Thank you so much."

Cindy removed the cape that had protected Mallory's clothing. "My pleasure. Nice to see you, and thanks again for the muffin."

Mallory gave her a quick hug. "You, too, and you're welcome. Ask that man out. The worst that can happen is he says no—and I doubt he will."

"I hear you."

After Mallory had paid and set up her next appointment, Cindy waved her off, while thinking about what Mallory had said. If Cindy asked Jace out and he said no, that'd make everything between them so awkward, she might feel that she couldn't hang out at the Beachcomber anymore. Since that had become her favorite part of the day, she'd hate to risk messing that up.

But the more time she spent with him, the more time she wanted to spend with him.

If only she knew if he felt the same way about her.

Ugh, this was like high school all over again—and that was bad enough the first time around. The last thing she needed was to mess up a nice friendship. If she'd learned anything in her life, it was to leave well enough alone.

CHAPTER 2

*A*fter his meeting the next morning, Jace sent a text to the number Mallory had given him from a flyer she'd seen about a room for rent.

Hi there, saw your flyer and would love to check out your place. I'm off tonight and can come by around six, if that works for you.

On his days off, Jace attended the morning meeting, did laundry at the Beachcomber, spent two hours at the gym and then went to the beach to swim and lie in the sun. He had to force himself to relax as his body buzzed with an overabundance of energy that he attributed to being locked up for years. Now that he was out, he wanted to fully experience every second of every day.

He'd texted Seamus to see if he could see the boys after school but hadn't heard back from him yet. That meant Seamus was probably captaining a ferry trip to or from the mainland. He'd reply when he could.

Jace had learned to be patient when it came to the man who was raising his sons. Seamus was extraordinarily accommodating to Jace when he certainly didn't have to be. They had come to an understanding of sorts, after Jace had promised to never do anything to disrupt the family Seamus and Carolina had created for his sons.

A mutual friend told him Lisa had died while living on Gansett Island. While processing the shock of hearing she was gone, Jace's first thought had been for his boys. Who was caring for them? Where were they living? Were they all right? He'd been frantic for information, and after a lawyer had helped him contact the O'Gradys, Jace had come to the island looking for answers. What he'd found had restored his faith in humanity—and broken his heart.

The boys were happily settled with good people who truly loved them. They were doing as well as could be expected after having lost their beloved mother and were thriving in school and in activities such as soccer and Little League baseball. He'd have to be a selfish jerk to do anything to disrupt the custody arrangement Lisa had brokered with the O'Gradys. Jace was determined to put his kids first, as painful as it was for him to acknowledge that Seamus and Carolina were better parents than he ever could've been to his own kids.

The truth hurt, but what did he know about raising kids? Especially kids who'd suffered the traumatic loss of their mother. They didn't even remember him, which had been crushing. In his heart of hearts, he'd been certain they'd know him. But when they'd looked at him with blank expressions on their adorable faces, his heart of hearts had shattered.

So now he was relegated to "friend" status and was forced to be content with whatever he could get where they were concerned. They'd told the boys he was an old friend of Seamus's, and they'd accepted him as such because they followed Seamus's lead on everything. They obviously adored the Irishman who'd stepped up for them, and Jace couldn't blame them for that. Seamus was a good man who was well regarded by everyone on the island.

Jace had asked around about the man who was raising his children. Of course he had, and he'd heard only accolades for Seamus as a person and as the man who ran the ferry company so competently for his wife, Carolina, and her son, Joe, who'd inherited it from Carolina's parents. He'd also heard nothing but praise for Carolina, who was quite a bit older than Seamus and had successfully raised Joe into a man people liked and respected.

Not only were they good people, but they were also loaded, as the ferry company was a total cash cow. The island community depended upon the ferries for everything, from passenger and automobile transport to deliveries of mail, groceries, gas, liquor, and medicine. The list was endless. One of the ferry boat captains was a regular at the bar and had blown Jace's mind one night describing the full extent of the operation.

Until he'd come to the island, Jace had never considered what it would take to keep the place going, and now that he knew, he'd concluded that his boys had fallen into a pot of gold. Since he barely had a pot to piss in, he could hardly compete with that. He was still paying off legal fees that would dog him for years to come.

So, yeah, the boys were way better off with the O'Gradys, and Jace was thankful to get whatever scraps Seamus and Carolina tossed his way. He was determined not to become bitter over it. What good would that do? He had only himself to blame for not being there when Lisa became sick and then passed away.

He would feel horrible about what he'd put her through for the rest of his life, but he was determined to do better going forward. Jace used his cup from the deli to make a sandcastle fort while hoping that maybe someday, Seamus and Carolina might trust him to take his sons to the beach. He wanted to know how to make a decent sandcastle in case that day ever came.

His phone chimed with a text, and he pounced on it, hoping it was Seamus. He'd seen the boys briefly yesterday, when he'd stopped by for the clambake Seamus and Carolina had hosted. But because he'd been due at work, he hadn't been able to stick around. The boys had been caught up with their friend Ethan, so he hadn't gotten any quality time with them.

Sure, come by between six and six thirty to see the place. The person at the other end of the text had included the address, which was two blocks from the Beachcomber. Convenient. He didn't own a vehicle, so finding a place in town would be perfect.

See you then, he replied.

He didn't bother to ask any of the usual questions—who are you, what's your story, do you care about living with a paroled felon? Asking for a friend… He laughed bitterly to himself, wondering if that detail would make it impossible for him to find anything he could afford on the island. Who wanted to live with a criminal, even if the person was an ex-criminal?

Shaking off the depressing thought, he got up, walked into the water and dove into a wave, letting the water wash over him in a frantic rush of power. Being in the ocean made his own problems seem trivial when stacked up against the vastness of the water and the sky. God, he'd missed the sky when he was locked up. Talk about things a person took for granted until they're gone.

Before prison, he'd never once acknowledged how much he enjoyed looking up at the sky, sun, clouds, moon and stars. Now he never missed a chance to look up and simply take it all in. Floating on his back, he looked for shapes in the clouds the way his mom used to do with him, Diana and Jess when they were kids.

His son Jackson resembled Jess. Realizing that had been another punch to the gut the day he first saw the boys. His fondest hope was that someday he might reunite his mostly estranged parents and sister with the grandsons and nephews they'd once adored. That might be a pipe dream, though, since a lot of things would have to happen to make that possible.

For now, Jace focused on the mantra of one day at a time preached by NA and AA and worked on keeping his life free of drama and things that might send him looking for the sort of relief he used to get from heroin and meth. Those days had to be over now, or he'd have no prayer of a relationship with his boys. It helped that he'd been clean so long that he had no desire to use. In that way, the years in prison had been beneficial, if you could call it that.

He napped on the beach until late afternoon, which was his favorite time of day there. Most of the people had left, but the sun was still warm and the beach inviting. Feeling refreshed from the afternoon off, he walked back to the Beachcomber to shower and change before his meeting with his potential housemate. He hadn't had a single other lead on a year-round place, so this needed to go well with only six more days until he had to be out of the Beachcomber housing.

They shut off the water in the off-season, thus the pending eviction.

His manager had told him he could stay in a room at the hotel for a reduced rate if he was unable to secure other housing, but he was hoping for something more permanent.

After showering, he put on a long-sleeved Henley in case his potential roommate was turned off by sleeve tattoos. People were weird about things like that. His chest ached a bit when he thought about having to be honest about his past. It wouldn't be fair not to tell him or her that he was out on parole, checking in weekly with a parole officer as well as the state cops who worked on the island, and would carry a felony record with him for the rest of his life.

When you considered all that, a few tattoos were probably the least of his concerns.

Jace laughed to himself. Who was he fooling thinking anyone was going to want to live with him? The thought of leaving the island, where his boys were, broke his heart, so he needed to make this work. Somehow. Maybe he'd encounter someone who understood that sometimes people screwed up, but that didn't mean they were bad or evil.

He studied his reflection in the mirror and saw a mostly handsome face with a few hard edges, golden-brown eyes, decent lips, a fashionable amount of stubble. Using his fingers, he arranged his light brown hair into a messy but stylish look and then shrugged. Having done what he could to make himself presentable, the rest was out of his hands. On the way out of his room, he nodded to a few of the younger guys who worked as bussers and waiters in the restaurant and did a fist bump with Chris, one of the barbacks he worked with frequently. He was a good kid, halfway through college and on his way to a career in engineering. He was heading back to school in Indiana at the end of the week.

None of the people Jace worked with knew about his past, except his manager, because he'd been forced to come clean about his record on the application. He'd promised her she'd never have any trouble with him, and she'd said she appreciated that because she had trouble with most of the young people she hired for the summer at one point or another.

She'd never had any trouble with him, and she wouldn't.

Trouble was in the past for him now. He was all about leading an upstanding life with one major goal in mind—to have a relationship with his sons. Everything else was secondary to that.

He walked the short distance through town, nodding to people he recognized from the bar and waving to Tiffany Taylor, who ran the Naughty & Nice boutique. She was a hot shit who came into the bar with her husband, Police Chief Blaine Taylor, his brother Deacon and Deacon's fiancée, Julia Lawry. The four of them cracked him up with their banter. Tiffany was always excited to have a night off from motherhood but couldn't drink because she was pregnant.

Julia's sister Cindy was another regular, and if Jace found himself thinking about her when she wasn't at his bar, well, he couldn't really help that. She was adorable, sweet, kind, sexy, easy to talk to and funny. He'd sensed an inner sadness in her, though, which made him curious, and she didn't drink because she suffered from migraines.

Jace loved watching her interact with Julia as well as her other sister, Katie, and her husband, Shane, when they came in, sometimes with their brother Owen and his wife, Laura, who was Shane's sister. It had taken him a minute to get his mind around a brother and sister marrying a brother and sister, but Cindy had drawn a picture for him on a Beach-comber cocktail napkin that had explained it, while insisting it was perfectly legal.

They were a fun bunch of people, and he enjoyed having them at his bar. He'd made a lot of nice friends on the island, but he didn't see them outside of work or anything like that. That said, it'd been years since he'd been part of a community, and he'd begun to feel at home here. He hoped he wouldn't have to leave any time soon.

He took a right onto Beach Street and walked to the small house at the end of the road. It wasn't much to look at, but the location was excellent. How much would it cost to live this close to downtown and the beach? he wondered.

Hoping for the best, Jace rang the bell and steeled himself to share his past with strangers for the second time in two days. Outside of NA and AA and his manager at work, he hadn't told his story to anyone since he'd been released from prison. Reliving the nightmare didn't come easily to him, but he'd learned to own his truth if he wanted to lead a sober life.

The inside door swung open.

Cindy.

Jace laughed, even as his heart ached at having to share his truth with her, of all people. "It's you."

CHAPTER 3

*C*indy couldn't believe it. Of all people to show up to look at the room she had for rent, it had to be the sexy bartender from the Beachcomber she'd been crushing on for weeks. She wished she'd spent some time on her appearance when she got home from work, rather than throwing her hair into a messy bun and putting on an old tank that sagged in the breast area.

"Come in."

She tugged the top up to make sure everything was covered as he walked by her, bringing a clean, fresh scent with him that made her want to lean in for a better whiff.

Don't be a weirdo, she told herself as Jace looked around the living room and kitchen. "It's not much," Cindy said. "Just this, two bedrooms and a bathroom. Oh, and a nice backyard. Check that out." She gestured for him to lead the way through the kitchen to the sliding door. "Kevin McCarthy and his sons lived here for a time, and they did the landscaping. They redid the patio and left the gas grill when they moved out."

"It's really nice." Jace walked across the yard for a closer look at the bushes. "Those are holly and boxwoods. I'm surprised the boxwoods are doing so well. They don't tend to like the salt air."

"You know your plants."

"My grandmother was a master gardener. She taught me."

Good God, Cindy thought for the thousandth time, but Jace was one of the hottest men she'd ever met. How in the world would she stand to have him as a roommate and not give in to the regular urge to lick him or kiss him or—

"What's the rent?"

Startled out of her salacious thoughts, she said, "Eight hundred plus utilities that are another hundred."

"Ouch."

"It's not cheap to live here year-round."

"So I've discovered. It's also not easy to find a place."

"Do you want to see the bedroom that would be yours?"

"Yeah, but first..." He pointed to the chairs Kevin had left. "Can we sit for a second?"

"Um, sure." Cindy's entire system had gone haywire with the same desire she felt for him while watching him tend bar, only it was enhanced by the fact that for once, she wasn't sharing him with numerous other customers.

He tugged on the sleeves of his Henley, revealing the tattoos that she'd stared at many a night at the bar. "I, um, I wanted to tell you... Before you decide to let me live here..."

She held her breath, waiting to hear what he would say and hoping it wouldn't ruin the first real crush she'd had on a man in years.

"I... I'm a convicted felon on parole for the next five years."

Like a pin hitting a balloon, all the air left her lungs in one deep sigh. "Oh."

"And a recovering drug addict. I've been clean for six years and have no desire to ever return to the life I led before my brother was killed right next to me during a convenience store robbery. I attend daily meetings and work the program to maintain my sobriety, which is one of the most important things in my life. You'd have absolutely nothing to fear from me if you allowed me to live with you, but I wanted you to know the truth before you decide anything."

"I, um... I appreciate your honesty."

He gave her a side-eyed glance that was the sexiest thing since Chris Hemsworth played Thor. "Is it a deal breaker?"

Her mind was racing. *I like him. I've liked him for weeks. I've started to*

17

think of him as a friend—as well as a crush. But I can't deny that I'm conflicted. "Would it be okay if I had a day to think about it?"

"Of course. I should also tell you that I'm here on Gansett because my sons, Jackson and Kyle, live here."

"Jackson and Kyle… The boys who live with Seamus and Carolina O'Grady?"

He nodded. "My ex-wife, Lisa, arranged for them to be the boys' guardians after she passed away."

"Oh gosh, yes, I heard about that from my sister Katie. She's a nurse and helped to care for Lisa when she was sick."

"I'll regret for the rest of my life that I wasn't there for them when they needed me. I wish more than anything that I could somehow make amends to her, but since I can't, I'm trying to be there for our boys and to be a friend to them."

Cindy's heart beat so fast, she was nearly breathless as she tried to get her head around everything he'd told her. "Would you… Would you like to see the room?"

"That'd be great, thanks."

Cindy got up to show him the way to the bedroom that included a queen-sized bed and dresser that had been left by previous tenants. "You may want a new mattress. I don't know the full history of that one."

"It's no different than a hotel, right? And better than what I'm sleeping on at the Beachcomber employee housing."

"That's probably true."

"It's definitely true. This would be perfect for what I need, but it's completely up to you. I'd understand if it's not a good fit."

Cindy followed him back to the living room. "It means a lot that you were honest."

He shrugged. "I can't change the story of my past as much as I wish I could. I'm working hard to have a better future, though. If you want to read the whole ugly story online, my last name is Carson."

"I want you to know…"

He tipped his head, his full attention focused on her.

It was a wonder she didn't melt on the spot. "I know you're just doing your job being nice to your customers at the bar, but your friendship has meant a lot to me this summer."

"Likewise, and being nice to you, Cindy, has nothing to do with my job. It has everything to do with you." On that startling note, he said, "I'll wait to hear from you. Either way, we're still friends. I promise."

"Thank you for understanding."

"No worries. Come see me tomorrow night."

"I will."

After she closed the door behind him, Cindy went straight to her laptop to google him. It took about five seconds to find the full story about his brother being killed as the two of them were holding up a store and how Jace had been convicted of armed robbery and other charges. He served six years of a ten-year sentence and was paroled six months ago.

She fell down a deep rabbit hole, reading every word she could find, including the report from the parole board that had deemed him a model prisoner who'd taken full advantage of every resource offered to him in prison to better himself, along with a recommendation that he be paroled early for good behavior.

An hour had passed by the time she came up for air. She sat back in her chair, thinking about everything she'd learned about him and trying to decide how she felt about it. After the upbringing she'd had with an abusive, narcissist father, she viewed every choice she made through the lens of having survived that nightmare. Sometimes that lens colored things unfairly, and for that reason, she needed outside opinions.

She reached for her phone to text Julia and Katie.

I need a sister meeting. Can you guys come by? I'll buy the pizza.

Coming! Katie replied right away.

Julia responded ten minutes later to say she'd be there after she finished her set at the Sand & Surf. She played the piano during standing-room-only happy hour at Stephanie's Bistro, their stepsister's restaurant. *Order the pizza, and I'll pick it up on the way over.*

After she called in the order to Mario's, Cindy got busy slicing some cheese and arranging it on a plate with crackers and grapes for her sisters. She got out wineglasses to go with the big bottle of chardonnay chilling in the fridge that she kept on hand for them. Cindy hadn't had a drink in years due to the migraines.

New medication had helped to keep them to one or two a month, but that was still far too many, and she avoided things like caffeine, chocolate and other foods that tended to trigger them. She'd rather live without wine than suffer through any more migraines than she already did.

Katie arrived thirty minutes after receiving the text, hugging and kissing Cindy like they didn't see each other all the time these days. Having all but one of her siblings around, as well as their mother and grandparents, was the best part of living on Gansett. The island had played a critical role in salvaging the Lawry siblings' childhood, as their summers had been spent at the Sand & Surf with their beloved grandparents. That'd been the only reprieve they'd gotten, other than their father's infrequent deployments, from their horrible home life.

The island would always have a special place in the hearts of all the Lawrys, and being close to most of her family again was wonderful, but the dilemma involving Jace weighed heavily on her.

She really wished she could have a big drink.

Since that wasn't possible, she chatted with Katie about her work at the clinic, Shane's night out with his cousins and how Katie was feeling after having suffered a miscarriage that summer.

"I'm fine physically." Katie tucked her blonde hair behind her ear and sipped from her wineglass as they enjoyed late-day sun on the patio. "It's the emotional element that's not quite there yet. I lost the baby before I even knew I was pregnant. The whole thing was just devastating."

"I'm sure it was horrible. It was for me, and I was just the aunt."

"Aw, you're so sweet. You, Julia, Mom, Gram and Laura... Everyone has been so good to me. I mean, I'm a nurse. I know how often this happens, but when it happens to you..."

"It's totally different."

"Yeah. And Shane has been so incredible. He's my rock."

"I'm glad you have each other to get through it."

"Maddie called when she heard the news and was so sweet sharing her experience losing a baby. We talked for an hour. Everyone has been so nice."

"The good news is, when you feel ready, you can try again."

"I know," Katie said with a sigh. "It's just different now that I know what it feels like when it goes wrong. Before that happened, it was just this abstract concept that happened to other people, so I didn't stress about it. But now... Hopefully, it'll be different next time."

"You and Shane are so strong and solid together. You'll be fine no matter what happens."

"That's what he says, too. That we've got this, no matter what."

"And he means it. You know that."

"I do. I got lucky with the best husband ever, and he's proven to me so many times that he truly loves me. I've even decided if we're never able to have children, we're still the luckiest people in the world because we have each other."

"You're going to have kids. I know it."

"You do?"

"I feel it. In my bones, and you know how my feelings are usually spot-on about things."

"I do know that. You're clairvoyant."

"I wouldn't go that far. I just have a sense for things and people." Cindy recalled the reason she'd asked her sisters to come over. "Although it doesn't always work as well as I'd like it to." When it came to Jace and the information he'd shared, there was a blackout where her intuition usually was found.

"I wish Julia would get here so you can tell us what's going on," Katie said.

"It's nothing bad. It's just a situation. I need your input."

"If there's one thing Lawrys have plenty of to offer, it's input."

Cindy laughed hard at that. "Truer words were never spoken."

Their family group chat was nonstop all day, every day. Cindy had to make time to catch up every night before bed because she always wanted to know what was happening with them.

If she told her brothers about the "situation," they'd flip their lids. Owen, protective eldest, would be there in two seconds to tell her he would not allow a felon to live with her, and John, the former cop, would be looking for ways to send Jace back to prison on the next ferry. The news about Jace wasn't going anywhere near their group chat.

Julia came rushing in the front door, her face flushed from the heat and the natural glow she got whenever she performed. She juggled the pizza box, the bag containing the salad Cindy had ordered and her dog, Pupwell, on a leash. He let out a happy squeak when he saw Cindy, who had a treat for him every time she saw him.

She picked up the dog, gave him a hug and said, "Does my sweet boy want a bone?"

Pupwell's happy yip made the sisters laugh.

"I swear he understands every word we say," Julia said, helping herself to a glass of wine. "What's up around here?"

"That's what I'm waiting to hear, too," Katie told her fraternal twin. The two of them looked nothing alike. Katie was as blonde as Julia was dark. Cindy fell somewhere in the middle, her hair a darker shade of blonde than Katie's. Her sisters looked more like Cindy than they did each other.

"I have a crush," Cindy said.

"*Ohhhh*, yes!" Julia fist-pumped the air. "Is it the sexy bartender at the Beachcomber? Jace, right? I told Deacon after the last time we were there that you liked him."

"And you say I'm the clairvoyant one," Cindy said to Katie.

"So, it is him!" Julia said. "I knew it."

"Before you get too excited, let me tell you the rest." Cindy led them outside to the patio and waited until her sisters were seated, needing the minute to get her thoughts together. "He's become a good friend. He never minds when I take up a seat at his bar and only drink water. He's super friendly and sweet and nice to everyone."

"Okay, so what's the problem?" Katie asked. "Because, if you ask me, he likes you, too. I've seen the way he looks at you."

Cindy's belly fluttered with butterflies when she heard that. "He answered my ad for a roommate."

"*Oh*," Julia said with a knowing look. "That could be a problem, or it could move things along very nicely."

"There's more." Cindy swallowed hard. "He's a convicted felon and recovering drug addict."

Her sisters stared at her, their expressions completely blank.

"You're not still thinking about letting him live here, are you?" Katie asked. "Tell me you're not doing that."

"I might be."

"Cindy!" Julia's high-pitched screech startled Pupwell. "He *cannot live here*. And you *cannot date him*."

Suddenly, she was overwhelmed with more sadness than she'd felt in longer than she could recall. She liked Jace—a lot. She wanted to know him better. She was attracted to him in a way she'd never been to any man. When he smiled at her, she felt the impact everywhere. Her nipples tightened, and she often had to cross her legs to contend with the throb of need—and all he'd done was smile at her.

What would happen if he touched her?

"Hang on, Jules," Katie said, eyeing Cindy. "Give her a chance to tell us how she feels."

"That's just it," Cindy said softly. "I feel something for him that I've never felt for anyone else."

"Not even Tyler?" Katie asked, referring to the boy Cindy had dated in high school and for several years after.

"Not even him. Or Chuck or Tim or Jose or any of the guys I dated in Texas. I went through the motions with them. I didn't feel *this* for them."

"What is it you feel for Jace?" Katie asked.

"When he's around, I'm excited. I want to hear everything he has to say. I want to know him, and I want him to know me. I'm sad on nights he doesn't work, because I don't get to see him."

"I didn't realize your Beachcomber habit had become an everyday thing," Julia said.

"It's a five-nights-a-week thing. He gets two nights off, and I don't see him on those nights, even though I'd love to if he asked."

Julia raised a dark brow. "Why haven't you asked him?"

"I've still got *his* voice in my head saying women who are forward with men are sluts."

"Oh, *fuck* him," Julia said. "He's dead to us. Do not let him dictate any decision you make about anything, but Cin… Seriously. You can't take up with this guy."

"Why?" Cindy gave her older sister a defiant look. "Because he has stuff in his past? We all do."

"Some of us have bigger stuff than others," Katie said in her always-gentle tone.

"I spent an hour reading everything I could find about what happened to him, and from what I was able to piece together, he and his older brother got into drugs when they were kids, and as their addiction grew, so did their need for money to pay for it. His brother pulled a gun on the owner of the store, who shot him to death right in front of Jace. He was arrested, convicted and sent to jail for ten years. He ended up serving six years. While he was in prison, he got clean and was paroled early for being a model prisoner."

Cindy paused to give her sisters time to digest what she'd told them. "He attends meetings every day and said his sobriety is one of the most important things in his life. And he told his story voluntarily, when he certainly didn't have to, so I'd have all the info I needed to decide whether I wanted to live with him."

"We do have to give him points for honesty," Katie said, earning a scowl from her twin.

"I don't like this," Julia said.

"I can see that," Cindy replied.

"Hear me out." Julia hesitated as she seemed to search for the words she needed. "After everything we went through with he-who-shall-not-be-named, all I want for us is peace in our adult lives. I want every one of you to have what I do with Deacon, what Katie has with Shane, what Owen has with Laura and what Mom has with Charlie."

"Who was also a convicted felon when Mom first met him," Katie said softly.

Katie's reminder of Charlie's past seemed to take some of the wind out of Julia's sails. "True, even if he didn't do the crime he was accused of."

"Right, but if we were to judge Charlie simply by the fact that he'd done time in prison, we'd be missing out on a pretty great guy who makes our mother happier than she's ever been," Katie added.

"Also true," Julia said with a sigh. She glanced at Cindy. "You know that all I want for you is peace, love and happiness, right?"

"I do know that, Jules. And I hear what you were saying about how we grew up and what we deserve as adults." It wasn't like Cindy to be so emotional, but this was important. "I want to give him a chance."

Katie and Julie exchanged glances.

"Tell her about Deacon," Katie said to Julia. "About what happened to him right before you met."

Cindy was immediately on alert for news she hadn't heard yet.

"He spent a night in jail for getting into a fight with a guy hassling his ex-wife, who was a friend of Deacon's. Blaine had to bail him out, and the cops cut him a break because Deacon used to be on the job in Boston. But they told Blaine to get him out of town. That's how he ended up here. Blaine thought he was reverting to the old days when Deacon used to get into a lot of trouble, but it wasn't like that at all."

"I bet you're glad you gave him a chance after you heard he'd been in jail."

"Our situation is a little different than someone who went to prison for six years for something pretty serious," Julia said.

"While in the throes of an addiction he's since beaten," Cindy reminded her. "People do all sorts of crazy stuff to feed an addiction."

"That's true," Katie said. "I used to see it a lot in my old job. Addicts in all kinds of trouble with the law for what they did to score drugs and the money to pay for them. I cared for many a person who was handcuffed to a hospital bed while they went through withdrawal."

"I hadn't really thought of it that way." Julia stroked Pupwell's fur as she considered what Katie had said. "That people would break the law to get the money for more drugs."

"They do things they'd never do outside the grip of their addiction," Katie said.

"Jace said he didn't know his brother had a gun, and the only reason he got caught was because he stayed with his brother after he was shot," Cindy said.

"Of course he stayed," Katie said. "I'm sure he could tell his brother was dying. Imagine witnessing that."

"He lost everything—his wife, kids, brother, parents, sister, his freedom. He used the time in prison to turn his life around, get clean and learn a trade. He's a plumber." She'd read about his work-release program in a story in the *Providence Journal*.

"That's amazing," Katie said. "Good for him."

"His kids… They're here, the boys Seamus and Carolina took in."

"Oh my God," Katie said. "He's Lisa's ex-husband. Wow."

"Yeah. He said he's sick with guilt over what he put her and his kids through and wishes more than anything he could make amends to her somehow."

"I hope he's not going to cause trouble for Seamus and Caro," Katie said. "They've been so good for the boys."

"He said he only wants to be a friend to them."

"This is all so *complicated*, Cin," Julia said. "I hate that for you after, you know, everything else."

"I know, but I like him. I've known him for weeks, and he's never been anything but kind, friendly and sweet to me—and that was before he knew I had a room for rent. I'd like to think I can trust my own judgment about people, but..." She shrugged.

Her sisters could certainly understand the legacy they'd been left with from their violent childhood. After discovering early in life that they couldn't trust their own father, knowing who they *could* trust had been a challenge.

"At some point, you have to take a chance," Julia said, "like we did with Shane and Deacon. I just wish you were taking a chance with a less complicated man."

"Who knows if he even likes me that way?"

"Sure he does," Katie said. "How could he not?"

"And you're not the slightest bit biased, right?"

"Not at all," Julia said. "You've always been the smoke show of the Lawry sisters."

Cindy tossed a pillow at her. "Shut up! I am not."

"Uh, yes, you are," Katie said. "I'd kill for your boobs and ass, and your face is a showstopper."

"You need to stop this right now. You guys are gorgeous."

"We're okay," Julia said. "You're stunning, and since Jace has eyes, he sees it, too."

Cindy covered her ears. "I can't hear any more of this. Don't you guys know I wanted to be you two when I grew up?"

"You grew up to be your own wonderful self, and we couldn't be prouder of you," Julia said.

"Couldn't have done it without you guys and Owen running interference for me and the boys." After they were of age, the three eldest Lawry siblings had moved along with the rest of the family to stay close for their younger siblings, who had still been stuck living with "the general," as they called the man who'd raised them—that was when they weren't calling him an asshole. It had driven the general crazy that Owen, Katie and Julia had moved wherever they went to help care for their younger siblings.

Cindy couldn't fathom what her life would've been like without them there to provide the only respite she and their three younger brothers had gotten, except their summers on Gansett Island. "I wonder sometimes... Who was there for you guys and Owen? We had you three. Who did you have?"

"Each other," Julia said. "And Gram and Pop."

"We got through it, and you did, too," Katie said. "Now we can have and do whatever we want. If you want this man to be your roommate and your friend, then I think you should try it. Ask him if you can have a month probationary period to make sure you're compatible roommates and go from there."

"I like that idea," Julia said. "I can live with that."

Cindy rolled her eyes at her sister. "As long as you're comfortable."

"You're our baby sister," Julia said. "There's no way you're doing anything we're not comfortable with."

"I'm twenty-eight," Cindy reminded her.

"So what?" Julia asked.

"That means I'm a fully grown adult."

"Again, I say, *so what?*"

"You can't treat me like a baby forever," Cindy said.

"Sure we can. You'll always be our baby sister, Cin. There's no escaping that."

"I wouldn't want to escape it, but I need you guys to support me in this. I honestly feel that he's a good guy who's made some big mistakes and is trying to start over. I want to give him a chance."

"Then you should," Katie said, "as long as you're willing to do what's best for yourself if it doesn't work out."

"I promise I will."

"Good," Katie said. "We want you to be safe and happy. That's all we've ever wanted for you."

"I'm happy to be here, where I can call my big sisters to come over any time I want to. I can see my big brother and my other brothers and my mom and get to know my wonderful new stepfather. I can't recall a time I've ever been happier."

"I know," Julia said on a long exhale. "Same for me. Remember how much we loved being here as kids? It's like a million times better now."

"Especially since you met Deacon, right?" Katie asked with a smirk.

"That's a big part of it," Julia said, "but it's being here with you guys, with Mom, Gram, Pop, Owen, Laura, their kids, all of it. It's like we're having the childhood we never got to have or something. I know that sounds weird, but..."

"I get it," Katie said, "and I agree. I feel like a little kid again whenever I'm with you all, except I'm a happy little kid this time."

"Yes," Cindy said, smiling. "That's it exactly."

"We deserve this," Julia declared. "We deserve every freaking good thing there is to be had in life."

The three of them touched their glasses in solidarity.

"I'll drink to that," Cindy said.

CHAPTER 4

*C*indy buzzed with nervous energy the next day as she cut hair, made conversation with clients, ran credit cards and booked follow-up appointments. It was like any other day at the salon, but nothing about it felt normal as she counted the seemingly endless hours until she could go to the Beachcomber and tell Jace what she'd decided.

Would he go for the one-month trial period, or would he hold out for something more definite? If she proposed the trial, would that change the easy groove of the friendship they'd formed over the last couple of months?

God, she hoped not. Her conversations with him had become such a source of enjoyment for her, and she looked forward to the time she spent with him, even if she had to share him with his other customers. She loved how he always made his way back to her once he'd tended to everyone else.

What if being roommates changed everything and not for the better?

Ugh, she couldn't bear that.

"Are you all right, Cindy?" Linda McCarthy asked after a long period of silence. "You seem distracted today."

"I'm so sorry, Mrs. McCarthy."

"I told you to call me Linda, and don't be sorry."

The comment resurrected a painful memory of her father backhanding her brother Josh for calling an adult by his first name, even after the man had told the Lawry kids to call him Tom.

"Thank you, Linda," Cindy said, undone by the recollection she'd much sooner forget. But that was the general's legacy. He was always there, lurking beneath the surface, ready to undercut any progress his children made in escaping him. "And I'm fine. Sorry to be quieter than usual."

"Don't you worry about that. You're not here to entertain me."

"Aren't I, though? I was taught a good haircut comes with a dose of gossip, or it's not a good haircut."

Linda laughed. "I love that."

"I learned everything I know about this business at a salon called Laverne's. It was right out of *Steel Magnolias*. You've seen that movie, right?"

"Of course. It's a classic, and I can picture your Laverne's based on the reference."

"It was such a great place, outside of Dallas. Everyone knew everyone, and there was no such thing as privacy of any kind."

"Sounds like Gansett."

"I guess it does," Cindy said, laughing. "So, what's the latest news on Gansett?"

"Well, let's see. With the season ending, everyone's looking forward to things slowing down, as it does every year in September. We're counting down to Big Mac's nephew Riley's wedding to Nikki Stokes in November, and the arrival of some more grandchildren this winter. Our sons Grant and Evan are both expecting with their wives, Stephanie and Grace. And then Adam and Abby are expecting quads in the spring."

"I was talking to Mallory about that. I can't imagine four babies."

"Abby couldn't either until there they were—and after she was told she probably couldn't have kids."

"It's a miracle."

"She's trying to see it that way, but they'll have five little ones all at once, counting their son, Liam."

"Wow."

"We'll be there to help, though."

"She's lucky to have family nearby."

"For sure. We'll also be working on the new spa at the hotel and the wedding venue at the old alpaca farm."

"You've got a lot going on."

"We wouldn't have it any other way."

Talking about other people's lives kept Cindy from obsessing about how many hours were left until she could see Jace.

Her mother was her last customer of the day, which allowed Cindy to relax a bit as she did color and a trim for her ageless mom. "I don't know how you do it," Cindy said.

"Do what?" Sarah asked.

"Look like you're forty when you're a little more than that."

"A little more," Sarah said, laughing. "Like twenty-five years more."

"You're wearing it well, Mama."

"Thanks to your efforts with those foils."

"Nah, it's all you. Tip of the hat to your ageless mother, too."

"She's a pretty spectacular eighty-five-year-old."

"Yes, she is. I guess good genes run in our family."

"On my side of the family, that is," Sarah said dryly.

"That goes without saying."

Cindy's youngest brother Jeff looked just like their father as a younger man. Julia had darker hair like he did, but the rest of them were blond like their mother, thankfully.

"You know what helps keep me young?"

"What's that?"

"Happiness. Being with Charlie has been life changing. I had no idea such a thing was possible, even growing up with my wonderful parents. If I'd known better, maybe I would've made some changes sooner. I wish I had. I wasted so much time that could've been spent being happy."

"I'm so glad you finally got there, Mom. No one in this world deserves it more than you do."

"We all do. That's what I've learned. Every single one of us deserves love and happiness. That's all I want for you kids now that I have it. Three down, four to go."

Cindy laughed. "No pressure, though."

"None at all. It'll happen when it's meant to, like it did for Owen, Katie and Julia."

"They definitely got lucky."

"You will, too, sweetie. I know it. That big heart of yours is going to make some man very lucky."

"We'll see, I guess."

"I hope you're open to the idea of finding someone."

"I am, but I'm holding out for something special. I see Julia with Deacon, and I think, 'I want what they have.'"

"They're adorable together."

"He's crazy about her."

"And vice versa. That's how it ought to be."

"I love that she's playing and singing again."

"Oh Lord, me, too. She absolutely shines onstage." Her mother's smile faded ever so slightly. "I hate what you all went through. I think about how I wish I had that time to do over, but if I did, I never would've married him or had you kids. And that would've been tragic. You guys make all the hard times worth it."

"We all hate what *you* went through. At least we got a break from it when we came here in the summers."

"I stayed far longer than I should have. I should've left him the minute Jeff moved to Florida with Gram and Pop. Your father kept promising things would be different. I should've known better by then."

"Enough about him," Cindy said. "Let's talk about you and Charlie and happy things."

Sarah's expression immediately softened. "Charlie is a very happy thing for sure. If you'd asked me a few years ago if I'd ever remarry, I would've laughed. But when the right guy comes along…"

"He's absolutely perfect."

"I'm glad you think so, because I worried what you guys would think of him being an ex-con covered in tattoos with a chip a mile wide on his shoulder when I first met him. I think all the time about what I would've missed if I hadn't taken the chance to get to know him, even after he told me about his past."

It occurred to Cindy that her mother would understand her dilemma with Jace better than anyone else ever could. After she blow-dried her mother's hair into a smooth, stylish look, she stood back to admire her handiwork.

"I love it, sweetheart. But I always do."

"You're my best customer, and it's my pleasure to have you in my chair." Cindy had lived away from her family for years, so it was a treat to be able to cut their hair again, the way she had when they all lived at home and first discovered she had a talent for it.

Her mother handed her a credit card.

"Don't be silly. No charge for you."

"You will take this and charge me what you would anyone else, and I'll tip you the way I would anyone else. I won't hear of anything but that."

Cindy rolled her eyes, took the card from her mother and charged her only for the color. "Happy now?"

"Very happy." Sarah added a thirty-dollar tip and signed her new name, Sarah Grandchamp, to the receipt.

"Can you stay for a minute?" Cindy asked. "There's something else I wanted to talk to you about."

"Of course. I have nowhere to be until later. Charlie and I are making dinner for Mom and Dad." Cindy's grandparents, Adele and Russ, lived in a cottage on the property Charlie had bought with the settlement money he'd received from the state for fourteen years of improper imprisonment.

Cindy turned the Open sign to Closed and locked the door before joining her mom in the reception area.

"Is everything all right?" Sarah asked with the old wary look Cindy had seen far too often growing up when nothing was ever all right.

"Yes, I'm fine, but I wanted to tell you I've sort of met someone. A man."

"Oh, Cindy, really? Do tell!"

"He's a lot like Charlie, and I only put that together when you were talking about what he shared with you when you first met him. Jace is an ex-con, a recovering addict and a very sweet man. In fact, he answered my ad for a roommate."

"What did he do?" Sarah asked, her tone guarded now.

"He and his older brother robbed a convenience store when they needed money for drugs. His brother pulled a gun, the owner of the store shot him, and Jace stayed with his brother, who died right there in the store. He did six years in prison and got clean while he was in there. He's here because his two little boys live here. Jackson and Kyle—"

"Chandler. Lisa's boys."

"Yes."

"They're doing so well with Seamus and Carolina."

"He's aware of that and is thankful to get to see them occasionally. He's not trying to upset anything."

"That's a lot to take on, Cin."

"I know. He said as much himself when he told me about it. But the thing is, I've already known him for a while. I pop into the Beachcomber for dinner a few nights a week, and he's the bartender there. We've become friendly, and well… I like him. I only found out his full story when he came to see the house last night."

"I give him points for being honest with you."

"I do, too. He didn't have to tell me what he did, but he said it wouldn't be fair not to."

"Charlie said something like that to me, too."

"Charlie was in prison for something he didn't do, though. Jace was there for something he *did* do."

"Yes, that's true, although he wasn't the one who had the gun, and he could've possibly saved his own skin by taking off after his brother was shot but didn't."

"I thought the same thing and feared I was trying to justify it all in my mind to make it work because I like him so much."

"It matters that he told you the truth and didn't let you hear it from someone else."

"I think I'm going to give him a chance as a roommate and friend."

"The ultimate irony is that my ex-con husband is a million times the man my decorated military officer husband was."

"Right?" The day Mark Lawry was sentenced to jail for abusing Sarah had been one of the best days of all their lives.

"It's funny that before Charlie, I would've freaked out about you living with an ex-con and recovering addict. But being with Charlie has taught me so much about grace and compassion and that everyone struggles in one way or another."

"That's so true. When I look at Jace, I see a sweet, kind, caring, sexy man who makes me feel things. I have no idea if he feels the same way, but he tends to give me extra attention at the bar, even when I'm only drinking water."

"I love that for you, sweetheart."

"But then there's this other part of me that worries about making a bad decision and bringing drama into my life."

"I get that. I was the same way when I first started to realize Charlie was interested in me as more than a friend. I wanted nothing to do with him. I'd been there, done that, and there was no way I was going down that road again."

"What changed?" Cindy asked.

"He kept showing up and was the same from one day to the next, no explosions of anger or temper tantrums when he didn't get his way. He was kind, loyal, funny, gruff, sexy... After a few months of seeing him every day and getting to know him, I could no longer think of a single reason to keep my distance from him—and that was the last thing I wanted to do anyway."

"I love that, Mom. It's such a great story."

Sarah shrugged. "It's hard to trust new people when you come from what we do."

"That's exactly it."

"If you like this man, if *you* trust him, then that's what matters."

Cindy leaned in to hug her mother. "Thank you for understanding."

"I do. Better than anyone. I worried so much what you kids would say about me dating Charlie because of his past. I hoped you'd take the time to get to know him before you judged him."

"He's wonderful. For the first time in my life, I feel like I have a father."

"Oh honey, that's a lovely thing to say. Do you mind if I tell him that?"

"Of course not. It's true. We all feel that way."

"I'll always be sorry I didn't choose a better man to father my children, but I'm forever thankful to your father for my seven marvelous kids."

They hugged again at the door. "Love you, Mom."

"Love you more, sweet girl. Keep me posted about your new friend."

"I will."

Cindy waved her off and then locked the door. She swept up the hair and ran a Swiffer over the floor. On Tuesdays, she also cleaned the mirrors and windows as well as the tiny bathroom in the back. She could've saved those chores for the next day, but the work kept her from watching the clock and thinking too hard about seeing Jace.

Her heart thumped and her pulse raced when she thought of him.

In the back of her mind, she feared setting herself up for a huge disappointment by getting so carried away over him. What if he was just doing his job and being nice to her because she was a customer? Was it possible she'd read too much into their subtle flirtation? Was it even flirtation or him just doing what he did with everyone?

As she scrubbed the bathroom floor, she drove herself crazy with those questions and others. She'd dated a lot when she was younger, but rarely allowed her interactions with men to go beyond the surface. It was safer there. If you didn't let people in, they couldn't hurt you.

The general had taught her that and many other lessons children should never have to learn from a parent. But after years of therapy and working on herself, she refused to let the scars from the past ruin the present and future. The Lawrys were survivors, not victims. They'd prevailed in the end. Mark Lawry's once-sterling reputation was in tatters, the worst kind of punishment for a man who cared more about his image than his own family.

Justice had been served, and she was determined to move forward without that dark cloud hanging over her life.

With the salon clean and fresh smelling, she tidied up the reception desk and shut down the computer that ran the appointment and billing systems. As she locked the door and began the short walk home, she was determined to remain positive no matter what became of her friendship with Jace. If he wasn't "the one" for her, someone else would be. She'd find him.

Eventually.

CHAPTER 5

*J*ace kept half an eye on the door while he chatted with customers, made drinks, placed food orders and kept his bar clean. One day after Labor Day, and the island pace had already shifted from the frantic level of summer to the slower off-season groove. He liked that groove, even if he'd make less money than he had in the summer.

Libby, the Beachcomber general manager, had warned him to be careful with his money if he planned to stay for the off-season. The summer, she'd said, paid for the rest of the year. With those words of wisdom in mind, Jace had banked most of what he'd made in the summer, which he hoped would keep him afloat during the long winter.

She'd also told him that he'd make an insane amount during the summer, which was exactly what'd happened. "People tend to go crazy when they're making big money," Libby had said. "They're not thinking about what happens in September when the tourists quit coming."

Thinking about surviving the off-season kept him from obsessing about whether Cindy would show.

When was the last time he'd wanted anything as much as he wanted to see her smiling face? If she didn't come, then he had his answer about the room—and their friendship, such as it was. While he waited, he unboxed the games he'd bought on the discount rack at the department store, thinking they'd be fun for the regulars during the winter months.

He'd gotten two checkerboards, a chess set and Yahtzee for ten bucks. As he set them out, musician Niall Fitzgerald took a seat at the bar, as he did every night that he worked. The Irishman had short dark hair and vivid blue eyes. "That's a fun idea," he said of the games.

"I thought it might be something to help pass the time in the off-season."

"The customers will love it, and it'll keep them coming in."

"Along with your music and my charming personality," Jace said with a grin for the man who'd become a friend.

"That goes without saying."

"Ready for the usual?" Jace asked.

"Yep."

"No point in telling you the specials, I suppose," he said, as he did every night.

"Nope. I'm in a burger-and-fries rut and staying there for now."

"Coming right up." Jace punched the food order into the computer and drew the single Guinness Niall allowed himself on a work night. He'd made an artform out of nursing that one beer for hours while he strummed his guitar and sang for the patrons. Listening to Niall was one of the most enjoyable aspects of the job for Jace.

Cindy was *the* most enjoyable aspect, though. She was like a ray of sunshine sitting at his bar, making everyone she encountered feel like they were the most important person in her world. Or maybe it was just him who felt that way around her.

She was late.

It was seven fifteen, and she was always there by seven.

He was crushed.

As soon as he'd seen that she would be his potential roommate, he should've taken a pass on the room, so she'd never have needed to know about his shady past. What woman in her right mind would take an ex-con, recovering drug addict into her home? If she were his daughter, he'd tell her to stay away from guys like him.

Her answer would be no, and he'd been a fool to hope otherwise.

After their AA meeting that morning, Mason had told him about a place for rent on his street. It was a full house, so probably more than he could afford, but Jace would check it out tomorrow.

He went to the kitchen to retrieve Niall's food and was returning to the bar when Cindy walked through the door. The relief he experienced at seeing her was similar to how he'd felt when he'd learned he was being paroled early for good behavior.

Somehow, he managed to complete the delivery of Niall's dinner and settle himself to greet her with his usual casual smile, even if nothing about this was casual. Not for him, anyway. He put a glass of ice water with a lemon on the bar for her. She'd told him she suffered from migraines. He had questions about that but hadn't gotten around to asking her. "How's it going?" he asked.

"Good. You?"

"Better now." He smiled at the way she blushed. God, she was adorable. "I thought you were ghosting me."

"What? Why?"

"You're late."

She glanced at the clock on the wall. "Oh, I was at the Surf listening to my sister and ran into my grandmother. We got to talking, and I lost track of the time."

"I'm teasing. How's your grandmother?"

"She's amazing, as always. The coolest woman I've ever known."

"You're lucky to still have her."

"I know! And my grandfather, too. They're the best."

"You want to hear the specials?"

"Sure."

He never took his gaze off her sweet face as he recited the details of the baked cod and brisket specials. "I recommend the cod. Had some earlier. It's good."

"That does sound good. I'll have that and chowder, please."

"Coming right up."

"What's with the games?" she asked as he put her order into the computer.

"I hear it's a long winter around here. Thought it might be fun."

"That's a great idea. I used to play checkers with my pop. I'm really good."

"Is that right?" He glanced at her. "Set up a game and show me how good you are."

She flashed a determined smile. "You're on, my friend."

Had two little words ever meant more to him? *My friend.* She knew the worst about him and was still there, still smiling at him and referring to him as her friend. He felt as if he'd been given a priceless gift in those two words.

As he waited on other customers, drew beer from the taps, rang up checks and mixed cocktails, he kept half an eye on Cindy as she chatted with Niall and then Kevin and Chelsea McCarthy when they arrived with their baby daughter, Summer. Chelsea used to have his job at the bar but was now a full-time mom and seeming to love every second with her sweet little girl.

He poured a beer for Kevin and a Sprite for Chelsea and put them on the bar in front of them. "What's Miss Summer drinking these days?"

"Still on the boob," Chelsea said.

"We don't have that spirit here," Jace replied, grinning.

"Only Mommy has that, right, my love?" Chelsea asked her daughter, who flashed a gummy grin.

"Oh, she's smiling," Jace said as a pang of memory hit him involving his own boys and their first smiles. That was one of the last milestones he got to experience with them before he was ripped from their lives. He was gone before Kyle, the younger one, had walked.

"That's a new development. Kev says it's gas, but we don't listen to Daddy when he says silly things, do we?"

"It is gas," Kevin, the doctor, said.

"Hush," Chelsea responded. "My beauty doesn't have gas. She's happy."

Kevin rolled his eyes. "She's happy, *and* she has gas."

"Do you know a good divorce attorney?" Chelsea asked Jace, her face glowing with delight.

"I'm not touching that one," Jace said over his shoulder as he headed for the kitchen to grab chowder for Cindy, Kevin and Chelsea. He carried the tray back and doled out the bowls, spoons and oyster crackers.

Then he leaned in, moved one of the black checkers Cindy had put on his side of the board and left her with a wink.

Her face flushed. She was so sweet and kind, and if he were a better man, he'd leave her the hell alone. The last thing a lovely young woman like her needed in her life was him and all his baggage. He should find a different living situation and stop flirting with her every chance he got.

However, despite all the work he'd done on himself over the last few years, he still wasn't a good enough man to walk away from someone who made him feel as good as she did. Being in her presence reminded him of what happened when the sun emerged from behind a cloud. Suddenly, everything was brighter, warmer, happier. Everything about her appealed to him, but nothing more than her heart, which was always on display in the way she interacted with others.

Case in point, while her own chowder grew cold, Cindy held Summer so Chelsea and Kevin could eat.

Jace retrieved her bowl of soup. "I'll warm it up when you're ready for it."

Her smile was a thing of pure beauty. "Oh, thank you."

The bar filled up with a lot of the regulars and a few lingering tourists. They kept Jace busy all night, but he made a move on the checkerboard every time he went near Cindy's seat. Judging by the stack of black checkers piled up next to her, she was about to beat him handily, but he didn't mind. He'd challenge her to best two out of three to keep her there until they could talk privately.

It was nearly eleven before things died down to just a few patrons other than Cindy. When they were tended to, he returned to her, frowning as he examined the board she was once again dominating in their second game. "Are you some sort of secret checkers champion or something?"

"Nope. You're just not very good at it."

"I am, too!"

"No, you're not," she said, snorting. "You make dumb moves. Like this. See how you moved this guy here?"

"Yep."

"That gives me an opening to do this." She triple-jumped him. "King me."

"Jeez. You're merciless."

She added his checkers to her stack. "You have to anticipate what the other player is going to do."

"Who taught you that?"

"My father. It was one of the few things he taught me that's done me any good in life."

"He wasn't a good guy, your dad?"

She shook her head.

Jace thought of the dimmer on his laptop and how it kicked in sometimes to save energy. That's what happened to Cindy when she talked about her father. All her brightness faded.

"I've been thinking about the roommate situation," she said.

"It's okay if it doesn't work for you. No pressure."

"I want you to know that I appreciate how you were upfront with me about everything when you certainly didn't have to be."

"You deserved the truth if you were going to let me into your home."

"A lot of people wouldn't have been thinking about me. They'd only be thinking about themselves. You didn't do that, and it matters to me. How would you feel about trying it for a month and seeing how it goes?"

"I can see why you'd want to do it that way, but the thing is, I need a sure thing. I want to spend the winter here so I can see my boys, and with everyone snapping up off-season housing this month, there won't be anything left if you give me the boot after a month."

"I suppose that's true."

"Listen, no hard feelings if you say no. I promise."

"I'm not saying no."

"Oh."

She bit her bottom lip as she gazed at him with more affection than he deserved. "I guess I'll have to just take you at your word that you'll be a good roommate."

"I will be. I'll do all the cleaning."

"Sold. I hate to clean."

"See? I'm already the best roommate you've ever had."

As he breathed a sigh of relief to know he'd found a place to live, he vowed to do everything he could to be the best roommate she'd ever have.

CHAPTER 6

*C*indy was again on pins and needles at work the next day, counting down until six thirty, when Jace would move into her house. He'd said he didn't have much more than clothes and a few personal items, so it wouldn't take long to move in. After her last client left, she cleaned up and headed for the grocery store to get some chicken to grill and vegetables for a salad.

She was walking home when it occurred to her that she might be trying too hard to properly welcome her new roommate.

Ugh, she'd been a red-hot mess all day, spilling a full container of hair color down the front of herself and ruining an apron, knocking a cup of hot tea over and just barely missing her own foot with the hot water and messing up the computer to the point that Chloe had to come do a rescue.

All this nonsense over a new roommate. Ridiculous. She'd also been plagued all day by memories of her father accusing her of being "easy" with boys just because she'd gotten a lot of attention from them when she was younger. How had that been her fault? Her dad had been incensed by the boys who'd called the house or surrounded her in public. It had been the same for Julia and Katie, who'd withstood his torture together.

By the time it had happened to her, her sisters had been out of the house and living on their own. She'd had to fend him off by herself, telling him all the time that she'd done nothing to encourage the attention she received. That hadn't mattered to a man who'd raged that he refused to have "sluts for daughters."

His words had done lasting damage. So much so that she was afraid she was going overboard by making dinner to welcome her new male roommate. She cringed to think of what her father would have to say about her living with a man she wasn't married to. It amazed her that, after years of being free of him, he could still have such a loud voice inside her head. It would please him endlessly to know his impact on her remained strong after all this time, which was why she refused to allow him to dictate how she led her life as an adult free of his abusive behavior.

She wished her mother's supportive voice could drown out her father's insults, but that had never been the case. The Lawry kids had lived under the dark cloud of Mark Lawry's tirades for so long, they'd all had trouble escaping the hold he had on them, even when he'd no longer been in their daily lives. Each of them had struggled in one way or another.

Cindy was convinced that her lifelong battle with migraines had come from living with unbearable stress for the first eighteen years of her life. They'd started when she was eight, shortly after she'd witnessed her father break Owen's arm in an altercation that her father lied about when he took Owen to the ER to have his arm set. That was the first time she vividly recalled realizing who her father really was. The migraines had started shortly afterward.

He'd told her to quit her whining and get her ass out of bed. She'd been forced to go to school with a migraine more times than she could count. Even when the school nurse had called home to suggest they come get her, the general had forbidden her mother to do so. Cindy had been forced to suffer through school, after-school activities, homework, dinner and chores before she could go to bed and find some relief.

It'd been torturous.

Once, she'd overheard the school nurse suggesting to someone that her parents be reported to child services, but that never happened, because of who her father was in the community. In the military towns where they'd lived, it was highly likely that the people who should've been helping Cindy and her siblings were married to someone who reported to the father who was abusing them. They'd run into that problem time and again. Every time someone should've done the right thing by them, they hadn't.

Owen had lied to the young officer who'd treated his broken arm, knowing the man's career would've been ruined if he'd tried to intervene.

Their long nightmare ended when their father was locked up like the criminal he was. All this time later, Cindy still had moments when she couldn't believe it was finally over. But days like today, when his voice was so loud in her head, she knew it would never truly be over.

"Cin?"

Cindy looked up to realize she'd nearly walked past Julia on the sidewalk. "Oh, hi."

"Jeez, where were you? I waved to you five minutes ago when I saw you coming, and you never blinked."

"I was actually stuck thinking about the bad stuff."

"What the hell for?"

Cindy shrugged. "Just sort of happened."

Julia took her by the arm and walked them to a park bench across the street that looked down over the ferry landing. Pupwell trotted along with them, in step with Julia as always.

"Don't you have to get to the Surf?"

"I've got time. What's going on?"

"Jace is moving in tonight."

"Okay... So why does that take you to the bad stuff?"

"Just thinking about the shit Dad used to say about boys and what he'd think of me living with a man I'm not married to."

"Once again, I say fuck him. Who cares what he'd say?"

"I don't care. It's just that sometimes I can *hear* him bellowing in my head, whether I want to or not."

Julia sighed. "Yeah, I know what you mean. His bellow drove me to an eating disorder when he would rage about having a fat daughter."

"And you were never fat."

"Try telling him that."

"I hate him so much, and I *hate* that I hate him."

Julia put her arm around Cindy. "I get that, too. It's a terrible thing to carry around. It's always with us, even in the good times."

"Exactly."

"It's not fair that he's messing up what might be the start of something lovely for you."

"He's not messing it up, and for all I know, this might just be a new roommate, not the start of anything lovely."

"Keep an open mind. You never know what might happen."

"I don't want to go into this new living arrangement hoping it'll be more than that."

"Even if you hope it'll be more than that?"

Cindy nudged Julia with her elbow, making her sister laugh. "I like him. I think he likes me, too. Beyond that, who knows?"

"Despite my initial reservations, I can see you have genuine feelings for this guy. I really hope it turns into something amazing. You deserve that. We all do."

"We'll see. Thanks for the pep talk. I needed it."

"I'm here for that any time you need it. Don't let the dark stuff drown out the light in your life, Cin. Don't give him that kind of easy victory. You hear me?"

"I do. Thank you for the reminder."

"Go welcome your sexy new roommate with my permission to fully enjoy anything good that may come of your friendship with him."

Cindy hugged her sister. "Thanks, Jules. Love you."

"Love you more."

"No way."

"Yes, way. I changed your diapers. That means I love you more."

Cindy laughed at the familiar comment. If Katie and Julia had told her once, they'd told her a million times how they'd changed her diapers, and since they were only a few years older than her, she doubted that had ever happened. She parted company with her sister, feeling a thousand pounds lighter than she had a few minutes earlier. Having family who understood in her daily life was such a blessing when the dark tried to smother the light.

Julia knew all too well what kind of damage their dad was capable of. She'd battled an awful eating disorder after hearing him tell her she was getting fat her whole childhood, when she'd never come close to being fat. He'd found a way to pick at each of them, homing in on their insecurities and working them as he tried to control them.

"Stop thinking about him," Cindy said out loud, as if that might help her put him in the past where he belonged. "Think about the good stuff." She rounded the last corner before her street and headed toward home, where a handsome man sat on her front stoop, swigging from a bottle of water.

Speaking of the good stuff.

He smiled when he saw her coming.

Cindy immediately added his sexy grin to the list of positive things in her life.

SHE IS SO DAMNED PRETTY. That was always Jace's first thought when he saw her, but she was even more so with the late-day sun shining on her, highlighting the golden streaks in her dark blonde hair. As she approached the small house they would share as of today, her smile lit up her face and filled him with a warm feeling of welcome.

He'd felt bad about having to reject her offer of a month trial period and had hoped that wouldn't make things awkward between them when he got to the house today with the two duffel bags that contained most of his belongings. If there was one "good" thing about spending years in prison, it was the ability to travel light.

He had no idea what'd become of his other possessions after he was arrested. Lisa had probably tossed his stuff in a dumpster, not that he could blame her. His most prized possession was the photo of the boys Seamus had texted to him after they first connected, which Jace had printed and framed to keep on his bedside table. That was the thing he'd grab in a fire.

It occurred to him as he watched Cindy approach that he'd also grab her.

"Sorry I wasn't here when you arrived. I ran into my sister in town and got to talking."

"No worries. I just got here a few minutes ago."

"Is that all your stuff?"

"That's it." He gestured to the plastic bag sitting next to one of his duffels. "I bought some sheets and a couple of towels at the department store. I can pick up anything else we need."

"Kevin left a lot of stuff when he moved in with Chelsea. He said she already had most of what they needed."

"That's nice of him." Jace stood and grabbed his stuff to follow her inside.

"Make yourself at home. You know where your room is."

"Thanks."

Jace dropped his bags on the floor of the room he'd call home. It had a queen-sized bed and a dresser as well as a small closet that had a few hangers. He used them to hang his work shirts. The rest he didn't care about. It took him ten minutes to unload his clothes into the dresser and stuff the canvas duffels under the bed. Then he broke open the package of sheets and pulled the tags off the white towels.

He'd bought white ones because he recalled Lisa saying they could be bleached if they got nasty, whereas colored ones couldn't. That random memory of her had come out of nowhere while he was in the store. Again, he'd been filled with sorrow to know she'd died before he could apologize for what he'd done.

He'd never seen or talked to her again after he was arrested. The only contact he'd had with her was through the lawyer who'd served him with divorce and custody papers that he'd signed, because what choice did he have?

She hadn't come to the trial or visited him in jail or sent him pictures of his kids. His letters to her had come back undeliverable, and his parents had said they had no idea where she was. She'd taken their little boys and disappeared to a place where no one knew who they were or what he'd done.

Jace couldn't blame her for doing what she had to do to survive the position he'd put her in. Armed robbery, of all things. In his right mind, he couldn't conceive of such a thing. In his drug-addicted state, the only thing he'd cared about was the next score. He hadn't given a single thought to his wife, sons, parents or anything other than getting more of what he needed to stay alive—or what he'd *thought* he needed. Turned out that was the last thing he needed. No one could've told him that then. The sad part was that even knowing how it would turn out, he probably still would've gone with Jess that night, because he'd needed a fix so badly.

That's how fucked up he'd been then.

He ran a hand through his hair and released a deep breath as he stood to go see what his new roommate was up to. Anything was better than reliving shit he wished he could forget.

Cindy was in the kitchen chopping vegetables, a tall glass of ice water next to the cutting board on the counter. "Are you hungry? I thought I'd make you a welcome dinner since you're always waiting on me at dinnertime."

"I enjoy waiting on you."

"Thank you, but tonight is my turn. I marinated some chicken for the grill."

"Want me to handle that?"

"Sure, if you'd like to."

"I used to be pretty good at grilling."

"Aren't most guys born with the grill gene?"

He took the plate she handed him. "Yep. It's in our DNA."

"I'm making salad to go with it, and I got a baked potato for you if you want it."

"I'd love it, but only if you share it with me."

"I avoid baked potatoes. Too many carbs."

He wanted to tell her she could afford some carbs, but he kept the thought to himself. Outside, he lit the grill and waited for it to warm up while admiring the patio and landscaping Kevin and his sons had done while they'd lived there. While his grandmother had taught him the names of a lot of the plants, Lisa had known *every* bush and flower and could've identified them in a matter of seconds.

Jace wished he'd paid more attention when she was constantly reciting the names of every bush, tree and flower she encountered. She'd dreamed of pursuing a career as a florist. That was another thing he'd ruined for her. He'd asked around about her on the island and had heard she'd worked two waitressing jobs to provide for their sons. Lisa and the boys had been about to receive one of the new affordable housing units being built on land a wealthy former resident had left the town when Lisa fell ill and died.

It made him so incredibly sad to think about how hardscrabble her existence had been after he went to jail.

"Are you okay?" Cindy asked, startling him out of his thoughts when she joined him on the patio, bringing glasses of ice water.

He took the one she offered him. "Thanks, and yes, I'm okay. Honestly?"

Cindy nodded. "I'm happy to listen if you want to talk."

49

Jace checked the grill and then turned toward her. "I have these moments... when I think of my ex-wife and what I put her through. She's the one person in my life I'll never be able to make amends to, you know?"

"I'm sure that's very difficult."

"It's nothing compared to what she went through raising two little kids on her own after her drug-addict husband got himself arrested and tossed in jail. But hey, that's not your problem, and I don't mean to dump it on you."

"It's fine. I don't mind. We all have stuff, you know?"

He gave her a side-eyed look. "You don't have stuff."

She snorted out a laugh. "Sure I do."

"Tell me." He put the chicken on the warm grill and glanced at her. "Only if you want to, that is."

"My father was a violent, narcissistic asshole who tormented my mom and us until we were able to finally get free of him. He's in prison now, convicted of beating up my mom."

"I'm sorry," he said. "That definitely counts as stuff."

"Like I said. We all have something."

"I guess so." He sat next to her and tipped his face into the late-afternoon sun. "Are you okay? Now, I mean?"

"I do all right, but every so often, something takes me right back to those years, such as wondering what he'd have to say about me living with a man I'm not married to."

"That gave you a rough moment today?"

"That's what I was talking to my sister about. Her exact words were 'fuck him.' I'm trying to take her advice."

Smiling, he said, "I like how your sister thinks."

"He did a number on all of us. We tend to stick together."

"I'm glad you have each other."

"I am, too. I don't know what I'd do without them." She looked over at him. "Do you have other siblings? Besides your late brother?"

"I have an older sister, Diana. She's married with two kids. She did everything right, unlike her brothers. I was never close to her, but I was super close to Jess."

"You must miss him."

"I do. I think of him every day. I go back in my mind to where it all went wrong for us and think about how I might've changed the story." He made a face that was a cross between a grimace and a grin. "It's stupid to think I could've done anything to change things."

"You were so young."

"I was old enough to be married with two little kids at home when I followed my brother into that store. When I think about how different our lives could've been if we hadn't gotten into drugs..."

"All we can do is live with it and move forward with the intention of breaking the cycle. In our case, we're intensely focused on living peaceful, loving lives. That's how we exact revenge on the man who raised us, by living completely differently than he did."

"I've learned the same thing about the past through NA and AA. That's one of the primary lessons that comes from both programs."

"I'm glad you've found comfort there."

"I have. Both programs saved my life. No question." He glanced over at her. "Where have you found comfort?"

"Mostly in my mom and siblings and watching them forge new lives for themselves. Two of them are married, and a third is probably getting married soon. The other three are doing so much better than they were. My youngest brother also had drug issues, but thanks to the emergency intervention of my grandparents, he was able to kick the habit and get through college. It was tough for him being the last one at home without the rest of us to run interference for him."

"I'm glad to hear he's doing well. What's his name?"

"Jeff."

"Ah, I think I know him."

"Right. From AA. He's been hanging out at my mom's the last month or so."

Jace nodded. "He's a fine young man."

"I'm glad you think so. We adore him."

"Your brother John is a good dude, too."

"He is. It's been so fun to have them here. We're hoping Josh will join us at some point, and then the gang will all be here."

"Why here?" he asked as he got up to check the chicken on the grill.

"My grandparents, who are my mother's parents, owned the Surf for more than fifty years, and we spent summers with them growing up. It was the only break we got from the madness at home. Except for when my dad deployed, that is."

"He was in the military?"

"A general in the air force."

"Oh damn. Wow."

"Which is why no one ever did anything about the bruises they saw on the Lawry kids or reported him to the authorities. He wielded so much power in every community we lived in."

"That's horrible. I'm so glad he's paying for his crimes now."

"We are, too. I still wake up every day and almost can't believe that justice was served, along with a heavy dose of humiliation. He would tell us all the time that our family's business was private, and we'd better never get caught 'telling tales out of school.' That was one of his favorite expressions. His trial got a lot of media attention. That was the best part for us. That he was publicly humiliated and the sterling reputation he was so proud of was ruined forever."

"That's the least of what he deserved."

Cindy smiled at him. "Thanks for listening to all that. I don't usually unload the whole story on new people."

"I'm happy to listen any time, and I'm not exactly new. We've been friends for weeks."

"True."

"I do think of you as a good friend, Cindy. I hope you know that."

"I'm glad, and likewise. I enjoy our chats at the bar."

"I do, too. Talking to you makes the night go by too quickly. I always want more time to talk to you." He absolutely loved the way her face flushed with color when he said things like that to her. "We need to have a new rule."

"What rule?"

"Nothing but fun in this house. None of the bad stuff, unless someone calls time-out to talk about something."

"I like that rule."

"We've both had enough of the bad stuff. It's time for good things." He held up his glass to her. "Here's to the good stuff."

She touched her glass to his. "Cheers."

CHAPTER 7

Sarah arrived home to dinner on the stove, a chilled glass of wine and a handsome husband waiting for her with a warm, welcoming smile. It was still such a wonderful surprise to be greeted that way when she was far more accustomed to being ignored or screamed at.

When she approached him at the stove to see what he was cooking, he put an arm around her and kissed her cheek. "How are things in town?"

"Pretty good. Jo and Jon had fevers this morning," she said of Owen and Laura's twins, "but they're feeling better now, and Holden has a new favorite word."

"Dare I ask?"

"No."

Charlie gave her a quizzical look.

"That's the word. No."

"Ah," he said, smiling. "I love it. It must be driving his parents crazy."

"It is, but they think it's funny, too. Not that they can let him see that. I told Owen how he had a 'no' phase, too. Of course, with his father, that didn't last long."

"I hate the way your whole demeanor changes when you mention him."

"I'm sorry. I have no business bringing him into our happily ever after."

"It's not that, love. I just hate to see him still hurting you after all this time."

"He's not. I swear. I hardly ever think of him, except when something comes up with one of the kids. Like with Cin."

"What's up with her?"

"She's found a new roommate."

"Oh yeah?" Charlie stirred the meat sauce he'd made with onions, peppers and mushrooms. "Who's that?"

"Jace, the bartender at the Beachcomber."

Charlie's entire body went rigid. "How does she know him?"

"Apparently, she's a regular at the bar."

"I thought she didn't drink because of the migraines."

"She doesn't. She goes in for dinner a few nights a week, and they've become friends. When she put up the notice for a roommate, she didn't know he was looking until he answered the ad and showed up to see the place. Do you know him?"

"I knew him inside."

"Oh. What kind of guy was he?"

"Kept mostly to himself, which I respected. I did the same. It's how we survived. Did he tell Cindy that he's the father of the boys Seamus and Carolina are raising?"

"Cindy mentioned that. Is Seamus unhappy that he's here?" Seamus and Charlie had become friends over the last year or so.

"I don't think he's thrilled about it, especially since Jace didn't tell him he was taking a job and moving here until he was already here."

"Oh wow."

"Yeah, it was a little unsettling for Seamus and Carolina. They're crazy about those boys and have bent over backward to give them a good home since their mother passed so tragically. He was a bit undone by the sudden appearance of their biological father."

"He's not angling for custody, is he?"

"According to Seamus, Jace could see the boys are doing well with him and Caro, and it was enough for him to just be able to see them occasionally. They've worked out a truce of sorts, I guess."

"Do the boys know who he is?"

Charlie shook his head. "They decided to wait until they're a bit older to get into that since they only lost their mom so recently and have settled into a new routine with Seamus and Caro. They've introduced Jace as a friend of Seamus's."

"I suppose that's for the best, but I can't help feeling a little sorry for Jace. That must be so difficult."

"He lost the chance to raise his kids when he went to prison. Did he tell Cindy that part?"

"He did, and that he's a recovering drug addict, too."

"Well, props to him for telling her the truth."

"That's what I said, too, knowing a bit about taking on a man with a checkered past."

Charlie gave her a gentle tap on the bottom that made her laugh. "The difference between him and me is he did the crime, and I didn't."

"True, but he was battling addiction, and that makes people do things they'd never do ordinarily."

"Prison might've done him a favor, forcing him to get clean. He might never have done that otherwise."

"Cindy likes him a lot. She said they've become friends over many weeks of nights at the Beachcomber."

"She's a smart young woman. If she has a good feeling about him, she's probably not wrong."

"She said something about you earlier."

"What's that?"

"She feels like she has a father for the first time in her life."

"Oh, well… That's very sweet of her to say."

"They all feel that way about you. I hope you know that."

"The bar was set pretty low," he said with his trademark gruff chuckle.

"True, but you've more than risen to the occasion with each of them. They adore you. Almost as much as I do."

"I adore them right back. They're all great people. I'm hoping to get the chance to know Josh a little better at some point."

"I'm working on getting him here when he has some time off."

"That'd be nice. I heard something that might interest John."

"What's that?" John asked as he came into the kitchen, wearing shorts and a tank top.

"The Wayfarer is hiring a director of security. I mentioned you to Big Mac McCarthy, and he said you ought to swing by the marina to chat about it if you're interested."

"That's amazing, Johnny," Sarah said. "What do you think?"

"Is it year-round?"

"It is, but you're on your own in the off-season. You can hire help in the summer."

"Huh. Well… That does sound interesting. Thanks for thinking of me, Charlie."

"Of course. No problem."

"I'm going for a run," John said.

"Dinner is at seven thirty if you're hungry," Charlie said.

"I am if you made enough. Whatever you're cooking smells awesome."

"I made a ton. Never know who's gonna show up for dinner around here."

"Thanks. See you in a bit."

When they were alone again, Sarah went up on tiptoes to kiss her husband. "You're the absolute best, and I love you so much."

He put his arms around her and kissed her again. "I love you even more."

"No way."

"Yes way."

"Such a good 'problem' to have, isn't it?" she asked, gazing up at him. "Fighting over who loves who the most."

Hugging her tightly, he said, "It's the best problem I ever had."

JOHN POUNDED the pavement on the road that looped around the outer perimeter of the island, thinking about the job possibility Charlie had mentioned. He was such a great dude that John sometimes feared he was too good to be true. But there was no sign of that. Rather, Charlie was exactly what he seemed—an honest, genuine guy who truly loved Sarah, as well as his daughter, Stephanie, and wanted the best for Sarah's children and parents.

Lawrys were predisposed not to trust people, thanks to their upbringing, but John couldn't find any reason not to trust the man his mother had married. He sure as hell made Sarah happier than she'd ever been. No one could deny that. Sometimes, John felt like he was just meeting the person his mother really was, having known only the stressed, anxious, miserable woman she'd been before she finally left the general.

She'd always been a wonderful mother under the worst of circumstances. Seeing her truly happy for the first time had been a revelation.

On the way out of the house, Charlie had told him he was making dinner if John was interested. If his own father had said that, it would've been a mandatory appearance, not that the general had cooked often. With Charlie, there was no such edict. It was there if John wanted it, with no obligation.

The job opportunity was intriguing, even if John wasn't sure he wanted to live year-round on Gansett. Summers on the island were the best. He suspected winters were a whole other story. What would it be like to be marooned on the tiny island in the dead of winter? The year-rounders loved it. John wasn't sure if he would. Having most of his family around would keep him from being lonely, so that was a plus. And the job sounded intriguing, although it'd probably be a nightmare during the season when he'd spend most of his time dealing with drunk and disorderly people.

Although, that was better than responding to domestic incidents, child abuse cases, murders, sexual assaults and other unpleasant things he'd encountered as a police officer in Tennessee. He'd lost that job after a romantic liaison with a superior officer had come to light, embarrassing them both. Despite all the progress that'd been made, the involvement of two male officers had been a scandal in their small town. John had been encouraged to resign rather than face disciplinary action for failing to disclose the relationship.

What he still didn't understand was why he'd had to quit when the other guy was a sergeant and should've been the one to disclose it. He was still working for the department, going on with his life as if nothing had happened—albeit with his personal life now under scrutiny by his colleagues. John was the one whose life and career had been left in tatters.

Life wasn't fair, but that was hardly news to a Lawry. They'd learned that lesson repeatedly growing up. In some ways, he'd been preconditioned to expect his life to be a shitshow. He'd been doing well before he'd made the mistake of getting involved with his boss. His career had been progressing nicely with regular commendations and the respect of his colleagues. Thank God he hadn't pulled the trigger on the fixer-upper he'd almost bought in town right before things had blown up.

It'd been stupid to get involved with Gary. He'd known it at the time, but loneliness and a desire to finally live his truth had won out over common sense. They'd vowed to tell no one about their relationship and had gotten away with it for months before Gary must've told someone. John sure as hell hadn't, even if Gary had accused him of blabbing. Knowing what was at stake, he hadn't told a soul and had trusted that Gary would do the same.

As he jogged along the scenic road, his gut churned as he relived the horrible week after the relationship was outed and the whole town was talking about them. In a way, it had been a relief to walk away from it all, to come home to Gansett, to be free of the judgment that had followed him around the town he'd once thought of as home. He'd put his life on the line more than once to protect the people of that town, only to have many of them turn their backs on him once they'd discovered his big secret. Even colleagues he'd considered friends had let him down, treating him like he was radioactive.

His only "crime" was living his truth. Granted, he should've lived his truth with someone who wasn't one of his supervisors, but why hadn't Gary borne the brunt of that lapse? Why had he been the one to take the fall? He'd thought about talking to a lawyer about that question, but the idea of following through with that process exhausted him.

With the general now in prison, John had felt free to fully explore his sexuality. Being with Gary in his first real relationship had been amazing. Until it wasn't. And now he was left heartbroken as well as unemployed. Did he really want to tear the scab off those wounds and air out the entire episode in court? Maybe the municipality would settle rather than allow it to go that far. If he didn't bother, he'd have little to show financially for the eight years he'd spent in uniform other than a small percentage of his pension that he planned to invest once he received the payout.

The dilemma weighed on him in a way nothing else had since his father's trial had dominated his thoughts. He hated being in that headspace and craved the mental and emotional freedom he'd experienced prior to the meltdown at work. After a lifetime of hiding who and what he was even from the people closest to him, was he ready to go fully public with the truth? Cindy had been shocked when he'd told her, but not in a bad way. Her reaction was proof that he'd done a good job of hiding himself from everyone.

His thoughts were all over the place when he jogged into the parking lot at the bluffs, planning to sit for a while and stare out at the ocean, as if the answers he needed might be found in the vast blue sea that crashed against the island's northernmost point.

This place calmed him like nowhere else could, tied as it was to beautiful childhood memories. He loved being on the island and was tempted to snap up the job at the Wayfarer so he could stay indefinitely.

As he approached a bench that overlooked the ocean, he noticed another man sitting there and recognized him as Niall Fitzgerald, the singer from the Beachcomber. "Hey." John wiped sweat from his face with the hem of his tank. Was it his imagination, or did he catch Niall checking him out as he dropped his shirt over his abdomen? "Is this seat taken?"

Niall slid over to make room for John on the bench. "Nope."

John let his gaze wander over Niall's long legs that were stretched out in front of him, crossed at the ankles. "I didn't realize you were a runner."

"I didn't realize you were."

"I suppose it wouldn't be obvious to either of us since we know each other from a bar."

Niall grunted out a laugh. "True."

"Not playing tonight?" John asked.

"Mostly weekends this time of year."

John could listen to his Irish accent all day. "What do you do the rest of the time?"

"I work at Island Breeze Studios as a backup musician."

"That's cool."

"I guess," Niall said. "I left a pretty big career back in Ireland to come here, hoping to break out in the US, but so far, it's not proceeding according to plan."

"I'm sure it just hasn't happened yet, because you're crazy talented."

"Thanks."

"How did I not know there was a recording studio on the island?"

"It's owned by Evan McCarthy."

"Ah, okay."

"He grew up here. His folks own the marina in New Harbor."

Evan's father was Big Mac, who wanted to see John about the security job. "My brother and sister are married to Evan's cousins. I knew them from when we came here as kids."

"That must've been fun."

"It was," John said wistfully. "It was the best part of our childhood. My grandparents owned the Sand & Surf. My siblings and I came every year the day after school ended."

"Your parents didn't come?"

John shook his head. "No, just us."

"How fun. Did the grandparents spoil you guys?"

"Like crazy." The only good memories John had from those miserable years were created on this island.

"Are they still living?"

"They are. They're living in a cottage at my mom's place and doing great in their mid-eighties."

"That's amazing."

"We've told them they need to live forever because we can't imagine life without them."

"That's very sweet. You're lucky to have them."

"And we know it. How about you? Is there a big family missing you in Ireland?"

"Not so much. I was adopted out of foster care when I was eleven, and my folks are getting on in years. I get home once or twice a year to see them, and FaceTime and such."

John had so many questions he wanted to ask about the first eleven years of Niall's life, but since he didn't offer more information, John didn't press him.

"Hey, would you be interested in a home-cooked meal?"

"Uh, is that a rhetorical question?"

John laughed. "My stepfather was cooking up something that smelled pretty good when I left the house. You're welcome to join us."

"I probably stink from running."

"There're like six showers in the house, and I can loan you some clothes."

Niall gave him a side-eyed look. "Are you sure they won't mind?"

In his past life, it never would've occurred to John to invite a friend home for any reason. In this life, he had no doubt his friend would be welcome. "I'm positive."

"Then I'd love to. Thanks for asking."

"Let's go."

They got up, stretched out the kinks from sitting and took off at an easy pace back toward the palatial house his mother now called home. Unlike the home he'd grown up in, this house was full of love and acceptance and peace. Perhaps in that home, he could finally and safely come out to his mother and the rest of the family.

He'd give that some thought, too. He had a lot to think about, but as he ran along with Niall, he pushed all his other worries aside to enjoy the sunset and the start of a new friendship.

CHAPTER 8

*J*eff came down the stairs to his mother's kitchen, his mouth watering at the scent of whatever Charlie was making. "What is that?"

"My own pasta sauce with sausage, peppers and onions."

"Wow, that smells good."

"Are you hungry?" Charlie asked.

"Starving, but I'm on my way out."

"No worries. I'll put some aside for you to have later."

"Oh. Thank you. That's nice of you." How long would it take, Jeff wondered, not to be shocked by the never-ending kindness of his new stepfather? Sure, he'd known fathers like Charlie existed, but having never experienced such a thing firsthand, it still came as a surprise to him.

"Where you off to?"

"Going to see my friend Kelsey. Today's her birthday."

"Oh, fun. What've you got planned?"

"I made a reservation at the Lobster House."

"Fancy. You need some money?"

Jeff stared at him for a second, wondering if he was for real.

Charlie pulled his wallet from his back pocket, tugged out a C-note and put it on the counter. "Put this toward it."

"I can't take that."

"Why not?"

"Because."

Charlie's laugh was a mix between a growl and a grunt. "I want you to have it, which means you can take it."

"You don't have to do that, Charlie."

"I know, but after years of bad luck, it's fun to share my good fortune with the people I care about, so take the money and have a nice dinner with your friend."

"Are you sure?"

"I'm very sure."

Jeff reluctantly took the bill, all the while waiting for Charlie to strike out, to tell him he was a loser for accepting it, to do something other than smile with pleasure that Jeff had accepted his gift. "Thank you."

"You're welcome."

"Thank you for everything, Charlie. Not just this, but for making my mom so happy."

"Making her happy is the most fun I've ever had in my entire life."

"I'm sorry if we can be a little skeptical sometimes. It's in the DNA."

"No worries. I get it." Charlie turned to face Jeff, making eye contact. "I swear on my life that what you see is what you get with me, and that's never going to change."

"You have no idea what that means to us."

"I think I do, and I mean it."

"I know you do. I'm starting to have faith in that."

"Good. Now go have some fun with your friend."

"Thanks again."

"You got it."

Jeff grabbed the keys to his mother's car, which he'd arranged earlier to borrow, and headed to Sweet Meadow Farm Road to pick up Kelsey at the house where she worked for Mac and Maddie McCarthy. As he drove, he was full of emotion over the kindness of his stepfather and what a balm it was on the festering wound on Jeff's soul. How lucky they were to have Charlie in their lives.

As he went up the stairs to the deck, the sound of babies crying filled the air. He had joked to Kelsey that working there was the most effective birth control ever.

She saw him at the door and waved him in as she consoled one of the wailing babies while Maddie dealt with the other one. "Sorry. We thought we had them down, but they had other ideas."

"No worries. Our reservation isn't for an hour yet."

"Hand her to me, Kelsey," Maddie said. "You're off duty."

"I don't mind staying a little longer to help get them settled."

"They don't seem to be having it today, and I hear baby Mac is up from his nap."

"I'll take her." Jeff reached for the baby Maddie was holding. "Go get Mac."

"Are you sure?"

"Yeah, no problem," he said, even though he had almost no experience with babies. He knew enough to hold her, support her head and not drop her, which seemed to be what was needed at the moment.

"Thank you so much," Maddie said. "I'll be right back."

"That was very nice of you." Kelsey smiled at him as they sat together on a sofa with the babies. "Poor Maddie hasn't slept in days. These girls are running their mama ragged."

"I can't fathom having twins."

"Me either, especially with three other little ones. Maddie's sister, Tiffany, took Thomas and Hailey to the beach after school, which helped a lot today."

"Five kids. Damn."

Kelsey laughed, and he lost his heart a little more to the magical sound. He'd never liked a girl more than he liked her and was seriously torn about what he was going to do next month when he was supposed to report to his first real job in Tampa. He'd recently signed a lease on an apartment there and had to pick up the car he'd left with a friend in Orlando.

When he'd arrived on Gansett for his mom and Charlie's house-warming party, he'd planned to spend a week, maybe two, before returning to Florida to hang with his college friends ahead of starting his job. Since he'd met Kelsey, all he wanted was to spend as much time with her as he could.

She wore her curly reddish-gold hair up in a bun when she was working and had warm hazel eyes that sparkled with amusement any time she was near the kids. Maddie referred to her as their "Disney princess" because she was so great with the children, who clearly loved her.

Jeff had known her for a couple of weeks now and had been waiting to see something in her he didn't like. That's what usually happened. A girl seemed so perfect for him at first, but after a while, he'd start to see her catty, jealous or mean side. Kelsey didn't have any of those traits. While Maddie thought of her as a Disney princess, Jeff considered her a unicorn, that rare young woman who wasn't all about her phone, her friends, her looks and chasing boys.

Kelsey had goals, such as owning her own daycare center someday, which was why she'd jumped at the chance to be a nanny. The job had given her experience that would be invaluable to her career goals. She hadn't said much about her plans now that Mac McCarthy's busiest season was winding down. Would the family want her to continue, or would she be free to pursue employment elsewhere? Like in Tampa, perhaps.

He almost laughed out loud at the direction his thoughts had taken. As if that was going to happen. She loved the kids and working for the McCarthys, and they were clearly in need of her help with two newborns, an eighteen-month-old, a four-year-old and a six-year-old. Besides, he hadn't told her much about his past, which would probably be a deal breaker for whatever fictional plans he might be making that included her. She was way too good for him. Hell, she was too good for anyone.

Maddie returned with baby Mac and put him down on the floor with his toys while he had a drink and a snack. "I'll take Miss Evie, Jeff."

He handed the baby over to her mother.

"Thanks for the extra hands."

"No problem."

"You're good with her," Maddie said. "Do you have babies in your life?"

"Just my brother Owen's kids. I was the youngest in my family. They all like to tell me how they changed my diapers."

Maddie and Kelsey laughed.

"To hear the oldest three tell it, all they did was change the diapers of the rest of us."

"Your mom had *seven* children," Maddie said. "She needed all the help she could get. I can't conceive of two more than what I have now."

"I can't conceive of one, let alone five or seven," Jeff said.

"We all say that until the time comes, and it makes perfect sense," Maddie said, "although we didn't plan on five." She held up baby Evie and made her chortle with baby laughter. "These girls were a big surprise. The best kind."

The slider opened to admit Mac McCarthy, drawing a shriek from baby Mac, who ran to his dad on unsteady legs.

"See how it goes?" Maddie asked. "It's Mommy, Mommy, Mommy until Daddy gets home."

Mac picked up his baby son and gave him a hug and kiss. "That's because Daddy is the coolest."

Maddie rolled her eyes. "Tell them that when they're hungry."

"Mommy is never more popular than she is at mealtime."

"Are they talking about breastfeeding?" Jeff asked Kelsey.

She giggled at the face he made. "I believe they are."

"Should I wait in the car?"

Maddie laughed. "You're off duty, Kels. Thanks for everything today. You kids go have some fun."

"You're welcome." Kelsey transferred the other baby girl to her mother. "I'll see you in the morning."

"We'll be here, and happy birthday again."

"Thank you for the gifts. I have no idea how you pulled that off—along with cupcakes."

"I had help."

"It's appreciated."

"Have a great night."

"Happy birthday, Kelsey," Mac said.

"Thanks!"

Jeff waited for her to get her things together. They said their goodbyes and walked down the stairs to the car. "Happy birthday to you," he sang.

"Thank you. Maddie got me the most awesome beach bag, coverup and a new towel. I love them."

"Glad you had a fun day. We're going to the Lobster Pot for dinner."

"Yum. I just need to run home and change first. Emma puked on me earlier."

"You say that so casually, as if it's no big deal that you got puked on at work."

"It is no big deal," she said, laughing. "She's a baby. That's what they do."

"Babies are kinda gross."

"And very adorable."

"If you say so."

"Don't you want kids?"

"I mean, sure. Someday in the far-off future."

"I want a lot of kids."

"How many is a lot?"

"At least six."

He looked over at her, astounded. "*Seriously?*"

"Yes, seriously. I longed for more siblings, but my parents couldn't have any more after me, so it was just my brother and me, and he was quite a bit older. You were so lucky to have six others."

"Yeah, for sure. They're all great." He couldn't imagine life without them—and didn't want to. "So, six kids, huh?"

"A girl has to have a goal."

"You'd be a wonderful mother. You're so good with the kids."

"I adore them."

Those three little words confirmed what he already knew—she wasn't going anywhere any time soon.

But he was, and sooner rather than later.

STILL HOLDING HIS YOUNGER SON, Mac sat next to Maddie on the sofa and leaned in to kiss his wife. "How'd the day go?"

"Not bad, all things considered. Tiffany took Thomas and Hailey to the beach after school, so that helped. She's bringing them home after dinner."

"Did Hailey have a good day at preschool?"

"She did. Ned said she didn't even cry this time when he dropped her off."

"That's progress. And how about first grade?"

"Thomas and Ashleigh had a good day, too, but the teacher separated them, so they won't talk to each other all day."

Mac laughed. "That's probably a good idea."

"Tiffany said she's praying they don't decide to play Naked-Boy-Naked-Girl in school."

"Oh my God, don't even say it!"

"I know! That's what I said to Tiffany, too."

"They'd be remembered forever for that."

"I'd rather they be remembered for being outstanding students or athletes or anything else, actually."

"Same."

"Your wonderful mother was here earlier and made dinner," Maddie said.

"God bless the grandmothers."

"You said it. How was your day?"

"Good. Busy as always this time of year shutting down the marina for the winter and getting my ducks in a row for off-season construction work."

"The summer goes by too fast, but this year, I'm thankful for that because we need you here."

"I'm here, love."

"I'm so glad Kelsey agreed to stay on until the twins turn one. She's such a godsend."

"The kids love her."

"*I* love her. I might even love her more than I love you."

"Ouch."

"Sorry, but it's the truth."

Mac smiled at her. "I get it, babe."

"I don't really love her more than you, but it's close."

Still smiling, he kissed her and then the two sleeping babies as Mac squirmed in his arms, trying to get free.

"I've decided he needs a nickname," Maddie said. "I can't have two Macs in this house plus your dad. Every time I say Mac, your mom asks which one. I think we should call him Trip. I read somewhere that's the nickname for boys who are the third to have a name in their family."

"Trip. I like that. What do you think, son? Do you want your nickname to be Trip?"

"Aye ya ya," he said.

"I'd take that as a yes," Mac said.

"Sounded like one to me."

"How about I take over for a bit so you can take a break?"

"I can't recall the last shower I had, so that sounds good." She transferred the sleeping babies to him and got up, waving her arms to get the blood pumping through them again. "I'll be quick."

"Take your time. Daddy is on the job."

After she went upstairs, Mac made sure his son was content with his trucks and *Paw Patrol* on TV before he leaned his head back and closed his eyes.

Just for a minute.

CHAPTER 9

*J*ace was already gone when Cindy got up to get ready for work after their first night as roommates. She wondered where he'd gone so early, but then she remembered he attended an AA meeting every morning. As she did first thing every day, she took the pill that helped to prevent migraines and then showered. She did her hair and makeup, always determined to look like she belonged in the beauty business.

Ms. Laverne in Dallas had hammered home that point time and again, a memory that made Cindy smile as she always did when she thought of the years she'd spent at that eclectic salon full of wise women and salty customers. Cindy had learned more about life there than in any class-room, and she'd carried those lessons with her when she came to Gansett.

The one downside to working alone on the island was that she missed the camaraderie she'd had with her coworkers. She kept in touch with many of them by email and text and was always happy to hear the latest news.

On Gansett, she heard the latest news from her customers rather than her coworkers. She was never lonely at work with a steady stream of delightful people coming in for haircuts and color. Cindy's workday began with Abby McCarthy, who was round with pregnancy and moving slowly as she came up the stairs into the salon.

"Morning," Cindy said.

"Morning." Abby's face was flushed, and she was breathing hard. "I thought it would be a good idea to walk over from the Surf. It wasn't."

Cindy grinned at the face Abby made.

"Quadruplets are no joke."

"I can't even."

Abby sat in the chair and exhaled a deep breath. "I was worried I wouldn't fit in the chair anymore."

Cindy choked back a laugh as she covered Abby with a cape. "Stop! You're nowhere near not fitting."

"Yet. Talk to me in a month or two."

"I'll come to the house so you don't have to worry about fitting in the chair."

Abby's eyes immediately filled with tears. "You'd do that?"

"Of course I would. Any time."

"Everyone is so nice," she said softly. "Whenever I start to panic about having five babies under the age of two, I remember how lucky I am to live here."

"You'll have more help than you know what to do with."

"I'll need it all."

Cindy rested her hands on Abby's shoulders and met her gaze in the mirror. "What're we doing today?"

"A few inches off the back and clean up my layers?"

"You got it."

Forty-five minutes later, Cindy held the door for Abby as she went down the stairs to the sidewalk where her husband, Adam, was parked in a white BMW SUV, waiting for her. Cindy had suggested that Abby text him for a ride, so she didn't have to exert herself walking back to her shop at the Surf.

As Cindy swept Abby's dark hair off the floor, she thought about what it must be like to be expecting quadruplets. Abby had shared her fertility struggles, so Cindy had initially assumed the babies had been conceived via IVF or some other treatment, but Abby had said they'd been a total surprise.

Five children under age two.

Cindy shuddered at the thought of how intense that would be, but with the McCarthy and Callahan families nearby to help, they'd get through it.

Hope Martinez came in a few minutes later, bringing news from Martinez Lawn & Garden and an update on her mother-in-law, Marion Martinez, who'd been the inspiration for the island's elderly care center that was now named for her. Hope was married to Marion's son Paul.

"Marion is recovering from a bout of pneumonia. We thought we were going to lose her, but she rallied three days ago and is doing much better now, thankfully."

"I'm so glad to hear that."

"It was a rough couple of weeks. I feel so sorry for the guys," she said of Paul and his brother, Alex. "They've been through so much since she developed dementia."

"By all accounts, they've taken beautiful care of her."

"They have," Hope said with a sigh, "but it's so hard for them to see her living this way."

"I'm sure. My father's mother had it. We weren't super close to them like we were with my mother's parents, but I vividly remember her not recognizing us and how shocking that was."

"It's an awful disease. It steals so much from the patient and their families."

"And how is Miss Scarlett doing?" Cindy asked of Hope's baby daughter.

"She's delightful." Hope called up some photos on her phone and showed them to Cindy as she applied foils to Hope's hair. "She's riding shotgun with Daddy this morning so Mommy could get her hair done."

"Aw, she's so cute! Who does she look like?"

"Her daddy. She's all him."

"I thought so, but I wasn't sure."

"Oh yeah, she's a Martinez through and through."

"How does your son like being a big brother?"

"He's wonderful with her, but he's busy with school and sports and his best friends, Kyle and Jackson."

Cindy perked up a bit at the mention of Jace's sons. "You must have pictures of him, too."

"Yep." She called up a photo of Ethan. "That's his school picture, which he hates. He says he looks like he's going to church."

Cindy laughed. "He's a handsome boy."

"Yes, he is. Soon to be nine years old. I can't believe that. Here's one with his best friends, Jackson and Kyle. The three of them are inseparable."

Curiosity had Cindy looking closely at the two cute blond boys with missing front teeth and freckles on their noses. She could see Jace in them. "They're so cute."

"They are, but holy moly are they *busy* when they're together."

"I'll bet."

"It's dogs and kids and chaos when they're around, but we love it. I'm so happy Ethan has made some wonderful friends and loves living here as much as I do."

"I'm so glad it worked out so well for you guys."

"It did. You have no idea how well. I don't tell a lot of people this, but Ethan's dad is in prison. He was a high school coach who became involved with a student."

"Oh, Hope. I'm so sorry. That must've been horrible."

"It was the worst time in my life. He's due to be paroled later this year."

"Does he know where you are?"

"Yes. We reached out to him a while back about Paul adopting Ethan."

"What did he say?"

"He was willing if I send him a yearly update on how he's doing along with photos. We've been waiting for him to sign the paperwork to get it moving, but he hasn't done it yet. Dan Torrington contacted his lawyer last week to ask about the delay, and I just heard from him on the way over here, which is why I'm rambling on to you about it."

"I'm happy to listen. What did Dan say?"

"My ex-husband is asking to see Ethan once before he signs the papers. He wants a chance to apologize to him and to let him know how much he cares for him. He wants to do that in person."

"Oh wow."

"I know. I didn't see this wrinkle coming. My hands are shaking so badly, it's a wonder I can sit still enough for you to cut my hair."

"What're you going to do?"

"I'm meeting Dan at Rebecca's after this to talk about it."

"Have you told Paul?"

"Not yet. I want to talk to Dan first and see what he thinks I

73

should do."

"I'm so sorry you're dealing with such a stressful situation."

"Thank you for letting me dump it all over you."

"That's what I'm here for, along with cuts and color."

Hope laughed. "You're part therapist."

"The woman who taught me everything I know about this business always said we were therapists as well as beauticians. What's your gut telling you to do?"

"I guess I have to let him see Ethan so we can be done with it."

"Perhaps you should let Ethan decide. He's old enough to make that call, isn't he?"

"Yes, I suppose he is. I'm preconditioned to want to protect him from this stuff, but you're right. It should be up to him."

"I have no doubt you'll figure it out and do what's best for him."

"Thanks for letting me air it out. I was losing it when I came in."

"You hid it well."

"Thinking about this stuff stirs up all the PTSD from when it first happened."

"I understand that."

"I guess you would," Hope said, her gaze meeting Cindy's in the mirror.

One of the benefits of living in Dallas had been that no one there knew her family's story. On Gansett, everyone knew. Cindy had found more comfort in that than anything else, but she'd been programmed by her father to be embarrassed about people knowing their business.

"I hope it's okay to say that," Hope added.

"It is what it is, you know?"

"I sure do, but everyone here is so thrilled to see your mom remarried to Charlie."

"No one deserves it more than they do."

"We all do. I hope this island spins its magic for you the way it did for your mom and me and so many others."

Cindy smiled at her. "I guess we'll see, won't we?"

Hope slid into a booth at Rebecca's and accepted a coffee from the owner. "Thank you, Rebecca."

"Just you?"

"I'm meeting Dan Torrington."

"I'll get another mug for him."

"Thanks."

Dan came in a few minutes later. His magnetic personality and dark good looks drew the attention of every person in the diner. Smiling, he slid in across from her. "Nice to see you."

"You, too. Thanks for making the time."

"I was in bad need of some caffeine."

"And a grilled corn muffin." Rebecca put the muffin on the table and poured his coffee.

"I might be a bit of a regular," Dan said with a sheepish grin.

"Anything to eat, Hope?"

"I'm good. Thanks, Rebecca."

"Just when we thought we had this all worked out, huh?" Dan said as he devoured the muffin like he hadn't eaten in weeks.

"I know! I can't believe he's throwing this at us at the last minute, but I suppose I shouldn't be surprised."

"You have a lot of anger toward him, and rightfully so. But asking a man, even one who's made huge, terrible, unforgivable mistakes, to sign away his paternal rights—permanently—is a big deal."

"So, you're not surprised by this."

"Not as much as you are. I've seen it before in cases like this, with a parent asked to do the right thing by their kid balking at the last minute."

Hope's stomach ached with worry. "Do you think he'll still go through with it?"

"He's already agreed to Paul adopting Ethan. This is one final step to get us where we want to be."

"I spoke to a friend about it, and she said it ought to be Ethan's decision."

"I tend to agree with your friend. He's old enough at this point to have some say in it."

"Ugh." Hope dropped her head into her hands, filled with despair at the thought of having to broach this subject with her son. "I hate that this is happening. Why can't he just leave us alone to live the lives we had to make for ourselves after he ruined everything?"

"All I can say is that you're asking him to legally terminate his paternal rights, and he's agreed to do so. Him asking to see Ethan once is a request, not a demand. I think that matters."

"Why do you have to be so sensible about this?"

Dan laughed. "That's my job—to get you to the finish line as painlessly as possible. This isn't what you wanted to hear, and I'm sorry about that, but it's nothing more than a wrinkle."

"It's going to be way more than that if it upsets my son's happy new life. Or mine."

"Don't let it, Hope. He's asking for an hour with Ethan. After that, he's out of the picture for good. That seems like a small price to pay toward the ultimate goal."

She agreed with him intellectually. Emotionally, however, the thought of seeing him even once was appalling to her. "I'll talk to Paul and Ethan."

"Let me know what you decide."

"If we say no, do you think he'll stop the adoption?"

"If it comes from Ethan, I don't see that happening. He's asked to see his son. If his son doesn't wish to see him, he can't exactly force him, especially with you having sole custody. Can he get vindictive and decide to withhold support of the adoption? Yes, that's possible, but from what his attorney has told me, he's concerned about Ethan's best interests."

"Then he ought to leave him alone."

"I think he will. After he sees him."

"Thank you for your advice, as always."

"I'm happy to help, but I hated having to call you with this news earlier. I knew it would be upsetting to you."

"It helps to know that you don't think he's going to pull the plug on the adoption. I'll talk to Paul and figure out our next step."

"I'm here if I can help."

"Thanks again, Dan." Hope signaled for Rebecca and insisted on paying their check over Dan's objections. "The least I can do is buy you a coffee and a corn muffin." She texted Paul to ask if he could pick her up in town.

Ms. Scarlett and I are on the way.

Hope couldn't wait to see them. Whatever happened next in this situation, she was thankful to have Paul's support as well as Dan's.

CHAPTER 10

*A*fter the AA meeting, Mallory, Quinn and Mason invited Jace to join them for coffee at the diner. Jace had realized over weeks of meetings that Mallory, Quinn and Mason were close friends, so he was honored to now be part of their group.

The others said hello to Hope Martinez and Dan Torrington and introduced them to Jace as they were leaving.

"How did that room-for-rent thing work out?" Mallory asked when they were seated.

"Very well. I'm now Cindy Lawry's roommate."

"Oh, that's great. Cindy's the best."

"Yes, she is. I'd already known her for a while. She comes into the Beachcomber for dinner a few times a week."

"That's a nice coincidence," Mallory said, smiling as she rested her chin on her upturned hand.

"Watch out," Quinn said. "I can tell when my wife has matchmaking on her mind."

"You hush," Mallory said. "Don't listen to him, Jace. I'm just saying Cindy is a lovely person."

Jace grinned, amused by her shamelessness. "I'm already aware of that, but thank you for the confirmation." To Quinn, he said, "Is this why she invited me for coffee?"

"Possibly, although we've been saying for a while now that we needed to get you to come with us, so the timing may or may not be coincidental."

"Good to know." Jace's phone chimed with a text from Seamus. He picked up the phone to read it.

Mate, we're finally going through the things that came from Lisa's place, and there are boxes with your name. Thought you might want them.

Yes, I do, Jace replied, surprised to hear she'd kept anything of his—and to have Seamus call him "mate." *When is a good time to come by?*

Assume you'd like to see the boys, so maybe around 3:30?

He had to work at five, so he wouldn't have much time with them, but he'd take what he could get. *That works. Thank you.*

See you then.

Jace put down the phone. "Sorry about that."

"Everything okay?" Mallory asked.

"That was Seamus. He found some boxes of mine in Lisa's stuff and asked if I wanted them."

"Oh, that's good, I guess. Right?"

"It's a chance to see the boys, so yeah, it's good."

"Is it awful for you to have them living with people you don't really know?"

"Mallory," Quinn said with a note of warning in his voice.

"It's fine," Jace said. "And no, it's not awful. Seamus and Carolina are great people, and by all accounts, they've been wonderful to my sons."

"But?" Mallory asked.

Jace shrugged. "No buts. They were there for them when I couldn't be, and I'll always appreciate that."

"What about you, though?"

"What about me? My mistakes cost me the chance to raise my kids. I don't blame Lisa for making the choices she did when faced with a terminal illness. It wasn't like she was going to call me in prison and ask if I'd become an upstanding citizen in the years since she'd seen me last."

"I just want you to know that there're people who feel for you in this situation," Mallory said, "and I'm one of them."

"I appreciate that, but I'm not looking to upset any apple carts around here. The boys are settled and doing as well as can be expected after losing their mom. I want what's best for them, and that's Seamus and Carolina."

"This may not be the right thing to say, but I'm going to say it anyway."

"Why am I not surprised?" Quinn asked with a grin for Mallory.

She rolled her eyes at Quinn. "You're still a young guy, Jace. There's time for you to have more kids while you continue to play whatever role you can in the lives of your sons."

"You're right, but that's not something I'm thinking about now. I'm just trying to rebuild my life and see my kids occasionally. Those are my only priorities."

"And stay sober," Mason added.

"That, too. In fact, that's first on the list, because nothing else is possible without that."

"That's right," Mason said. "I'm glad to hear you say that. I find myself rooting for you, too. Maybe not as cheerleaderly as Mallory, but I'm on Team Jace."

"Cheerleaderly?" Mallory asked him, brow raised, while Quinn cracked up.

Mason waved pretend pom-poms. "Rah, rah, rah."

Jace laughed at their banter. "I appreciate the support, you guys. It means a lot. It's been a long time since I had friends."

Mallory reached across the table to put her hand on top of Jace's. "You have friends, and we're pulling for you."

"Thank you."

After he parted with the others on the sidewalk outside the diner, Jace walked home to change before heading to the gym. Working out had saved his sanity in prison, and it was a routine he'd stuck to since his release. He ran into the same guys there every day, and they spotted each other through a series of lifting sequences that kept up the muscles he'd built in prison.

Billy, the owner of the gym, as well as Duke from the tattoo studio and Seamus's cousin, Shannon, who worked on the ferries, were some of the regulars. Over the last few weeks, they'd become friends, too.

Life on Gansett was full of a rich array of people he interacted with every day, most of whom had no idea he was an ex-con. They didn't know he'd screwed up his life so badly that other people were raising his sons, and he hoped to keep it that way.

It'd been a relief to go somewhere that no one knew about his past, which was why it had taken him weeks to share his story at the AA meeting. He didn't want his new friends to view him differently. He was thankful that after sharing his story, he felt even closer to the meeting regulars. They'd had their own struggles and didn't judge others the way those who hadn't been through what they had often did. People heard *ex-con*, *prison*, *felon*, *drug addict* and automatically assumed he was a bad person. He wasn't. He'd made mistakes he deeply regretted, but those mistakes didn't make him a bad person.

As he was leaving the gym, his phone rang with a call from a 401 number he didn't recognize.

"Hello?"

"Is this Jace?"

"Yeah, who's this?"

"Mac McCarthy. I run a construction company on the island. My sister Mallory told me you've done some plumbing?"

"Yes, but I'm not licensed or anything."

"On an island, we can't afford to be picky. Would you be interested in some work?"

"Sure, as long as I'm free by four to work at the Beachcomber at night."

"We can accommodate that. Can you meet me at the old alpaca farm on North Point Road on Tuesday around noon? If you head out on the west side, you'll eventually see the sign for the farm."

"That works. I'll call you if I can't find it."

"Sounds good. See you then and thank you."

"Thank *you*. I appreciate the call."

"You got it."

The line went dead, and Jace stood in the gym parking lot as the September sun beat down on him, marveling at the way things worked around here. He certainly knew the McCarthy name and had seen the signs for their marina and hotel in North Harbor, but he hadn't expected a call from Mac McCarthy about work.

He owed Mallory a big thank-you tomorrow morning for referring him to her brother. Walking the short distance to his new home, Jace felt more settled than he ever had before. It'd been years since his life was as well ordered and uncomplicated as it was in this beautiful place. A man could put down roots here, surrounded by new friends who didn't know all his dirty secrets. And even if they did know, they didn't care.

Six months after being released from prison, he was still figuring out who he was in this new life he was creating for himself. His only goal had been to locate Lisa and the boys, which had taken some time. And then he'd learned that Lisa had died, and his boys were being raised by her friends. That's when he'd contacted an attorney, who'd helped him navigate the thorny path to contacting the boys' guardians.

He understood he'd shocked Seamus and Carolina when he'd reached out via the attorney and that they would've been perfectly within their rights to tell him to go to hell. But that wasn't what they'd done, and he'd be forever thankful for the arrangement that allowed him to see his sons —not as their father, but as a friend of Seamus's—until they were older and further removed from the trauma of losing their mother.

This wasn't the time to introduce their long-lost father or to explain where he'd been all this time or why he hadn't come when their mother was sick. He couldn't bear to think of when they would learn the truth about him and his past or how terribly he'd let them down when they were babies. Would they forgive him? He wouldn't blame them if they didn't.

Those thoughts were still on his mind later that afternoon when he jumped on the bike he'd borrowed from a colleague at the Beachcomber and rode to Seamus and Carolina's house. Already, there was a September chill in the air that had been warm only a week ago. He remembered his mother saying it was like someone flipped a switch on Labor Day, and summer in Rhode Island became autumn overnight. That was especially true on Gansett with the ocean breeze cooling things considerably.

Island roads that had been clogged with traffic and mopeds during the holiday weekend were now clear and far less treacherous for a bicyclist. When he turned the bike into the driveway that led to Seamus and Carolina's place, he heard the delighted voices of two boys released from the confines of school and the barking of their beloved Burpy, who was always with them.

Seamus, who'd driven the boys home in his Gansett Island Ferry Company truck, waved to Jace when he saw him there, gesturing for him to come in. Jace would never have the words to tell the Irishman raising his sons how thankful he was for the grace he'd shown him.

Having recently turned seven and eight years old, Kyle and Jackson were now in second and third grades. Both were missing teeth, and Kyle had a scab on his chin. They were blond and freckle-faced, just as he and Jess had been at their age. They reminded him so much of him and Jess, giving him a pang of regret and longing for the brother he'd lost so senselessly.

Kyle saw him first and came running over. "Mr. Jace, look at the picture I drew in art class today. It's Burpy!" The little boy held up the paper with the drawing.

"I can see that. It looks just like him."

Kyle looked up at him with big golden-brown eyes that reminded Jace of Lisa. "You really think so?"

"I do. For sure."

Kyle ran off to find Jackson, yelling as he went. "I told you it *does, too*, look like him. Mr. Jace said it!"

"You really saw Burpy in that drawing?" Seamus asked, brow raised.

"I saw the start of what might eventually be Burpy."

Seamus grunted out a laugh. "Well played, mate. Boys! Get your backpacks and go inside to do your homework and get a snack."

With much grumbling about the stupidity of homework, the boys returned to Seamus's truck to get their backpacks and ran inside, with Burpy following them.

"They're like an energy tornado after being trapped in school all day." Seamus gestured for Jace to follow him to a barnlike structure about a hundred yards from the main house. He rolled open a huge door and flipped on overhead lights that illuminated a vast space used for storage. A musty smell filled the air. "Caro and I have had good intentions about cleaning out all this junk, but with the two tornadoes underfoot these days, that job is taking a lot longer than it should've. We figured we should do something with the boxes that came from Lisa's place, though."

He pointed to them. "The ones on the left have your name on them. The rest are hers. Caro went through it all and set aside some clothes, photos and other personal items the boys might want someday. Do you know of any family that might want the rest of her things?"

"She was estranged from her family after they told her not to marry me." He glanced at Seamus. "Turns out they were right."

"I wonder if they're aware that she passed. Dan Torrington would know. He handled her estate."

"I met him in town earlier. I could check with him and see if there's anyone who might want her things."

"That'd help. Thanks."

"I'll let you know what I find out." Jace opened one of the boxes that contained clothes he hadn't seen in years.

"We can put them in my truck, and I'll give you a lift to town when I go back to work."

"Thanks." The two men carried the ten boxes to Seamus's truck. "Can I ask you something?" Jace said when the last of the boxes had been loaded.

"Sure," Seamus said, a little wary, as he always was around Jace.

"Do you know where Lisa is buried?"

Seamus nodded. "She's in the town cemetery. I could show you if you'd like."

"I'd appreciate that."

"Let's spend a few minutes with the boys first, if you have time."

"I do, and I'd love to hang with them."

They went inside to join the boys, who were seated at the kitchen table. Carolina supervised snack time, which consisted of carrot sticks and cheese cubes with milk for Kyle and water for Jackson.

"What's this?" Seamus asked. "No cookies?"

Carolina gave him a withering look. "Not until they eat the healthy stuff."

"Should we help them out, Jace?" Seamus asked, his eyes twinkling with mischief as he snagged a carrot from the napkin in front of each boy.

Jace did the same as the boys grinned at them.

"Look, Caro, the boys ate all their carrots," Seamus said as the boys giggled. "I think that earns them a cookie."

"You guys think you're so sneaky," Caro said as she gave each of the boys a chocolate chip cookie that they devoured.

"What about us?" Seamus asked of himself and Jace. "We don't deserve cookies, too?"

"I suppose you can have one since you ate their carrots."

"We did not!" Seamus said, making the boys giggle madly.

Their laughter was such a wonderful sound.

"You're like an evil leprechaun," Carolina told her husband.

"She likes to give me sweet compliments," Seamus told Jace.

"I see that," Jace said, amused by them.

"It's how she tells me she loves me," Seamus said, stealing a little block of cheese from Kyle.

"You have to be on top of your game when you're married to an Irish charmer," Carolina said.

"Indeed, you do, love. What's the homework situation, lads?"

"I have a *massive* math worksheet," Kyle said glumly.

"I have to do spelling," Jackson said.

"I'll trade you math for spelling," Kyle said.

"No trading," Seamus said. "Just get it done so you can play outside for a while."

"Are you going back to the office?" Jackson asked.

Seamus nodded. "For about another hour or so, and then I'll be home to wrangle boys."

Jace envied him fiercely, but he'd never let on to that. How he wished he'd made better choices so he could be the one to wrangle his own sons.

"Will you come back to play again soon, Mr. Jace?" Jackson asked.

"I'd love to. You let me know when, and I'll be here."

"We'll tell Seamus to text you," Kyle said.

"Perfect," he said, unreasonably touched that the boys wanted to spend time with him.

"Welp, we'd better get going. Mr. Jace needs to get to work, and so do I." Seamus ruffled two blond heads and kissed Carolina on the way out the door.

"I'll see you again soon," Jace said to the boys.

He tossed the bike into the back of Seamus's truck and got in the passenger side. "Thanks for the lift."

"Woulda taken you a while to get all that stuff home on a bike."

"For sure."

"You got a place to keep it?"

"I just rented a room in a house in town for the off-season. I'm living with Cindy Lawry."

"She's good people. All the Lawrys are."

"She's great. We've known each other awhile from her coming into the Beachcomber."

Seamus glanced over at him. "She's to be handled with kid gloves. You know what that means, right?"

"I do."

Seamus shook his head. "No one in this town would take kindly to someone hurting her."

"I like her a lot. I'd never hurt her."

"See that you don't."

The comment put Jace on edge, but he supposed he ought to expect a warning like that from one of the people on the island who knew his story—and Cindy's. Right before they reached town, Seamus took a left turn that led to the cemetery. He drove through the gates and hung another left.

Jace took note of two other turns before Seamus parked along a row of headstones and got out of the truck.

"Are you coming?" he asked Jace before he closed the driver's door.

"Yeah." Jace followed him through several rows of stones before Seamus stopped next to a flat stone with Lisa's name, the dates of her birth and death and the words DEVOTED MOTHER engraved below the dates. The sight of her name engraved in stone brought tears to Jace's eyes as he squatted for a closer look. With his left hand, he brushed away some dirt. "Did a lot of people come to the service?"

"Hundreds."

"That's good. She deserved that." He pulled a couple of weeds near the stone. "Do you bring the boys here?"

"We've come a few times, but only when they've asked. We don't force it on them."

Jace stood. "They seem to be doing really well."

"They are. Still have a rough moment or two, usually at bedtime, when the grief catches up to them. Jackson told me he's afraid he's going to forget her."

"God, what did you say to that?"

"I told him he'll carry her in his heart for the rest of his life, and even if he can't remember every detail, he'll never forget how much she loved him."

"That's nice, Seamus. Did it seem to help?"

"For that moment, but there'll be others, and we'll keep reminding them that their mum loved them more than anything. Because she did. They were her only concern after she was diagnosed."

"I hate that I wasn't here with them when that happened, that I haven't been there for them at all."

"I'm sure that's a bitter pill, but you're here now, and that'll matter to them."

"You have no idea what it means to me to be able to see them, even if it's just as a friend."

"I think I know. They're great kids. I'd be bereft if I couldn't see them every day."

"You and Carolina are just what they need right now. I wouldn't have had an answer as good as yours for Jackson."

"I appreciate you saying so. They mean the world to us."

"I understand this arrangement of ours is a lot to ask of you—"

"It was at first, before I had the chance to get to know you. I'm not losing any sleep over you anymore."

"I'm glad to hear that. I wouldn't want you to worry about me. I'm not going to disrupt their lives or yours, but I'm deeply grateful to be able to see them."

"Their fall baseball league is starting up soon if you want to come to the games."

"I'd love to. Thank you for asking me."

"No problem. I'll text you the schedule."

"Thanks. Will they think it's odd that a friend of yours is coming to their games?"

"I don't think so. They like you. I could say I invited you to come, and that would be enough of an explanation for them."

"Is it going to bite us both in the ass someday that we weren't straight with them from the get-go?"

"I really hope not. I'm trusting my gut that this isn't the right time to tell them the truth about you, so soon after their lives were upended. I hope I'm right about that."

"I think you are. The truth will keep until they're old enough to handle the full story about why I disappeared from their lives—and their mother's."

"Let's hope we're both right about that."

CHAPTER 11

Cindy had felt it coming on all day Friday as she cut hair and tried to make conversation with customers while fighting the nausea that always accompanied a migraine. By the time she shut the door behind the last customer and flipped the Open sign to Closed, she was about to pass out from the pain.

Though she took a daily preventive medication, the migraines still struck out of nowhere, although not as frequently as they had before the daily meds. She forced herself to sweep the floor, turn off the computer, lock the door and walk home as carefully as she could, trying not to jostle her throbbing head. *Thank God for sunglasses*, she thought as the afternoon sun lit up the downtown area.

As she got closer to home, she feared she might vomit on the public sidewalk, so she picked up the pace. That made everything hurt more than it already did. Her preference when in the throes of a migraine was to move as little as possible. She'd made it to her front yard when she lost her lunch in the bushes outside.

The act of vomiting was akin to a knife to the skull, and for a second, she feared she might faint. That'd happened before.

Above her, the front door opened, and then Jace was there, holding her hair back as she vomited.

"No, you don't have to…"

MARIE FORCE

"Shhh, it's fine. What can I do?"

"Nothing," she whispered because anything louder might've killed her.

"Let me help you inside."

She wanted to tell him she could get herself inside, but his strong arms around her felt too good as she rested her splitting head on his chest.

He lifted her gently, seeming to get that she needed that.

Cindy closed her eyes, only for a second, and startled awake when he lowered her onto her bed. Then he closed the blinds, which was just what she needed. She wanted to ask him how he knew to do that but posing the question would take energy she didn't have.

Jace left the room and returned a minute later with a tall glass of water, the cold compress she kept in the freezer for when the headaches struck, a plastic bowl/puke bucket and a throw blanket from the living room that he put over her. "What else do you need?" he asked in a whisper.

"Meds in the bathroom cabinet." She told him the brand name of the drug, and he got the bottle for her.

"How many?"

"Two, please."

He put the tablets in her palm and held the water for her to drink. "Anything else?"

"There's a Coke in the fridge. Would you mind getting that for me? Sometimes a little caffeine helps.

"Coming right up." He returned a minute later with the mini-can of Coke and a straw that he held for her while she took a few sips.

"Thank you so much, Jace. I really appreciate this."

"No problem. Can I get you anything else?"

"No, thanks."

"I have to go to work. Is there someone I should call?"

"No, that's okay."

"Will you be all right alone?"

"I'm fine as long as I don't move."

"Text if you want me to bring some food home."

"I will. Thanks."

"Sure."

She could tell he didn't want to go. "It's okay. I deal with this by myself all the time. Don't worry."

"I will worry, and I'll miss you at the bar tonight. You owe me a game of checkers when you're feeling better."

"Sounds good." Cindy closed her eyes because she couldn't bear to keep them open for another second. "See you later."

That was the last thought she had until she heard the door open and close, which startled her, as she was accustomed to living alone.

Jace was back.

He knocked softly on her bedroom door. "How're you feeling?" he asked in the same whisper as before.

It took her a couple of seconds to realize it was hours later and she felt much better. Thankfully, this headache wouldn't be a multiday event. "Better, I think." She needed to pee urgently but couldn't tell him that. Rather, she sat up slowly, closing her eyes when the room spun.

"Let me help you." He was there with an arm around her and a strong body to lean against as he helped her to the bathroom without having to be told what she needed.

After she took care of business, she stood at the sink and splashed cold water on her face, trying to shake off the sickening malaise the migraines always left behind after one of their attacks. She ought to be used to the routine by now, but it was the usual shock to her system to be felled out of nowhere by one of the monster headaches.

"You okay in there?" Jace asked from outside the door.

"Yeah. I'm coming."

"Take your time. Just checking."

She brushed her hair and teeth, and when she felt presentable, she opened the door and found him leaning against a wall in the hallway, checking his phone. He put it in his back pocket and reached out a hand to her.

"I'm okay."

"Let me help you anyway."

Because he was so solid and smelled so good, she was more than happy to have him help her to the sofa. He disappeared for a second and returned with the throw blanket he'd brought into the bedroom earlier, as well as the unfinished Coke. "You want me to put this on ice for you?"

"Do you mind?"

"I'm a bartender. If there's one thing I can do, it's ice."

She smiled at how cute and funny he was, not to mention thoughtful.

He returned with the icy glass of Coke. "Are you hungry? I picked up a pizza at Mario's earlier, but I don't want to heat it up if the smell will make you sick."

"Pizza actually sounds good if you have a slice to spare."

"I do. Coming right up."

Bringing two plates, he handed her one and then sat on the sofa next to her. From under his arm, he retrieved two paper towels.

"Excellent service as usual. Thank you."

"My pleasure."

Cindy's mouth watered at the smell of the pizza. She swallowed a small bite, hoping it would stay down. When the first bite landed without a problem, she took a second. "Now tell me how you know all the steps to take for a migraine."

"My grandmother had them. She trained me on what to do at an early age. I'm so sorry you get them, too."

"Thanks," she said, sighing. "They've been the bane of my existence since I was about eight and got the first one. I was in school when it came on. I thought I was dying."

"That must've been terrifying."

"It was. My mom took me to the doctor. He diagnosed migraines and put me on medicine that didn't always work that well. I started getting them a lot, like once or twice a month, and missed a ton of school. That was a problem for my dad. He made me go, even when I could barely function."

"Why would he do that?" Jace asked, sounding appalled.

"Because he believed in bucking up and not giving in to weaknesses."

"A migraine isn't a weakness, but of course you know that. What the hell was wrong with him?"

"So many things it would take me all night to tell you."

"Is it okay to say I already can't stand him?"

She laughed and immediately regretted it when her head throbbed. "It's okay. No one can stand him, least of all his ex-wife and children." Cindy glanced at the beer bottle he was holding. "Are you allowed to have that?"

"It's nonalcoholic, but alcohol was never my problem."

"Is it okay that I asked that?"

"You can ask me anything you want. My life is an open book these days. It's recommended that we stay away from all of it, not just our drug of choice."

"Is that where you were this morning?"

Nodding, he said, "I go to the AA meeting at eight." He raised his bottle in toast to the statement. "They don't have Narcotics Anonymous here, so AA keeps me working the program. After that, I went to coffee with some friends from the meeting and then to the gym. Before work, I went out to Seamus and Carolina's and got to see my boys and picked up those boxes." He pointed to a corner of the living room.

Cindy hadn't noticed them.

"They were with the stuff that came from my ex-wife's house after she passed away. Seamus also showed me where she's buried."

"Was it hard to be there?"

He nodded. "Seeing her name on a stone was so final, you know?"

"I'm sorry for your loss."

"It wasn't really my loss."

"Wasn't it, though? You were married to her when everything went wrong. Did you ever see her again?"

"Nope. The only contact I ever had with her was when I received divorce papers in prison that also gave her full custody of our kids. Since I was serving a ten-year sentence, I signed the papers."

"What about you?"

"That didn't matter. I wanted the best for them, and me being out of their lives was for the best."

"You made a mistake, Jace. You shouldn't have to pay for that for the rest of your life."

"What I did was more than a mistake. I'll pay for the choices I made back then for the rest of my life because my brother is dead, and I'll always be a convicted felon."

"That doesn't have to define you, though. You can write a whole new chapter for yourself now that you're out of prison and starting over."

"Are you always this positive and optimistic?" he asked, smiling.

"Not always. That mindset took some work, but it's how I try to look at things these days."

"It's a good way to look at things. Are you happy here on the island?"

"I love it. It's my favorite place in the whole world. We looked forward to the summer here all year long. My grandmother would put us to work the minute we arrived, but we didn't care. We were so damned glad to be here."

"That sounds like a great way to spend a summer."

"It was awesome. We've always loved Gansett. It's great to have everyone here now, except for my brother Josh."

"Where's he?"

"In Virginia. We're trying to get him to come to the island, but he's dating someone there, and it's going well." She shrugged. "Six out of seven is pretty good."

"I'd say so." After he devoured three pieces of pizza to her one, he stretched his long legs out in front of him and crossed them at the ankles. "Tell me more about the others. I've met them, but I don't know all the details."

"Owen is the oldest. He's married to Laura McCarthy. They have three kids, Holden, Jonathan and Joanna, and are now the owners of the Sand & Surf."

"I love that place. The building is so unique."

"It really is the coolest building on the island. Julia and Katie are next —they're fraternal twins. Katie is married to Laura's brother, Shane, and yes, that's I'm still sure that's legal," she added with a teasing smile, recalling the night they'd discussed it at the bar.

"So you guys have told me, but I'm not convinced."

"Most people question it when I tell them how my brother and sister married a brother and a sister. You know what's so cool about it?"

"What's that?"

"Their kids will be double cousins and genetic siblings."

"Wow, that's wild."

"I know! Then there's Julia, who's an amazing singer and piano player."

"She plays at Stephanie's, right?"

"That's her."

"I've seen her a few times. She's so talented. And her little dog is cute."

"Pupwell. He's the cutest. She's living with and engaged to Deacon Taylor, the harbor master, and they're deliriously happy. Next is me and then Josh, John and Jeff, who has a job in Tampa that starts in October."

"Seven kids. That must've been fun."

"It could be. At times." Like when her dad had been deployed. "They're my best friends."

"You're lucky to have them."

"I'm sorry. I wasn't thinking when I said that."

"It's okay." He placed his hand on top of hers as if it was perfectly routine for him to touch her. But if the way her body reacted to him touching her was any indication, there was nothing routine about it. "I love that they're your best friends. Diana was a bit older than us, so we didn't hang out much, but Jess was my best friend, until it all went so wrong."

"I'm sorry that happened to you—and to him."

"Me, too. We should both be married with kids, houses, mortgages, car payments, Sunday dinners with the parents." He shrugged. "Living the dream."

"Was he married, too?"

Jace nodded. "With a baby on the way that neither of us ever got to meet."

"You could still live the dream, you know. It's not too late."

"You're the second person to remind me of that."

"How old are you?"

"Thirty. What about you?"

"Twenty-eight."

"Never been married?" he asked.

"Never even came close."

"I find that hard to believe. You're so pretty and sweet and kind."

Cindy fanned her face, which suddenly felt warm. "That's a lot of compliments in one sentence."

"I've got more where those came from."

"Is that so?"

"Uh-huh."

"Like what?"

"Smart. Funny. Sexy. Good at checkers but possibly cheats."

She didn't hear anything after sexy. "Are you, um, flirting with your new roommate by any chance?"

"What if I was? Would that be all right?"

"As long as it doesn't make things weird between us."

"Does it feel weird to you?"

"Not at all."

"Me either. Haven't we been kinda flirting at the bar for weeks now?"

"I wasn't sure if that was flirting or your usual routine with customers."

"That was just for you."

His blunt honesty flustered her. She felt her face heat as he kept his gaze on her, seemingly without blinking. "Oh," she said, her brain wiped clean of thoughts that weren't focused on his sexy lips.

"That's all you've got?" he asked, smiling. "Oh?"

"I, uh, well... I'm glad it wasn't just me."

"What wasn't just you?"

"The flirting."

"Definitely not just you. I find myself watching the door, waiting for you to arrive to brighten my night. And when I found out you were the one looking for a roommate, I wasn't sure I should move in here because of the crush I already had on you."

"I wasn't sure I should let you move in for the same reason."

Flashing a lethally sexy grin, he said, "And yet, here we are."

"And yet."

For a long, charged moment, neither of them said anything. And then he turned their hands, linked their fingers and gave her hand a squeeze.

"Do you promise that if we do... *this*, it won't be weird here?" she asked hesitantly.

"I promise, although," he said, his expression darkening in an instant, "your family probably wouldn't approve of you going out with me or even living with an ex-con."

"They know."

"They do?"

She nodded. "My mom is married to an ex-con."

That clearly shocked him.

"Although, he was falsely imprisoned for fourteen years for a crime he didn't commit and has since been exonerated. His stepdaughter, Stephanie, worked for all that time to get him out."

"Is your stepfather Charlie Grandchamp?"

"Yes, why?"

"I knew him. Inside. Wow," Jace said on a long exhale. "I had no idea he was living here and married to your mom."

"Don't forget my father is also in prison. As an air force general, he was respected and revered by everyone, even people who knew the truth about how he abused his wife and children. That finally caught up to him just over a year ago, when he was convicted, finally, of assaulting my mother. He nearly killed her that time. So, you don't need to worry about the Lawrys judging you for things you did years ago, especially since you're all about leading a more productive life now." She glanced at him. "You are all about that, right?"

"God, yes. I never want to go back to who or what I was back then. I lost everything that mattered to me in the span of five minutes."

"Then we shouldn't have a problem." Cindy forced herself to tug her hand free and stand so she wouldn't do something rash like kiss him. "I have an early morning. Will you lock up?"

"Sure."

"Thanks for the pizza, the ice pack and everything else."

"I'm glad you're feeling better."

"Me, too. Good night."

"Night."

CHAPTER 12

For a long time after Cindy went to bed, Jace remained seated on the sofa, thinking about what she'd told him about her father and stepfather. It surprised him that Cindy would be connected to men who'd been inside—or who were still inside. He'd known about her dad, but learning that her stepfather was Charlie Grandchamp stunned him. That guy had been a legend in prison. Everyone had revered him.

When Jace thought about little Cindy being forced to go to school with a debilitating migraine, it made him happy to know her father was locked up where he belonged. Earlier, when he'd heard a noise from the yard, he'd been shocked to find her bent over the bushes. Only when he'd gotten closer had he realized she was vomiting, and when she'd looked up at him, she'd been pale as a ghost. Even her lips had lost all color, and her eyes had been filled with pain he'd recognized right away as a migraine.

He'd hated seeing her suffer and had worried about her all night at work, especially when she hadn't answered any of the texts he'd sent checking on her.

She emerged from her bedroom, holding her phone. "Sorry I didn't answer your texts. I was out cold."

"That's okay. I'm just glad you're better."

"Thanks for checking on me."

"Sure. Sleep well."

"You, too."

Jace wasn't sure how he'd sleep at all with thoughts of her filling his heart and mind. He'd noticed the way she'd stared at his lips as if debating whether she should take what she clearly wanted—what they both wanted. He'd been *this* close to making the decision for them when she'd abruptly pulled away, ending the charged moment.

It'd been so long since he'd dated anyone that he'd almost forgotten how it was done. Unlike most guys fresh out of prison, he hadn't run right out and slept with the first willing female. No, he'd been too busy trying to figure out where his wife and kids had gone and looking for a job, a place to live and acquiring a cell phone, as required by his probation officer.

Sex had been the last thing on his mind until Cindy Lawry started coming into his bar every night, making him want things he hadn't had in years. He'd understood early in their friendship that she was special and wasn't the kind of woman he could use to sate years' worth of pent-up desire and then move on. More than once, he'd thought about finding someone else to take care of the pent-up issue, but his thoughts kept coming back to Cindy.

She didn't know she was the reason he hadn't gotten busy with someone else. It seemed the only woman he wanted was her. When and how that had happened was a mystery to him, but now that he knew their crush ran both ways, he was determined to see where it might lead.

In the back of his mind, he was aware that he had no business wanting a woman who'd endured the things she had. Cindy deserved a nice, sweet, uncomplicated guy who could give her the life she deserved, not a jaded ex-con, recovering addict with kids being raised by other people because their father was in jail when their mother died.

If he was any kind of man, he would stay away from Cindy and find someone else to focus his interest on. Except... He'd tried that and just kept coming back to her time and again. Once, he'd even gone out with a coworker from the Beachcomber, fully intending to invite her back to his room at the end of the night. But when the time had come, he couldn't summon the interest because his mind was so full of thoughts about the one he really wanted.

And now she was his roommate.

He'd wanted nothing more than to call in sick to work earlier so he could take care of her, but he couldn't afford to do that in the off-season, especially with rent to pay now.

His probation officer, Darrell, had been after him to figure out his plan now that his summer job was petering out to occasional shifts. After he talked to Mac about the job on Tuesday, he would report to Darrell with his new address and, hopefully, a more solid job.

Cindy came out of her room, holding a glass. She'd changed into a tank and short shorts that put her full breasts and long legs on full display.

Jace nearly swallowed his tongue as he tried not to react to her, which was almost impossible. He'd have to be dead not to react to her.

"You're still up," she said.

"Yeah, just thinking about some stuff."

"Are you okay?"

"Yep. You?"

"Uh-huh. I just wanted some water."

As she went into the kitchen, he allowed himself to watch her go, his gaze fixating on the gentle sway of her perfect ass. Goddamn but she was sexy. And the best part? She didn't even seem to know that. She was so unaffected and normal. In his experience, women who looked like she did were so full of themselves as to be ridiculous. Not Cindy. She wasn't like that at all.

In fact, she reminded him of Lisa that way. She'd been a knockout, and everyone knew it but her. She hadn't given the first care about her hair or makeup or clothes. If anything, she'd been more tomboy than princess.

While Cindy was always well put together, Jace sensed it was more out of professionalism than vanity. She didn't come across as fussy about her looks, and he liked that about her. Hell, he liked everything about her.

She came out of the kitchen and glanced at him again. "You sure you're all right?"

As he looked at her, he realized he was better than he'd been in years, and a lot of that was due to her presence in his life. "Yeah, I'm great. Sweet dreams."

"You, too."

Jace couldn't wait to see her tomorrow.

. . .

ACROSS TOWN at Sweet Meadow Farm Road, the McCarthy family had gathered for dinner and a farewell of sorts, to Mac McCarthy's fertility. He would leave on the morning boat to have a vasectomy on the mainland. He'd been lucky to score a Saturday appointment, so he didn't have to miss work. Maddie had thought it would be funny to have a send-off party for him and his boys. While juggling twins, his diabolical wife had somehow managed to put together a basket full of not-so-funny items, such as Goldfish crackers labeled as "swimmers," donuts relabeled "Nonuts" and a pair of the sharpest scissors he'd ever seen. Ha. Ha. Ha.

Mac didn't find any of this funny. Not one bit. But as he and Maddie managed newborn twins, an eighteen-month-old, a four-year-old and a six-year-old, there was no question it had to be done.

"What if something goes wrong?" Mac asked as the others talked around him. "Has anyone considered that?"

His brother Grant, that bastard, laughed. Of course he thought it was funny. His boys were still needed for making babies. "They do vasectomies by the dozen every day. Stop thinking your package is special."

Mac was offended on behalf of his package. "It's very special to me."

Maddie patted his hand. "And me."

Mac glared at her. He wasn't at all sure whose side she was on in this situation.

"What?" she asked, laughing. "It *is* special to me."

"And yet, you're sending it to be sliced and diced like it's just another piece of worthless meat."

"Oh my God, Mac," his mother said. "Will you please stop being so dramatic?"

"That'll be the day," Evan said. "Mac has always been dramatic."

"Shut up," Mac said to his brother. "Wait until it's your turn to get the snip."

"I'm not getting it. Grace wouldn't let a knife go near my vessel of love."

The entire family groaned at that.

Grace held up a steak knife. "I'll do it myself if I have to, but your vessel of love will be getting a snip as soon as I'm done with it."

"The women in this family are ruthless," Adam said.

"You better believe we are," his wife, Abby, replied. "When you're capable of doing this to me," she said, gesturing at her huge belly, "you'll be getting snipped very soon so there's no chance of a repeat performance."

Adam puffed out his chest. "I do hold the McCarthy record for most babies in one shot."

Abby walloped him in the stomach, which deflated him.

"Ow." He rubbed his wounded belly. "That wasn't necessary."

"Yes, it was. While you're prancing around like a fool, all proud of yourself, I'm carrying *four* babies!"

"You have to admit that's a singular spermatic accomplishment," Adam said to groans from the entire family.

"That is *so* gross," Grant's wife, Stephanie, said.

"You're all a bunch of windbags." Linda glanced at her husband. "They get that from your people."

"Kevin is a bit of a windbag," Big Mac said of his younger brother. "I'll agree with that."

"So are you, dear," Linda said. "And now we've created four monster windbags who can't stop talking about their packages, their prowess, their baby-making abilities and their spermatic accomplishments."

The entire table lost it laughing.

"It's so much grosser when Mom says it," Evan said, wiping tears from his eyes.

"You have to admit we are rather accomplished in the spermatic department, Mom," Grant said. "Currently, there are six babies on board right at this very table and five others running around this place."

"And I'm responsible for four of them all at once, lest any of you forget," Adam added.

"Oh my God," Abby said. "Will you please shut your stinking piehole?"

"I love her so much," Evan said, laughing. "She shuts you right down."

Adam grinned at his wife. "She loves me."

"Someone's gotta," Mac said.

Adam and Abby's son, Liam, perked up in his high chair. "Piehole," he said as clear as day.

"*Stop it,*" Abby said, horrified. "*That cannot be his first word!*"

"This family is certifiable," Stephanie declared, "and I love every minute of it."

Mallory and Quinn laughed so hard, they held each other up.

"Take it back, Liam! Say *Mommy* like a good boy."

"Piehole."

Abby shrieked. "I can't!"

Liam's face lit up with delight. "Piehole, piehole, piehole."

"Make it stop, Adam! Right now!"

"Buddy, Mommy said a bad, bad thing, and you shouldn't say what she says, okay?"

"Piehole."

Moaning, Abby dropped her face into her hands. "Shoot me right now."

"Get out the baby book," Linda said. "First word 'piehole.'"

More moaning from Abby. "How am I going to handle *five* of them?"

"I'd recommend keeping them away from these people," Grace said. "They seem to be the source of all the trouble."

"Yes!" Abby said. "I've never used that expression in my life until I was married to Adam McCarthy, and he drove me to it."

"You love my piehole," Adam said. "I can list numerous examples when—"

Abby's hand over his mouth shut him down. For the moment, anyway.

"Back to my vasectomy," Mac said, appreciative of his family taking his mind off his worries for a few minutes.

"We've fully covered that topic, son," Big Mac said. "It's no big deal. One quick pinch, a little tugging, and it's over in fifteen minutes."

"That one quick pinch is a *shot to the ball sack*, Dad."

Big Mac waved a dismissive hand. "It's over in a second."

Mac hoped he didn't pass out during that one second. The thought of a needle in the balls had kept him awake at night for weeks now. More than once, he'd broken into a cold sweat as he imagined the moment needle met flesh. He wasn't afraid of any other part of this procedure, but that shot was the thing of nightmares.

As they left, each of his family members hugged him and wished him —and his package—well in the morning. He was glad to entertain them, he thought, as he locked the doors, finished cleaning up, shut off the lights and headed upstairs. Maddie was emerging from the nursery they had made for the twins in the smallest of the bedrooms. She placed a finger over her lips and pointed to their bedroom.

He followed her in and closed the door. Each of the kids' rooms had monitors so they could hear anyone who woke in the night—and someone always woke in the night. Since the twins had joined them, it wasn't unusual for *everyone* to wake during the night when the babies were crying.

Good times.

The best of times.

After the first three—and after losing Connor before he was born— Mac knew the craziness wouldn't last forever, and since the twins were the last of their babies, he'd decided to relax and enjoy the chaos. Losing Connor had given him perspective he wouldn't have had otherwise.

"Why the pensive expression?" Maddie asked when he stood next to her in the bathroom to brush his teeth. "You can't be seriously upset about the vasectomy."

"I'm not."

"Then why the pensiveness?"

"I was thinking about Connor and how much I wish he was here with us."

"I do, too," she said on a sigh.

Mac knew better than anyone how deeply she'd grieved the loss of their unborn son.

"Even with all the chaos and lack of sleep," Maddie said, "I wouldn't trade any of it."

"Me either. We know all too well what the alternative to chaos is."

"Yeah, for sure."

"And you're a hundred percent positive we're done having kids?"

She glared at him, attempting a sinister look that failed miserably. "I am *one thousand percent* positive I'm done having kids."

"If you're sure, then."

"Mac! You can't possibly be having second thoughts about the vasectomy."

He was having second, third, fourth and one hundredth thoughts about the vasectomy. "Not about that. Just whether we're sure we're done. What if we get a hankering for more babies in a year or two?"

"I'll find someone else to father them if that happens."

He gave her his darkest scowl. "That's *not* funny, Madeline."

"Neither is you thinking I might want more than *five* children! We're going to have *ten years* of teenagers! I am done, done, *done!*"

"So, what you're saying, is that you're *sure* about this."

She rolled her eyes and went to get into bed.

He was right behind her.

Even when she was exasperated with him, which was most of the time, she still curled up to him in bed every night, resting her head on his chest while he wrapped his arms around her. "How about one final visit with my boys when they're still packing a punch?"

"Absolutely not. With my luck, I'd get pregnant with triplets."

"You can't get pregnant again yet."

"Yes, I can. Besides, it hasn't been six weeks, and I'm still sore as hell from the twins. So put that thing away, cowboy."

"He's very sad that no one is paying homage to him in his time of need."

Maddie lost it laughing. "Do you *hear* yourself?"

"I'm advocating for someone who has no voice of his own."

"You've lost what was left of your mind."

"I'm losing what was left of my fertility, which isn't fair when you get to keep yours."

"I have no plans to ever use that equipment again."

"But you get to *keep* it."

"Stop acting like you're having your dick chopped off."

Recoiling, Mac covered his package with his hand. *"How can you even say such a thing?"*

Maddie laughed. "You're such a baby."

"We're in the biggest fight ever right now."

Maddie ran her hand over his chest and down to push his hand out of the way so she could get to his insulted member, which hardened immediately. "It seems you're the only one who's mad at me."

"He's a slut."

"He is rather easy."

"Only when you're around."

"Sure. That's the only time he ever stands up and takes notice of anything."

It'd been so long since they'd done anything that he was immediately on the verge of coming, and she'd barely touched him. "You're the only one he notices."

"I want him to know how much I appreciate the beautiful babies he's given me. Will you let him know that?"

"I'll be sure to tell him as long as you don't stop—" He gasped when she squeezed him, and then he flooded her hand with his release, his eyes rolling back in his head from the overwhelming pleasure.

"I'm sorry I can't give him a proper sendoff. Hopefully, that will suffice."

"Yeah, that suffices. As soon as my heart stops pounding, I'll get a towel." He took another thirty seconds to get himself together before he got up to retrieve a towel that he used to wipe her hand clean. Then he kissed the back of it. "I love you, even when you're mean to me."

Smiling, she said, "I love you, too, and I appreciate you taking one for the team tomorrow."

"Will you nurse me while I convalesce?"

He could tell she was trying not to roll her eyes again. "Of course I will."

"Did you know it takes *twenty* ejaculations after a vasectomy for all the baby-making boys to go away?"

"Twenty, huh?"

"That's what they say. You're going to have to help me with that if you want to be *absolutely sure* there won't be any more babies."

She rolled her eyes to high heaven. "I'll jack you fifty times if that's what it takes to make sure there're no more babies."

"Can I get that in writing?"

Maddie laughed so hard, she had tears in her eyes. "Go to sleep, you fool."

CHAPTER 13

or the second time that week, Jace raised his hand when Nina asked for volunteers at the meeting the next morning. "I've met someone," he said, cutting to the chase. "Someone I really like."

"That's wonderful, Jace," Nina said. "But you seem troubled."

"I've been sober more than six years, so it's not that it's too soon. It's more that I worry I'll somehow mess up her life the way I did my former wife's, and this woman has already had more than enough crap to deal with."

"Why do you think you'd mess up her life?" Mason asked.

"Because that's what happened the only other time I was seriously involved with someone. I created a nightmare for her and left her to raise our two kids alone."

"You can't really compare who you were then with who you are now, Jace," Quinn said. "You were a drug addict then. You're in recovery now and have been for years."

"The damage I did to Lisa went far beyond my issues with drugs."

"Is it possible," Mallory said, seeming contemplative, "that you haven't made peace with her yet, and that's keeping you from being able to fully commit to a new relationship?"

"I can't make peace with her. She died."

"Which leaves you with unfinished business with her that might be holding you back from moving forward with someone new," Nina said.

Jace considered that. "Yeah. I suppose that's possible."

"Do you know where she's buried?" Jeff asked.

His presence at the meeting had given Jace pause about whether he wanted to bring up his new relationship with Cindy. He'd decided he needed their advice badly enough to risk it. "I do. She's here on the island."

"Then maybe you go have a talk with her, tell her what's in your heart where she's concerned and clear the air with her," Jeff suggested. "Short of being able to speak to her in person, that might be the next best thing."

Surprised by the younger man's insight, Jace said, "I suppose I could try it. I owe her the biggest apology, but if I'm able to do that—even symbolically—that doesn't mean I won't screw up with Cindy, too."

"My sister Cindy?" Jeff asked, eyes big.

Jace nodded.

"Oh, well..." Jeff said. "You do need to be careful there."

"I know, and it's why I'm so worried. I like her a lot, and I think she likes me just as much, and now we're roommates, too, so the stakes are even higher. I can't mess up with her. I just can't."

For the sake of the others, Jeff said, "I've mentioned some of what our family went through with my father."

While Jeff had talked about their father at meetings, Jace had learned most of the details from Cindy. "Yes, and Cindy has talked to me about it some. She's sweet and kind and strong, but there's an underlying fragility to her that she tries to keep hidden," Jace said, aware of her brother hanging on his every word. "I couldn't bear to ever hurt her."

"Then don't," Quinn said, blunt as always. "Just don't. Show up, be there, don't disappoint her. That's how you avoid hurting her."

"You make it sound so simple," Jace said.

Quinn took his wife's hand. "It is." He paused before he continued. "Look, we've all been through some shit, or we wouldn't be here every day talking it out and trying to stay sober. We've disappointed people we cared about, we've fucked up, we've done things we're not proud of. But that doesn't mean we can't do better going forward. It takes effort every day to be worthy of someone's love, but it's effort well worth making."

Mallory stared at him with the start of tears in her eyes.

"What?" he asked, seeming slightly annoyed.

"I've never heard you say that much at one time."

"Yes, you have. I said more than that at our wedding."

"I guess you did, and PS, Dr. James is very good at showing up every day and being present in our relationship. But it wasn't always that way for either of us. We had to work at it to get to where we are now."

"If you're willing to put in the work," Mason said, "the rewards can be incredible."

"And he ought to know." Mallory grinned at him. "He's happy as a pig in shit with Jordan."

"Oink," Mason said, making the others laugh.

"You guys all have your lives so together."

"So do you, Jace," Nina said. "You shouldn't sell yourself short."

"I'm an ex-con bartender with two kids someone else is raising. I'd hardly consider my life in any way together."

"Look at where you were six years ago," Mason said. "Think about how far you've already come rather than how far you have to go to get where you want to be."

"Mason makes a good point," Nina said. "For what it's worth, I find that the people who tend to do the best in this program and in a sober life are the ones who have genuine regret for what's happened in the past and want to do better in the future. They're the ones who tend to work the hardest to maintain their sobriety and to chart a better course for the future. I see those qualities in you."

"I'm glad you do," Jace said, moved by her words, "but I feel like a work very much in progress."

"We all are," Mason said. "When I was first with Jordan, I couldn't imagine what a woman like her saw in me. I almost messed it up by having so much self-doubt. You need to think of yourself as a clean slate, like a dry-erase board wiped clean with a new set of markers that you can use to create a whole new picture."

"That's very profound, Mason," Nina said.

Mason rolled his eyes. "If you say so."

"I do say so," Nina replied. "What do you think of that metaphor, Jace?"

"I like it."

"To continue Mason's metaphor," Mallory said, "you could put the mistakes of the past in a box off to the side, stored in a safe place to remind you not to make them again."

"You guys are good at this," Jace said, grinning.

"We've all been where you are," Mallory said. "We understand how hard it is to rebuild, but we've found the effort is worthwhile. The rewards can be enormous."

The others nodded in agreement.

"Thank you for listening to me and for the outstanding advice."

"We're here every day, same time and place," Quinn said, smiling.

"I'm very thankful for that." Jace was amazed at how much lighter he felt after airing his worries with the group that had become so important to him. When Mallory, Quinn and Mason invited him to join them for coffee again, he was pleased to accept.

After the meeting, Jeff pulled him aside. "I heard what you said, and I respect the effort you're making, but please… My sister is so special. Please be good to her."

"I promise you I will. She's very special to me, too."

Jeff nodded, seeming satisfied by what Jace had said.

Jace extended his hand to Jeff, who shook it. "Thanks for looking out for her, and maybe don't tell her I was talking about her at an AA meeting?"

Jeff smiled. "I won't."

They parted company in the church parking lot, where Quinn, Mallory and Mason waited for him. When they were seated at Rebecca's with coffees and muffins in front of them, Jace thanked them again for the insight they'd shared at the meeting.

"You're doing all the right things," Quinn said. "That's what matters—and it'll matter to Cindy, too."

"Part of me feels like I should just leave her alone. She's been through so much. More than I even know about, I'm sure."

"It's a lot," Mason said. "Her dad is a piece of work and got away with his shit for years because he was a high-ranking officer."

"I hate that for her. For all of them. She deserves a nice, uncomplicated guy who's an accountant or something."

Mallory snorted with laughter. "Why does everyone shit on the accountants?"

"You know what I mean. A doctor or a firefighter would be good for her, too."

"We're all taken," Mason said, smiling.

"You're a hardworking guy," Mallory said to Jace. "That's what matters to any woman. Cindy isn't the type to care that you're a bartender."

"Thanks to you, I might also be a plumber."

"*Oh*, did Mac call you?"

"He did, and I'm supposed to meet him next week. Thank you so much for the referral."

"You're welcome. He's going to the mainland today for a vasectomy, but don't let on that I told you that. He's acting like he's the first guy to ever get one."

"Be nice to your brother, babe," Quinn said. "Anything with the penis is traumatic for our kind."

"You heard him last night," Mallory said. "He's insane."

"We knew this about him long before last night," Quinn replied.

"Don't worry, though," Mallory added for Jace's sake. "He's a great businessman. He's only insane in his private life."

"Good to know," Jace said, amused by their description of Mac.

"I'm glad it might work out for you working for him," Mallory said. "He's got big plans to remake the old alpaca farm into a wedding and event venue, our latest family business venture."

"I'm looking forward to checking it out."

After they parted company, Jace hit the gym and then went home to shower. He was surprised to find Cindy there. "Not working today?"

"I'm between appointments and came home to grab lunch."

"How're you feeling?"

"Much better, but I'm taking it easy today. I'm always wiped out for a few days after a migraine."

"You couldn't rearrange your appointments?"

"No, I never do that if I can avoid it. People count on me, and I don't want to let them down."

"But if you're sick…"

"I've powered through worse than a few haircuts and some color treatments."

"Is there anyone who can cover for you if need be?"

"I could call Chloe, but I try to save that for dire circumstances. This was a mild one."

"Didn't seem mild to me."

"Trust me, that was nothing compared to what can happen. It's been a few years since I had one like that. I'm on better meds these days, and they work most of the time."

"I hope you never have a really bad one again."

"Me either. They're the worst and usually last multiple days during which I literally can barely function. Anyway, enough about me. How's your day been so far?"

"Great. I probably stink, though. Just came from the gym."

"I don't smell anything."

"Maybe I should get a little closer," he said with a wicked grin.

Cindy laughed and held up a hand. "I'll take your word for it. If I wanted to go to the gym sometime, would you show me what to do there? I'm terrible at that stuff."

"I'd be happy to train you. Any time you want."

"I'm off on Sundays and Mondays."

"Either of those days work for me. Just let me know."

"I tend to talk more about the gym than actually go, so we'll see if it ever happens. You want a sandwich?"

"Sure, if you don't mind."

"I don't mind."

"I'm just going to grab a quick shower. Be right back."

"I'll be here. My next appointment is at one thirty."

They had an hour to spend together. Jace intended to make the most of that.

THE UNEXPECTED LUNCH on the patio with Jace was the highlight of Cindy's day. He smelled so good after his shower that all she wanted to do was breathe him in.

"How about I trade you a haircut for training at the gym?" he asked.

"Sure, we can do that. When do you want to do it?"

"Whenever you have time."

"I'm off tomorrow."

"Tomorrow works. Thank you for the sandwich. Not sure what you did to bread, turkey and cheese, but it was the best turkey sandwich I've ever had. If cutting hair doesn't work out for you, you've got a career in the sandwich industry."

"Whatever you say, charmer."

"Hey, Cindy?"

"Yes, Jace?"

"I heard what you said last night about your dad and all that, and I want you to know… I'm going to do my absolute damnedest to never hurt you. And if I do? I want you to tell me, okay?"

"I, uh… Yeah, I'll tell you."

"I hope it's okay to put that out there."

"It's okay." And refreshing, she thought, but didn't say. Over the years, she'd gotten so tired of men and the games they played that she'd begun to avoid dating and everything that went along with it. It'd been years since she'd had anything resembling a boyfriend. The girls in the Dallas shop had always tried to fix her up until she'd said no so many times, they'd finally given up on her. That'd been a relief. "I'd better get back to work."

"Will you be in to see me later?"

"I'll see how I feel when I get home."

"Hope to see you, but only if you feel up to it."

"Gotta run. I've got my favorite client due in—my grandmother."

"Enjoy that."

"Always do."

Cindy left him with a smile and a wave and headed back to work, feeling energized after spending time with him. And what he'd said about not hurting her… He had no way to know what an enormous gift those words had been to her. There'd been so much hurt in her life that all she wanted now was peace and harmony, even if that meant being alone.

She vastly preferred that to the drama that seemed to accompany relationships.

As she approached the doors to the salon, her grandmother waved from across the street.

Cindy looked both ways before watching Adele cross the street with a spring in her step.

"I parked at the hotel." She hugged and kissed Cindy. "I hope Owen and Laura don't have me towed."

Cindy laughed. "They wouldn't dare."

Her grandmother's calming presence was a balm on Cindy's soul, as it had been for as long as she could remember.

"I couldn't wait to get here. This hair of mine is ridiculous." She ran her fingers through her snow-white hair. "Grandpa said I'm growing a mullet."

Cindy sputtered with laughter. "It's not a mullet, yet, but it's heading in that direction. Not to worry, I'll fix you right up."

"Spin your magic, my love, and tell me everything that's going on."

CHAPTER 14

Cindy put a cape over her grandmother and snapped it into place. "Let's see... I had a migraine last night, but I feel better today."

"Thank God for the new meds, huh?"

"You said it. I've got a new roommate named Jace, and he's... well... I like him a lot."

Adele's eyes went wide with surprise. "He must be very special. You never like them a lot."

"I know, and he is. Special, that is." Cindy turned the chair so she could wash Adele's hair.

When her grandmother was seated upright again, she said, "Tell me everything about this man you like."

"Some of it might upset you."

Adele waved a hand dismissively. "Once upon a time, I was absolutely thrilled to see my daughter marry a dashing young military officer. Look how that turned out. I'm much less concerned with things like appearances and credentials these days."

"Jace did time in prison." She filled her in on the details and mentioned the two sons being raised by Seamus and Carolina O'Grady.

"You know... I remember thinking about their father when the boys' mother died and wondering whether he'd resurface at some point."

"He's determined not to upset their lives any more than they've already been. For now, they're explaining him as a friend of Seamus's."

"I give him credit for doing what's best for the boys rather than what's best for himself."

"I do, too."

"Says a lot about his character."

"I agree."

"Is he sexy?"

"Gram!"

"Well, is he? And don't get all flustered and act like that doesn't matter when we both know it does."

"He's very good-looking in a bad-boy kind of way, with sleeve tattoos and muscles on top of muscles."

"He sounds yummy," Adele said.

Cindy giggled madly at the face her grandmother made.

"Your grandfather was a bad boy back in the day."

"He was not!"

"Oh yes, he was, too. All the girls wanted him, and he led them on a merry chase."

"I cannot picture that if I try my very hardest." Her grandfather was a sweet, gentle, old man with a heart of gold.

She pointed to her purse. "Grab my phone."

Cindy got it for her.

While her grandmother found what she was looking for, Cindy gave her a trim that would rid her of any semblance of a mullet.

"Look." Adele held up her phone to show Cindy a photo of young Russ leaning against a car, arms crossed over a bare, muscular chest, hair messed up and his jaw sprinkled with whiskers. "Total hottie, right?"

"I, uh, well... Yes, I suppose he is."

"He was—and is—the sexiest man I've ever known. If you're going to spend a lifetime with a man, make sure he does it for you that way, or you'll have nothing but trouble."

"You're not advocating premarital sex, are you, Gram?"

"You wouldn't buy a car without test-driving it, would you?"

"Gram!"

"Well, would you?"

Cindy wanted to die from laughter and embarrassment. "No, I wouldn't."

"Then you shouldn't shackle yourself to a man without making sure he's bringing his A game in every possible way, especially in the bedroom. Or the backyard. Or wherever floats your boat. Just don't get caught by the police if you're outside."

"Have you had a stroke I didn't hear about?"

Adele's laughter echoed through the shop. "Don't be a fuddy-duddy, Cynthia."

"Does Mom know you had a stroke and didn't tell us?"

"Your mother is well aware that her mother may be an old lady, but she's still got gas in her tank." Giving Cindy a saucy look in the mirror, she added, "Your grandfather is also aware."

"Lalalalalala, I can't hear you."

"Take your sexy Jace for a ride and thank me afterward."

"What are you hearing about the weather forecast?"

That brought more laughter from her incorrigible grandmother.

As Cindy blow-dried her hair, she thought about what Adele had said and had to admit, she had a point. And Cindy certainly wasn't opposed to getting busy with her new roommate. Her biggest concern since he'd moved in had been awkwardness at home if she took a romantic chance on him and it didn't work out. But she had options if that happened. She could always move in with her mom and Charlie for a short time until she found a new place to rent.

The legacy of her upbringing was that she always had an exit strategy if she found herself in an uncomfortable situation. No matter where she was or what she was doing, she kept her back to the wall with an eye on the door so she could leave if necessary. Metaphorically speaking, that was. Walking away was almost second nature to her. It was almost too easy, and other men she'd dated had accused her of giving up without a fight.

That was the problem. She had no fight left in her. If there was going to be a fight, she was gone. Once, back in Dallas, an argument had broken out in the shop between two of her coworkers that had had Cindy's heart racing and her hands shaking in a matter of seconds as the old trauma resurfaced to remind her it was always there. She'd walked out the back door and straight to her car to go home.

Laverne had called later to apologize and tell her the two women involved in the screaming match had been fired. It'd taken Cindy all night to recover from the altercation and start to feel like herself again.

She shut off the hair dryer and ran the brush through her grandmother's soft white hair. Then she added the curls on top that Adele always asked for and brushed it out again, adding some spray. "What do you think?"

"You're a magician."

"Only when I have a beautiful subject to work with." She kissed her grandmother's cheek, unsnapped the cape and brushed some stray hair off Adele's neck.

Adele got up like she was sixty rather than eighty-five and enveloped Cindy in a warm hug, the scent of Dior perfume bringing back a thousand memories of the best times of Cindy's life. "Thank you, my love."

"My pleasure, as always, and a reminder that this one is on me. I let you pay last time."

"You can't give away your talents for free," she said, as she did every time Cindy refused payment from her.

"I can give away my talents to you any time I wish to, and that's that."

"So fresh to your old granny."

"My granny is not old."

"But my granddaughter *is* fresh."

Cindy laughed and hugged her again. "Love you so much."

"Love you more."

"No way."

"When can I meet your Jace?"

"He's not my Jace."

Adele raised a brow. "But he could be?"

"I suppose. Maybe."

"Great, so when can I meet him?"

"Soon."

"I'll hold you to that. And remember what I said—take him for a ride, love. You won't know if you don't try." With that, she kissed Cindy's cheek and gave a jaunty wave as she headed out the door.

Cindy wondered how she would think of anything other than taking Jace for a ride now that her grandmother had put that thought in her head. Not that she hadn't already had it on her own, but Adele's "permission," for lack of a better word, made it even more enticing than it already was.

THE SHOT to the balls had been every bit the nightmare that Mac had feared. As he sat in his truck on the ferry ride home, ice pack on his wounded junk, he wondered how long it would take before he didn't break into a cold sweat when he recalled that needle coming for him. His father had offered to come with him and drive him home, but Mac had assured him that wouldn't be necessary.

He should've let him come. He'd had to wait hours for the light sedation to wear off before they'd let him leave. Driving had been much more complicated than expected with every part of him feeling like Jell-O after the procedure.

And yes, he understood he was being a big, fat baby who had nothing to complain about when chalked up against Maddie delivering babies, including giving birth to twins on a helicopter with no pain meds. This was a breeze compared to that, except it hurt like a mother-effer.

He needed to get his shit together before he got home. Maddie wouldn't stand for him being a whiner over what was a minor procedure compared to what she'd been through to have their children. This was a fine time to realize he probably should've stayed at Joe's place on the mainland for the night so he could whine to his heart's content without an audience to mock him.

Speaking of Joe, he put through a call to his brother-in-law and life-long best friend. He and Mac's sister Janey were living in Ohio with their kids and pets while Janey finished veterinary school.

"Is this the eunuch?" Joe asked when he answered.

"It didn't go quite that far, thank you, Jesus."

Joe's laughter rang through the phone. "Hurts like fuck, doesn't it?"

"Yes! Why didn't you tell me that?"

"Because you would've chickened out if I had, and Maddie would've divorced you."

"Ugh, I hate you for not telling me how bad this was gonna suck."

"It's only for a day or two, and then you're fine. Where are you?"

"On the ferry back to the island."

"You drove yourself?"

"Yeah."

"That wasn't the best idea you ever had."

"I know. I found that out the hard way."

"Don't say 'hard.'"

Mac laughed even as he winced. "I'm never going to be hard again after this."

"Yes, you will, and you can get busy with no worries about more babies."

"That's true."

"Although you have to do the sample in six weeks to make sure it took."

"Wait, what? It's possible it didn't take?"

"Didn't you read the discharge instructions?"

"Not yet."

Joe laughed. "You have to check in six weeks to make sure all the swimmers are gone."

"What if they aren't?"

"You have to go back for further treatment."

Mac groaned. "I'm never going back there again, swimmers or not."

"You have to make sure it took, or you run the risk of another pregnancy, and I fear your long-suffering wife will kill you if that happens."

"I hate to agree with you, but…"

"Then you jack in a cup to make sure you're good to go. They can probably do that right at the clinic for you."

"I don't want to even think about that today."

"Yeah, hands off until the boo-boo heals."

"The things we do for these women."

"As your marital advisor, I'd recommend you keep that thought to yourself when you get home."

"You don't need to be enjoying this so much."

"Why not? I knew you'd be a big baby over it. We all did."

"Who all did?"

"Your entire family. There's a Mac's Vasectomy group chat."

"There is not!"

"Yes, there is."

"Who started that?"

"Um, well, I'm sort of afraid to say."

"I bet it was Janey."

"She did say she was sorry she didn't think of it, but you need to look for the culprit a little closer to home."

"*Maddie?*"

"You didn't hear it from me."

"That traitor."

"You can't honestly be surprised."

Mac grunted out a laugh. "Not really."

"I love how she's so perfect for you."

"Yes, she is, even when she's busting my bruised and battered balls."

"Especially then."

"Shut up. You're supposed to be *my* best friend, which means you're always on my side."

"I am on your side, but she's funny."

"You can't be on my side and think she's funny, too. That's not how this works. I'll remind you we've been friends since kindergarten."

Joe was laughing so hard, he wheezed. "You're such an idiot. I love that she gives you such a run for your money."

"She's a brat, and she's going to pay for this."

"I'm sure she's very afraid."

"The ferry is pulling into port. I need to go home and get my woman under control."

"Let me know how that goes."

"You'll be the first to know."

"I hope your pee-pee feels better soon."

"I do, too."

"You'll survive. I promise."

"Good to know."

"I'll check on you tomorrow."

"See ya."

CHAPTER 15

ac groaned as he leaned forward to start the engine, that small movement enough to make him nauseated from the pain. The doctor had said it would hurt once the numbing medicine had worn off and had advised him to start on pain pills right away. But Mac wanted to get home first. Now, he was desperate enough—and close enough—to pop a pill on the drive to Sweet Meadow Farm Road.

He winced when he thought about the kids being all over him and how that wouldn't be possible tonight.

As he took a right into his driveway, he noticed every light in the house was on, which meant business as usual. His mother had once said that was a sign of a house well lived in. To him, it was also the sign of a huge electric bill. He was working with Thomas to be his ally in conserving electricity, making shutting off lights part of his weekly allowance. Clearly, his oldest was failing at that job today.

Mac parked, shut off the engine and breathed a sigh of relief to be home. He sent a quick text to his parents to let them know he'd survived and was back on the island and then moved slowly and carefully to get out of the truck, bringing his ice pack with him. Every step up to the deck hurt worse than the one before, and he was in a full sweat by the time he reached the top. He slid open the slider and stepped into chaos.

Thomas was chasing Hailey around the room while baby Mac, also known now as Trip—he would never get used to that—toddled behind them while Maddie juggled screaming babies. The house was a total wreck, with toys strewn from one end to the other.

Hailey saw him come in and let out a shriek as she ran for him.

Mac put his hands out to keep her from colliding with him. "Easy, honey. Daddy is hurting."

"What did I tell you, Hailey?" Maddie said. "We have to be gentle with Daddy tonight."

"Sorry, Dada."

Mac leaned in to kiss the top of her head. "That's okay. Will you take care of me?"

His baby girl nodded and reached out her hand to lead him to the sofa, releasing him so she could move the dolls, trucks and Legos on the cushions and throw them on the floor with the rest of the toys. "I'd ask how it's going around here, but I can see," he said as he lowered himself gingerly to the sofa.

"It's been that kind of day," Maddie said, holding Emma as she brought him a bag of frozen peas.

"What's this for?" he asked of the vegetables.

"I read online that they work well as an ice pack."

"Ah, gotcha. Thanks." He placed the peas on his lap. "Where's Kelsey?"

"I knew you were on your way home, so she left twenty minutes ago. She cleaned up before she left, and this is what they've accomplished since then."

"Yikes," he said of the mess. "Could I borrow your phone for a sec?"

"Sure." She pulled it out of her shorts pocket and handed it to him. "What's wrong with yours?"

He punched in her code. "It doesn't have the Mac's Vasectomy group chat on it, because I wasn't invited to participate."

She lunged for the phone. "Mac! Give that back to me!"

Despite the pain, he held it out of her reach. "Not until I see what my lovely wife has been saying about me."

"It's all in good fun."

"There is nothing good *or* fun about what I endured today."

"Was it anything like pushing an extra-large pumpkin out of your vagina? Asking for a friend."

"Since I don't own a vagina, I can't say for sure. All I can tell you is having a needle in the balls is the stuff of nightmares."

She ran her fingers through his hair. "My poor, poor baby."

"You're not even trying to be sincere."

"I am, too! I'm sorry you're hurting, and I got the frozen peas for you."

"Whatever. Go tend to our children. I have some reading to do."

"Mac, come on. We were just joking around. How did you find out about it anyway?"

"I'll never reveal my source. This is some interesting reading. It's good to know that you predicted I'd have to spend the night in the hospital afterward because I'd be crying too hard to drive myself home."

"I was *joking!*"

He looked up at her, brow raised. "Were you?"

"Mostly. I mean, you must admit you've been a little... *over the top...* about the whole thing."

"You mean about having someone slice into my balls with needles and knives?"

"How is that different from having my vagina sewn back together four times? Oh wait, it was three more times than you. That's how it's different."

"You took a bigger hit for the team than I did. I concede that."

"It's good to know you can see that, because the way you've been going on about a quick procedure has made me wonder if you did."

"I do. Of course I do, but that *quick* procedure totally sucked, and I feel like shit."

"Shit," Hailey said, grinning at him.

"That's a bad word, and Daddy shouldn't have said it." He tried to be stern with her, but that was impossible. She was so cute.

"Shit, shit, shit," she said as Thomas joined in her chorus.

Maddie scowled at him. "Lovely. Thank you."

Mac hoped that pain pill kicked in soon, because this was already shaping up to be a long night.

JEFF FLOATED next to Kelsey in the water behind the Sand & Surf as the sun dipped toward the horizon. He had so many memories of moments just like this one during the magical summers they'd spent here. Now, like then, he didn't want to leave when the summer ended.

He had a pit in his stomach when he thought about getting on the ferry and heading back to Florida to start the job he'd once been so excited about. That'd been before he met the perfect girl, or he should say *woman*, since neither of them were kids anymore. Now, all he wanted was more nights like this, with her by his side, making him feel like he was the king of the world.

That was the best feeling he'd ever experienced, and he had no idea how he was going to give it up at the end of the month. He had to tell her he was leaving. It was unfair that he hadn't yet.

Jeff reluctantly let his feet drop to the sandy bottom as he stood.

When Kelsey saw him get up, she followed.

They made their way to where they'd left their towels and wrapped up in them, sitting on the sand to watch the sun set in an explosion of red, orange and purple.

"It's so pretty here," she said. "Prettier than anywhere I've ever been."

"I agree."

"Prettier than Florida?"

"Florida has nothing on Gansett." That had never been truer than it was now. "Speaking of Florida..." He looked over at her, noting once again how pretty she was. "I have to go back soon."

"I wondered how long you were going to be here."

"I start a new job in Tampa in October and move into my apartment on the first. I need to go back soon to get myself together to move."

"Oh."

"I'm sorry I haven't said anything about that before now. I kept hoping something might come up to make it possible for me to stay."

She looked over at him. "Why would you stay when you have a job lined up in Tampa?"

"Um, because you're here?"

"I, ah, well..." She released a deep breath and a laugh. "Sorry, you're making me stammer."

"Why's that?"

"Because I wasn't sure what this was," she said. "If we were two buddies hanging out at the end of the summer or something more."

"It's definitely something more for me, so much so that I've actually thought about quitting the job I haven't started yet and breaking my lease so I can stay here with you." He glanced at her and found her staring at him. "Was that too much?"

"No, not at all. I just... I wasn't sure."

Jeff held out his hand to her, barely breathing as he waited to see what she would do. Their relationship up to now had been platonic, and he wasn't sure she wanted the same things he did.

As she joined her hand with his, the look she gave him was full of vulnerability and maybe a hint of excitement.

"Is there any chance you might want to move to Tampa?" he asked in a teasing tone, even though he was serious.

"I promised Mac and Maddie I'd stay for the year, at least. They really need me."

He kissed the back of her hand. "I do, too."

"Jeff..." She released a nervous laugh. "Don't say things like that."

"I mean it. I *really* like you, Kelsey. Like, a lot, and I hate to think about leaving here and not seeing you for months."

"I like you, too, and I'm sorry you have to leave. I'll miss you."

"You will?"

"Of course I will," she said, laughing. "We've spent every minute we could together for weeks."

Everything about her did it for him—her smile, her pretty face, her curly reddish-gold hair and her sexy body—but more than anything, he was attracted to her sweetness. She was the nicest person he'd ever met, except for maybe his mom and grandmother. In a way, she reminded him of them and how they never had a bad word to say about anyone. Well, except for his father, that was, but they all had bad things to say about him.

"There are things you should know about me," he said, feeling deflated as he broached a subject he'd studiously avoided until now.

"What is it? You seem so serious all of a sudden."

"It is serious."

"Whatever it is, Jeff, it won't change how I feel about you."

"How do you feel?"

"Interested, excited, happy—and sad now that I know you're leaving."

He was relieved to know she had feelings for him, too, but hoped he wouldn't spoil everything by sharing the truth with her. "I, um, I told you I'm the youngest of seven, right?"

"Yes, and I feel like I know your siblings from the way you talk about them."

"They're all great, but we went through a lot growing up. Our dad, he wasn't a good guy, and it was hell. It got even worse when everyone else moved out, and it was just me. I got messed up with drugs, and when I was fourteen, I tried to kill myself because I honestly felt there was no way out of the addiction and depression with *years* ahead of dealing with him."

"Oh God. Oh, Jeff. I'm so sorry you went through that—and when you were so young."

"It was an awful time, but thanks to my grandparents and some intensive rehab, I've been clean for years, and I'm in a much better place than I was then. My grandparents moved me to Florida where they were living and got me back on track. I owe them everything. I take my recovery very seriously and actively attend meetings and help others who are just starting their journey through recovery." He realized he was saying more than he'd intended to, and as he glanced over at her, he wasn't sure what to expect. "So, yeah. It's a lot."

She gazed at him with what might've been respect and admiration. "I'm proud of what you've overcome."

"It's not a deal breaker?"

"Not at all."

"What would your family say if they knew about my past?"

"My brother had a drinking problem in high school. He went to rehab three times before he finally kicked it. They don't judge people who've battled addiction."

"I'm sorry you guys went through that."

"It was rough, and he struggled so much to get to where he is now. We're proud of him, and I know they'd be proud of you, too."

"That's nice to hear. It may sound weird, but in some ways, I'm thankful for having been through everything that I have. I feel like I'm better prepared for life than I would've been without the struggles."

"I can see that. My brother is full of gratitude, too, not so much for the alcoholism, but for the journey he took through recovery and AA."

"Narcotics Anonymous and AA are amazing programs. I can't imagine where I'd be without all the support I've found there—and continue to find there."

"Thank you for telling me about it."

He released her hand and put his arm around her. "I should've told you sooner, but I was afraid of what you might think. I should've known better."

She rested her head on his shoulder. "You told me when you were ready to. That's the right time."

"And you wonder why I like you so much."

"I don't wonder."

Jeff laughed and kissed the top of her head as he tightened his hold on her. He wanted to hang on to her forever. With that thought in mind, he pulled back from her and looked down, studying her gorgeous face while trying to commit every detail to memory. Although he already knew he'd never forget a thing about her. He moved in slowly, hoping he'd be welcome to kiss her like he'd wanted to for weeks now.

As their lips came together in the sweetest, most perfect kiss of his life, she placed her hand on his face and kissed him back with the same ardor he felt. Was it possible for one kiss to change everything? He wouldn't have thought so before now. After one taste, he wanted to gorge. The need was so great that when she pulled back, he moaned.

"I think," she said softly, "that we ought to put this on hold for now."

"That's the worst idea you ever had."

Smiling, she shook her head. "It's not what I want, but if we let things get even more involved, it'll be that much harder when you go."

"Leaving you here will already be the hardest thing I'll ever do."

"Don't be silly. You just told me you've been through much worse."

"This is going to be harder than that. I already know it."

"Now you're being dramatic. We can FaceTime and talk every day. You'll visit me. I'll visit you. If it's meant to be, it'll work out."

"You're very mature about all this."

"One of us has to be."

Laughing, he nudged her with his shoulder. "You'll really FaceTime with me every day?"

"Yes."

"And you won't date anyone else?"

She glanced at him. "Will you?"

"Nope."

"Then I won't either."

"Promise?" he asked playfully.

"Yes, Jeff, I promise."

CHAPTER 16

*J*ohn helped his mom and Charlie clean up after dinner. After he cleared the table, Charlie said he was going out to the garage for half an hour to finish a job he'd started earlier. He gave Sarah a kiss on the cheek before he went out through the mudroom door.

"You two are cute," John said. "It's nice to see you so happy."

"It still feels like a dream."

"Good for you. You deserve it, Mom."

"Yes, I do."

John laughed at the emphatic way she said that. No one had ever deserved happily ever after more than she did.

"What about you?" she asked in the casual tone mothers everywhere used when they were looking for information from reluctant offspring.

"What about me?"

"Are you going to see Niall again? He seems like such a nice young man. I was so glad you brought him to dinner the other night."

Unsure of what she was really asking, John continued to wipe the countertop. "He is nice."

"Johnny."

He stopped what he was doing and turned to her, shocked to find her watching him with a knowing look on her face. "What?"

"Do you *like* him?"

"Yes, of course. We're friends from the Beachcomber. I met up with him when I was out running and…"

"It's okay. You don't have to explain anything to me. It's just that I think he's great, and it seems like maybe you do, too."

"We're friends."

"Are you ever going to tell me the truth?"

John felt like he'd been hit by a hot arrow to the chest. "About what?"

She tipped her head and raised her brows. "About everything. Do you think I don't know what you're trying so hard to hide from me? Or that I won't understand or won't support you the same way I always have?"

John was so shocked, he had no idea how to respond.

She came closer to him, put her hands on his shoulders and looked up at him. "We're no longer living in Mark Lawry's house."

"Thank God for that," John said with a nervous laugh.

"That means we're all free to be who and what we are, including you."

He heard what she said, understood the deeper meaning behind the words, but couldn't bring himself to reply. It had become second nature to him to hide from the truth, which meant he had no idea how to broach the subject, even with the opening his mother had given him.

"If you want to talk about it, I'm here. I love you unconditionally, now and forever."

She would never know what those words meant to him.

He stood frozen in place as she went back to wiping down the stovetop. The words he wanted to say burned on the tip of his tongue. *Just say it. Tell her what she seems to already know.* He wanted to so badly, but all he could hear was Mark Lawry's voice in the back of his head saying none of them had better be gay, that he'd rather be dead than have a gay child.

His father's hateful words were burned on John's soul in permanent ink. They'd forced him to live a lie for most of his life, until he finally took a chance on what he wanted and had it blow up in his face in spectacular fashion. He hadn't even told his mother why he'd quit the department. It might be better, for him, for everyone who loved him, to keep the truth buried, and he might've done that if his mother hadn't told him he wasn't fooling her.

"I, uh… Mom."

"Yes, Johnny?" she said as she turned to him, her expression open, loving and accepting.

"You already know."

"I always have."

Incredulous, he said, "*How* is that possible?"

She shrugged. "I just knew. I'm so sorry for the things *he* said and what I put you through by not getting you kids away from him."

"We don't blame you."

"I blame myself enough for all of you."

Her sharp retort stunned him.

"I'm sorry," she said. "I don't mean to snap at you."

"You didn't."

"For the rest of my life, I'll regret that I wasn't strong enough then to do what needed to be done, that you and the others went through what you did at his hands. Every one of you carries scars from how you were raised, but you're the one I've worried about the most."

That shocked him. "Why me?"

"Because."

That one word spoke volumes.

"Do you think he knew about me, too?"

"No," she said. "Not at all. It never occurred to him. I'm sure of that."

"I guess we ought to be thankful for that, because as bad as it was, that would've made it a thousand times worse. I went so far out of my way to hide it from him, dating girls and saying stuff to keep him from suspecting."

"I know you did, and I'm so sorry, Johnny," she said tearfully. "I'm so damned sorry for the things he said and did."

He went to her and hugged her tightly. "You don't need to apologize for him."

"Yes, I do, and you have to let me. I should've done more."

"You were terrorized, Mom. Please don't take the blame. I saw so much of what domestic violence does to people when I was on the job. What matters now is that he can never hurt us again."

"He continues to hurt us if we don't live our truth."

"I hear you, and it means everything to me that you understand."

"I do, and I love you. No matter what."

He hugged her again, fully aware of how lucky her support made him.

"Now, talk to me about Niall."

John laughed. "What about him?"

"Do we like him as more than a friend?"

"Maybe." It was still strange to admit such a thing to his mother when he'd spent his entire life hiding the truth from everyone around him—and apparently failing if his mother had known all along.

"What're you going to do about it?"

"Haven't decided yet."

"Perhaps you ought to give that some thought, huh?"

"Perhaps I will."

"Excellent. How about the job at the Wayfarer? What do you think about that?"

"I think it might be perfect for me. Work hard for four months and get paid an annual salary while coasting the rest of the year? That probably wouldn't suck."

"Probably not, and we'd love to have you here with us year-round."

When John had first come back to Gansett for the housewarming party, his entire life had been a mess. He'd lost a job he'd put his heart and soul into, his first real relationship had imploded, and he'd been living a lie for as long as he could remember. Now, though... Things were looking up, and he couldn't wait to see what happened next.

HOPE WAITED until she got Scarlett down for the night and then went to find Ethan and Paul. On the nights when Paul, a town councilman, didn't have a meeting in town, the two of them could be found enjoying a bowl of ice cream while they watched some form of sports on TV. Tonight, they had a Red Sox game on and were talking about how to identify the various types of pitches.

"See that curve?" Paul asked. "Right at the end? That's how you know it's a curveball."

Hope would be forever thankful to Paul for treating Ethan like a son, long before she and Paul had admitted their feelings for each other. Her son hung on Paul's every word, followed him around like a puppy, and even imitated some of Paul's mannerisms. She couldn't think of a better man for her son to look up to. She ached at the thought of anything disturbing their harmonious life, especially the man who'd caused them so much pain in the past.

"Can I talk to you guys for a minute?"

Since they'd planned this conversation earlier, Paul muted the TV. "Sure."

"I wanted to talk to Ethan about his dad getting out of jail."

"Oh," Ethan said.

"As you know, he's agreed to allow Paul to adopt you."

"That's still happening, right?" Ethan asked, seeming unnerved.

"It is," Hope said, "but your father has requested the opportunity to see you, just once. I believe he'd like the chance to apologize for everything that happened. Paul and I have talked about it, and we think the decision should be yours."

Ethan thought about that for a minute. "Do I have to see him?"

"No, you don't."

He looked at Paul. "What do you think I should do?"

Hope wasn't at all surprised that he wanted Paul's opinion.

"If I were you, I'd want to see him and hear him out so I could move on with my life without any regrets, but I want to add that if you think it would be too upsetting for you, then you shouldn't do it."

"What about you, Mom? What do you think I should do?"

"The part of me that still has a lot of feelings about what he put us through wants you to tell him to go to hell."

Ethan laughed at her unusually harsh language.

"However, the part of me that will always be grateful to him for giving me you thinks that maybe we could give him an hour and then close the book on that chapter of our lives for good."

"An hour is really no big deal, right?" Ethan asked.

"It's nothing in the grand scheme of things," Paul said.

"As long as you know that *you're* my dad, that you always will be, I'll see him," Ethan said.

Paul took Ethan's empty bowl and placed it on the coffee table. Then he put his arm around the boy. "I'll always be your dad. Nothing could ever change that, and nothing could ever change how much I love you. If you want to see him, now or any time in the future, you should."

"You promise you wouldn't be mad?"

"Swear to God," Paul said.

"When would it happen?" Ethan asked Hope.

"He doesn't get out until later in October, so after that sometime."

"Can we go back to watching the game now?"

"You bet, buddy." Paul unmuted the sound on the television and looked up at Hope, his eyes full of emotion.

She smiled at him and mouthed the words *love you* to him, and he did the same back to her.

The luckiest day of her life—and Ethan's—was when she came to Gansett Island to interview for a job helping to care for Marion Martinez. She never could've imagined that job would lead to a whole new life for herself and her son.

They were blessed beyond measure to love and be loved by Paul Martinez.

THE BAR WAS BUSIER than Jace had expected for a post-Labor Day Saturday night. He kept an eye out for Cindy while pretending not to save her usual seat by putting his jacket on it. Niall was playing later, and the bar was full of regulars who'd come out to reclaim their island, as one of them put it.

Piper, who worked the front desk at the Sand & Surf, was playing a game of checkers with Niall before he began his first set.

Jace approached Oliver and Dara Watson, who'd arrived with another woman a few minutes ago, and put Beachcomber coasters in front of each of them. "Let me guess, a rum and Diet Coke for Dara, a Sam Adams for Oliver and..." He took a measuring look at the newcomer. "Vodka and soda with a twist of lime."

The woman's smile lit up pretty brown eyes. "Close. Make the lime a lemon and the vodka Ketel One, and we've got a deal."

"Just a soda water with a lemon for me," Dara said.

"Sure thing. Are you guys eating, too?"

"Yep," Oliver said. "This is Dara's sister, Monique. We told her the Beachcomber has the best food in town."

"I won't argue with that." Jace placed a menu on the bar in front of her. "These two know it by heart."

"And we get the same thing every time," Dara said.

"They're boring that way," Monique said to Jace.

"I'm not getting dragged into this argument," Jace replied, grinning as he prepared their drinks.

"Monique just got divorced," Oliver said. "She ought to come with a warning label for single men. Crazy lady back on the market and on the make."

Laughing, Monique gave her brother-in-law a playful shove. "Shut up with that. It's not that bad. Yet."

"I stand warned," Jace said gravely.

"Don't listen to him." Monique smiled as she brushed away Oliver's comments. "It's not quite that bad."

"But close," Dara said.

"The last few years with the husband weren't great," Monique said with a shrug. "I'm excited to get out and meet new people and start over. I hear Gansett is a good place to do that."

She was gorgeous and vivacious. Jace doubted she'd have any trouble meeting new people. Oliver and Dara were two of Jace's favorite regulars. One night, they'd shared the story of how they'd lost their young son in a tragic accident and had come to Gansett to be the new lighthouse keepers, hoping for a fresh start.

They seemed to be doing better, and he was glad to see them smiling and laughing with Dara's sister.

"Cheers to a fresh start," Jace said when he delivered their drinks.

He'd almost given up on her when Cindy came in, smiling at him as she pointed to the barstool he'd saved for her. "Is someone sitting here?"

"You are. That's my jacket."

When she realized he'd saved her seat, the affectionate look she gave him filled him with an unreasonable feeling of joy. The only time he'd felt anything close to that was when he'd seen his sons after years away from them.

He poured her usual glass of ice water and topped it with a slice of lemon. "How're you feeling?"

"Much better, thank goodness."

"Glad to hear it."

"And ready for a couple of days off."

"What've you got planned?"

"I'm seeing Owen, Laura and the kids tomorrow for haircuts."

"On your day off?"

"That's fun, not work. I can do yours, too, if you want."

"That'd be great. Did I tell you I'm talking to Mac McCarthy next week about doing some plumbing for him?"

"No, but that's wonderful. My sister Julia works for him and says he's booked two years out."

"That's what I hear." He handed her a printout. "Tonight's specials. Be right back." He went to pour another glass of wine for Piper and Niall's Guinness before returning to take Cindy's order.

"I'll do the seafood casserole with a house salad, please."

"Hold the onions," he added.

"You know me too well."

"Not as well as I'd like to."

CHAPTER 17

*J*ace dropped that bomb and walked away to punch her order into the computer.

"Girlfriend's been holding out on me," Piper Bennett whispered to her. "You and sexy Jace the bartender. Making some progress, huh?"

Cindy shrugged, even as her entire system went haywire over his not-so-subtle comment. "We're friends. And roommates."

"Since when?"

"He moved in earlier this week."

"Convenient. He's not only sexy, but he's nice, too. Good for you."

"We'll see."

"I like you two together. It works for me."

"As long as it works for you," Cindy said, laughing. "What's going on with your friend Jack?" Piper had engaged in a summer-long flirtation with Jack Downing, one of the two state troopers stationed on the island.

Piper groaned. "He's been on the mainland for two weeks. Supposedly, he's coming back next week, but I'll believe it when I see it."

"Have you talked to him?"

"We've texted a few times, but nothing major. I'm starting to wonder if the *thing* between us was one-sided."

"It wasn't. I've seen you two together. He's into you, too."

"You really think so?"

"I do. He never takes his eyes off you."

"Kinda like someone else we know with you." Piper used her chin to point to Jace. "He's always got eyes on you."

"Does he?"

"Yes," Piper said, laughing, "and you know it."

"He gets me all flustered."

"That's a good place to start."

"If you say so. What's your plan when Jack gets back to the island?"

Piper shrugged. "I have no plan. Part of me wants to just skip the whole thing. I'm so over guys." Weeks ago, she'd confided to Cindy about how her fiancé had called off their wedding and dumped her and how she'd been attacked by a guy she met on the island earlier in the summer.

"You can't let a few bad apples ruin the entire barrel for you, as my grandmother would say. Jack is a good guy. He's nothing like the others."

"And I know that, but I have zero energy to put toward anything with him."

"Because he's not here. You might find some energy when he gets back."

"Eh, we'll see. I'm not counting any chickens where he's concerned. In other news, I heard yesterday that the guy who assaulted me pleaded guilty to a felony charge, so I won't have to testify against him. That's a huge relief."

"I'm so glad it worked out that way."

"Me, too. Your sister-in-law, Laura, has been such a great friend to me through all of it, from the day it happened."

"She's the best."

"Yes, she is. I'm thankful that one of the worst days ever brought me to her and a job at the Surf."

"She's thrilled to have you. She's told me more than once what a huge help to her you were during the busy season."

"She's got a lot on her plate running the hotel with three little ones."

"And yet, she makes it all look so effortless," Cindy said, filled with admiration for Owen's wife. "I'm glad we'll get to work together a little in the off-season."

"Me, too! She told me you're coming over to help out once in a while." She'd taken Laura's offer to help change linens for the winter and other tasks that needed to be done in the off-season. Cindy was thankful for the chance to make a little extra money.

"I'll be there tomorrow for haircuts for Owen and the kids."

"That'll be fun."

"If you consider trying to get at a squirming little one with sharp scissors fun…"

Piper laughed. "Let me know if I can help."

"Between their parents and my mom, we should be able to corral them."

Jace returned with her salad and nodded to the checkerboard. "Set us up with a game. I'm out for retribution."

"If you ask me," Piper said when he'd walked away again, "that's not all he's out for."

Cindy laughed as she nudged her friend. "Stop it."

Piper left a short time later, and her seat was taken by Cindy's brother John.

"I'm shocked to see you here," he said with the dry wit that always made her laugh.

"No, you're not."

"At first, I thought it was the chowder that brought you in, but now I think it might be the bartender."

He'd no sooner said that than Jace came over to put a draft beer in front of John and make his first move in the checkers game.

"Dinner, John?" he asked.

"No, thanks. I ate with my mom and Charlie."

"Gotcha," Jace said before moving to tend to other customers.

"It seems to me," Cindy said to her brother as she slid a red checker forward, "you're usually here when a certain man is performing." John had told her about the blowup over his relationship in Tennessee a while ago, and which had surprised her at the time. But with hindsight, a lot of things made more sense since she'd had that conversation with him.

"Maybe. Maybe not. So, something kinda huge happened earlier."

Cindy looked over at him. "What?"

"I came out to Mom, or I should say, she asked me when I was going to."

"*She did?* Oh my God! So, she already knew?"

"She said she's always known."

"Wow, Johnny. That's amazing. What did she say? What did *you* say?"

"The other night, I ran into Niall when I was out for a run and invited him back to the house for dinner. We had a nice time with Mom and Charlie, and she asked if I'm going to see him again. She said it like it was no big deal when I was shocked."

"I'm sure you were."

"She said..." His eyes filled, and he quickly looked away.

Cindy put her hand on his arm. "What did she say?"

"That she loves me unconditionally, now and always."

"Aw, of course she does. We all do."

"Do you have any idea what a relief it is that she knows and doesn't care?"

"I can only imagine."

"I've been carrying this huge secret my entire life, and now..." He shook his head. "Now, I don't have to do that anymore."

"No, you don't."

"It's been so hard, Cin. I never wanted to disappoint anyone, even Dad, as weird as that might sound."

"I get that. When he wasn't being a thug, he set high standards for us that we've all struggled to live up to in one way or another."

"Yeah, for sure."

"I'm so glad you had that conversation with Mom and that it went as well as it did."

"Me, too. I'm still kind of stunned that it happened at all. I wasn't planning to go there with her, at least not then."

"She could tell you've been struggling and wanted to help."

"She really shocked me by coming right out with it."

"I'm sure that was a huge shock, but a good one, right?"

"Definitely."

"Will you tell the others?"

"Eventually."

"Maybe you ought to just send a text and get it over with in one fell swoop."

"Like, just text them and say, 'Oh, by the way, I'm gay and always have been'?"

"Why not? It won't change anything for them, and it'll change everything for you."

"You really don't think it'll change anything for them?"

"Johnny," she said. "We love you. We always will. I haven't a doubt in my mind about that. Just do it. Get it over with once and for all so you can get on with living your best life."

He pulled his phone from his back pocket and stared at the screen for a second before he found their family group chat and began typing as Cindy read over his shoulder.

Talked to Mom tonight, and Cindy says I have to tell the rest of you what Mom already knew when I talked to her earlier... So I'm gay. That's all I wanted to say. Love you guys. Hope you still love me. Johnny

"What do you think?" he asked Cindy.

"It's perfect. Send it. Be done with it."

John took a deep breath and held it as he pressed Send on the message.

Julia responded first. *So what else is new? Have known that for years. Glad you're doing you, boo. Love you always.*

John ran a hand over his mouth as he teared up reading Julia's message.

How did I miss this? Owen responded. *No matter, good for you, love you.*

Katie: *Love you so much, Johnny.*

Jeff: *Duh. Carry on, bro.*

Josh: *I'm with you, O. Didn't know, but whatever. Love you, J.*

"There," Cindy said. "All good just like I told you it would be." She put her arm around John and brought his head to her shoulder.

"Thank you for the push. I suppose I should tell Gram and Gramps, too."

"They won't care either. I was with her earlier, and she was urging me to take Jace for a spin because, and I quote her in horror, 'You wouldn't buy a car without test-driving it, would you?'"

John sat up straight and laughed. "She did not say that."

"Yes, she did, and you know she did."

"She's becoming more irreverent all the time. I love it, and I'll talk to them. After that, I don't care who knows."

"That's the way to be."

On a break, Niall came up behind them. "What's going on over here? Are you okay?"

"I am," John said, smiling at the other man. "Better than ever, in fact."

"And what brought this on?"

"A little coming-out party, you might say."

Niall raised a brow. "You weren't out yet?"

"Not officially."

"And you are now?"

"To almost everyone who matters."

"Great. You want to grab dinner some night?"

"Yes, I do."

"Excellent."

Watching them exchange phone numbers filled Cindy with an incredible feeling of pride in her brother and the courage it had taken for him to share his truth with their family. John left an hour later, and the bar crowd slowly dwindled until Cindy was left alone with Jace, who'd offered to walk her home after his shift.

"Everything all right with your brother?" Jace asked as he washed the last of the glasses.

Cindy reached for a towel he'd left on the bar and gestured for him to pass her the glasses for drying. "It is now. He came out to our family tonight."

"Oh wow. How'd that go?"

"As my friend in Dallas would say, it was a nothingburger in the grand scheme of things. My mom said she already knew, and the siblings were very supportive. A couple of them said they've known for years, too."

"It might've been a nothingburger for all of you, but I'm sure it was a big deal for him."

"It was huge. He was shocked when my mom said she already knew."

"Mothers are spooky that way."

"Yes, they are, and when you're a mother of seven, you have ESP."

"I suppose you'd have to have something extra to survive seven kids. You and John were cute sitting with your heads together plotting whatever you were up to."

"He was texting the others with the news after he talked to my mom. I encouraged him to do it and get it over with. Now he just has to tell our grandparents, and then, as he said, everyone who matters will know."

"How will they take it?"

"They won't care. They're very hip, and they love us more than anything. My mom is an only child, so she and the seven of us are their family. And besides, after what we endured with our father, all they care about is that we're healthy and happy."

"I guess that brought some perspective."

"It did. When the whole story finally came out, they were sick over what'd been happening right under their noses, as they put it. But he went to great lengths, especially by threatening us, to keep our family's business private. We never breathed a word of it to them. Owen, who's the oldest, has said how badly he wanted to, but he feared making things worse rather than better."

"Would it have? Made things worse, I mean?"

"Very possibly. Because of my dad's rank, people were deferential to him. They looked the other way. Once, when Owen was about fifteen or sixteen, my dad broke his arm during an altercation."

"Seriously?"

"Yep. The young doctor who saw him at the clinic, a junior officer, got Owen alone and asked a bunch of questions that led Owen to believe he suspected my dad had done it. Owen lied to him because he knew my dad would ruin the other guy's career for trying to help."

"He protected the doctor at his own expense. That's wild."

"That's how it was for us. People were afraid to call out my dad for fear of reprisals. So, we were abused in plain sight, and no one ever did anything about it because they were afraid of him, too. Until the trial, when the wife of one of my dad's former subordinates came forward, willing to testify that she knew, that everyone knew, who and what Mark Lawry really was. She was just what we needed—someone from outside the family to confirm our account. The minute my dad saw her in the courtroom, he took a plea deal because he knew she could bury him."

Jace had stopped what he was doing to listen to her.

"Sorry, I didn't mean to go on about it."

"Don't be sorry. I want to hear whatever you want to tell me, but I hate that you and your family went through that with him."

Cindy shrugged. "It happened. We survived it, and we're all doing well now. That's what matters."

Jace shut off the lights over the bar and came around to where she was still seated on one of the stools, with only the light from outside illuminating them. He turned her stool toward him and tucked a strand of hair behind her ear. "That's not all that matters."

Cindy's mouth had gone dry. "What else matters?"

"You do. You matter. What you endured growing up... It's made you strong and resilient, but you still hurt on the inside, don't you?"

His insight startled her almost as much as his nearness did. "Most of the time, I'm okay, but yeah, it's always there."

"Yeah, it is. I think of my final minutes with Jess every day. It'll never stop hurting."

"I hurt a little less when you're around," she confessed, looking up at him as she said the words without taking even a second to consider whether she should.

"Likewise," he whispered in the second before his lips met hers in a soft, sweet, undemanding kiss that would go down as one of the most perfect moments of her entire life. He cupped her face and stroked her cheek as he kissed her.

Still seated on the chair, Cindy strained to get closer.

Jace put his arms around her and lifted her right off her seat and into his embrace.

This, she thought in a second of complete clarity, *is why I was born*. He *is why I was born*. If a friend had told her that was what they thought the first time a guy kissed them, Cindy would have laughed at them for being dramatic.

But it didn't feel dramatic to her. It simply felt true.

She looped her arms around his neck and opened her mouth to his tongue, which brushed against hers in a suggestive rhythm that immediately had her trying to get even closer.

His arms were like a vise around her, keeping her trapped against him as he kissed her until she was breathless from wanting more of him.

Best. First. Kiss. *Ever*.

CHAPTER 18

*J*ace had wanted to kiss her since the first time she took a seat at his bar and smiled at him. He'd wanted to kiss her before she said a single word to him, and the more he got to know her, the more he'd wanted to kiss her. When he'd realized she was the one advertising the room for rent, he'd been torn because of the overwhelming attraction he felt for her.

What the hell, he thought. Why not tell her that?

"I almost didn't move in because I've wanted to kiss you since the first time we met."

"That long?"

"Yep, and every minute since then." He kissed her again, because they had a lot of time to make up for now that the kissing portion of the program had begun.

"Jace?" a voice called from outside the doors to the bar. "Are you still here?"

He released Cindy so quickly that they both stumbled as they parted. Taking hold of her arm, he helped to steady her. "I'm still here," he called to Matilda, the night manager. "Just leaving now."

"Ah, okay," Matilda said when she came into the room. "I was going to lock up."

He took Cindy's hand and headed for the door, handing a bag of cash and credit card receipts to Matilda. "Have a good night."

"You do the same."

This was already shaping up to be the best night of his life since his kids were born, and it wasn't over yet. At least he hoped it wasn't.

Still holding hands, they walked through a dark, quiet town that they had mostly to themselves at that hour. He wanted to say something to her, but he wasn't sure what, so he stayed quiet while wondering what she was thinking and feeling. Had that kiss rocked her world the way it had his? Was she dying to do it again the second they got home?

It'd been years since he'd been anywhere close to something like this. The last time had been when he was first seeing Lisa and had been completely overwhelmed by feelings he'd never experienced so intensely. Unfortunately, those feelings had been exacerbated by his rampant drug addiction. He'd screwed that up royally, which worried him as he started something with Cindy. She'd already had more than her share of grief. The last thing she needed was more.

"You're very quiet all of a sudden," she said when they were almost home.

"So are you."

"That's your fault."

"How's that?" he asked as they approached their place.

"You kissed me senseless."

"Did I?"

"You know you did."

"You did the same to me." Jace used his key in the door and stepped aside to let her go in ahead of him.

During the summer months, when the doors to the bar were open, he would've wanted a shower immediately after sweating his balls off for hours. But with the weather turning cooler, the doors had been closed, and he hadn't worked up a sweat.

Now that they were in the house, he felt uncertain about how to pick up where they'd left off in the bar. Until Cindy turned to him, dropped her purse on the floor and put her arms up around his neck.

"Okay, then," he said, smiling.

"Are we going to pretend that we don't want to continue the conversation from the bar?"

He placed his hands on her hips and smiled down at her gorgeous face. "I'm not pretending."

"Neither am I."

"And this is what you want? I'm what you want, even with everything you know about me?" he asked.

"You're what I want *because* of what I know about you."

"I'm not sure I deserve you," he whispered against her lips.

"Yes, you do. You deserve me, and I deserve you, and we both deserve to be happy."

"How happy are we gonna get?"

"I think we're going to be very, *very* happy."

Smiling, he kissed her with the abandon he hadn't been able to surrender to while at the Beachcomber.

Pressed against him, arms tight around his neck, Cindy was right there with him, making him see stars, he wanted her so badly. It'd been so long since he'd been close to a woman that he was afraid he might scare her. He couldn't let that happen. He *wouldn't* let that happen. She wasn't just anyone. She was special, and he wanted to show her that.

"Tell me to stop if it's too much."

"It's not." She tugged at the long-sleeved Henley with the Beachcomber logo on the chest. "Take this off."

He pulled the shirt over his head and gave thanks for the hours in the gym as her eyes went wide with appreciation.

She ran her hands over his biceps, making him shiver from the excitement of her touch.

"What about this?" he asked, giving her sweater a gentle tug.

"Take it off."

Jace kept waiting for her to call a halt to this madness, but as long as she didn't, he was all in. And *madness* was the only word to describe the way he felt being close to her this way. As the sweater cleared her head, he gazed down at her, taking note of the tan lines on her chest and the rise and fall of full breasts.

Reaching behind her, he released the clasp on her bra and watched as the fabric fell away. "You're pretty everywhere, Cindy."

Her hands skimmed over his back. "So are you."

He cupped her ass and lifted her, hoping she'd wrap herself around him, which she did. "Your place or mine?"

"My bed is bigger."

"Yours it is." As he carried her to the bedroom, he was still waiting for her to say, *Hang on, this is happening too fast.* But she only continued to kiss his face and neck, making him even crazier than he already was. When he lowered her to the bed and came down on top of her, he held himself up on his elbows. "You're sure about this?"

"Are you?"

"Very sure."

"That makes two of us."

Gazing down at her sweet face, he said, "And we're not going to regret this afterward?"

"I'm not planning to if you're not."

"No regrets. Just pleasure."

She ran her fingers through his hair, sending more shivers down his spine.

"I ought to warn you that it's been a while for me."

"How long is 'a while'?"

"Like seven years?"

"Oh. Well…"

"Yeah, this is apt to be quick."

Smiling, she said, "Are you good for only once?"

"Um, no," he said, laughing.

"Then quick is fine."

"You haven't taken leave of your senses or anything, have you?"

Cindy laughed. "Why, because I'm not freaking out or pretending like I don't want this as much as you do?"

"Yeah, all that."

"My grandmother told me I should take you for a ride, so I'm doing what she told me."

"Have I mentioned that your grandmother is the coolest granny ever?"

"She is." Cindy's hands moved over his back and arms, making him shiver from her touch. "I can't wait for you to meet her."

"I can't wait to thank her for putting ideas in your head." He bent to touch his tongue to her nipple, making her gasp. She was so responsive, sweet and sexy. What he wouldn't give to know what else her grand-mother had said to her. Then another thought occurred to him that had him groaning and pulling back from her. "Shit. I don't have condoms."

"You really haven't done this in seven years?"

"I really haven't."

"I'm on birth control, and it's been ages for me, too."

"So, what you're saying…"

Cindy laughed at the face he made that probably conveyed torture as much as excitement.

"When I said fast before… what I really meant was over before it starts."

She shocked the shit out of him when she reached between them to cup his erection. "Maybe we should take care of that, so you don't have to worry about it."

"So, what you're saying…"

Her laughter was quickly becoming his favorite thing. "Turn over, cowboy."

"Um."

Still laughing, she gave his shoulder a push.

Jace turned onto his back and looked up at her, waiting to see what she would do.

She bent over him and began placing light kisses on his chest and abdomen.

After going so long without a woman's touch, the sensations were nearly excruciating, the desire overwhelming. He trembled helplessly as she outlined each of his abs with her tongue. "Cin…"

"Hmm?"

He exhaled a laugh. "You're driving me crazy."

"Am I?"

"You know you are."

"Is crazy good in this case?"

"It's not *bad*."

Laughing, she continued the torture until he was on the verge of begging for relief.

When she tugged on the button to his jeans, he held back a whimper. He helped with the zipper and lifted his hips so she could pull his pants and boxers down. Then her hand wrapped around his cock as her lips brushed against the head.

"Cindy, *stop*," he said, his tone full of warning.

She didn't stop. Rather, she slid his cock inside her mouth and lashed it with her tongue.

He came so hard, he saw stars and comets and a few random asteroids behind his tightly closed eyes.

"There." She ran her tongue over the length of him. "All better now."

Jace was trying to remember how to form words.

"Are you okay down there?"

"Mmm." He settled her on top of him, loving the feel of her breasts pressed to his chest. "So good. You wiped me out."

"I bet I can wake you up again."

"I have no doubt that you can." With his hands on her face, he studied her for a moment before he kissed her. "You're the best thing to happen to me in a very long time. I hope you know that."

"Likewise."

"Nice how that works out, huh?"

She nodded and smiled as she kissed him.

Jace surprised her when he suddenly turned them over and got busy returning the favor she'd granted him. He kissed her everywhere, removing the last of her clothing and spreading her out before him as he ran his tongue up the inside of her thigh.

She raised her hips in invitation, which he happily accepted, burying his tongue inside her and teasing her until she was panting. He pushed his fingers into her heat and ran his tongue over her clit, making her explode in a screaming release. Moving quickly, he changed positions and pressed his cock into her, riding the last waves of her orgasm.

He grasped her hips as he moved carefully, giving her time to adjust as he went. "Is this okay?"

"Mmm, *yes*." She arched into him as her fingers dug into his back muscles.

It was a good thing she'd taken the edge off, or this would've been over the minute his flesh connected with hers. During the long years of his incarceration, he'd survived by not thinking too much about the things he was missing. He'd stayed focused on working out and learning a trade and turning his life around.

This was the payoff for all that hard work. Cindy was the payoff, and as he lost himself in her, he felt almost reborn into a whole new life free of his painful past. The trauma of his brother's death and the price he'd paid would always be part of him, but maybe it didn't have to define him.

No, he was beginning to think that this gorgeous woman might define him.

CINDY SLEPT LIKE A DEAD WOMAN. She woke facedown, sun streaming in the window and the smell of coffee filling the air. When she stirred, her body objected, muscles she hadn't used in a while reminding her of a wild, almost-sleepless night.

How was he functioning after being up most of the night?

She turned on her side, moaning.

The bed dipped, and she opened one eye to find him there.

"Is someone not a morning person?"

"I'm a morning person when I actually sleep."

His low rumble of laughter made her smile, which had her realizing her lips were sore. "You don't drink coffee, right?"

"Normally, no, but today is not normal." Grasping the sheet to her chest, she used her other arm to sit up and took the mug from him. She hadn't had coffee in years and hoped a few sips wouldn't ruin her day. Today, they were apt to save her day.

"Are you okay?"

She opened her eyes to look at him. "I am. Are you?"

"I'm great."

"Even though you barely slept?"

"I can sleep when I'm dead."

She handed the mug to him. "Don't say that."

He took a sip and gave it back to her. "Okay, I won't."

"Why are you up so early?"

"Got to hit my meeting at eight."

"Oh. Right."

Jace reached out to caress her face. "Last night was amazing."

"Yes, it was."

"And it doesn't feel weird this morning."

"Not for me."

"Me either." He leaned in to kiss her. "I've got to go. Are you going to be around later?"

"I have to see Laura and Owen at the hotel in a bit, but nothing after that, although I did promise you a haircut today."

"We can do that any day. Let's go to the beach or something before I have to work."

"That sounds good."

He kissed her again and handed the mug of coffee to her. "I'll be back in a bit."

"Okay."

Jace made it to the doorway before he turned around and came back, bending over the bed to kiss her one more time. "There," he said. "That ought to hold me until later."

Cindy watched him go, smiling like a kook as memories from the most sensual night of her life played like a dirty movie in her mind.

CHAPTER 19

*A*fter she heard the door close as he left, she reached for her phone to text her sisters. *I need a sister meeting. I'll provide the coffee. Bring me something decadent to eat. It's that kind of morning.*

Katie wrote back immediately. *Color me intrigued.*

Likewise, Julia said. *Pupwell and I are on the way. Will stop at the diner for the decadence.*

Yessss! Cindy replied.

How lovely was it to have her sisters nearby when she needed them? She had to tell someone about her night with Jace, and there's no one she'd rather tell than them. After two more sips of coffee, she reluctantly put the mug aside and forced herself out of bed, groaning as she walked on aching legs to the shower.

"Girlfriend is out of shape," she muttered.

The hot water on her aching muscles was blissful. After the shower, she felt a tiny bit more alive than she had before but was still dragging when her sisters arrived twenty minutes later.

Katie took one look at her and said, "You look like something the cat dragged out—all night long."

"It wasn't quite *all* night, but damned close."

"Oh!" Julia put a bag from the diner on the table. "Do tell!"

Cindy poured coffee for her sisters and ice water for herself. "Jace kissed me, and one thing led to another, which led to pretty much all damned night, and now I can barely walk."

"*Girl!*" Julia did a little happy dance around the tiny kitchen. "It's about freaking time!"

"Tell us everything," Katie said. "Was it good?"

"If it was any better, I might not have survived it."

"That's the best kind of good," Julia said with a knowing grin. "That's how I knew Deacon was the one for me. I never get tired of it with him. In the past, I'd be mentally composing my grocery list after twenty minutes. With him, I'm not thinking of anything else."

"You did not make a grocery list!" Katie said.

"I did, because I was so bored."

"I wasn't making any grocery lists last night," Cindy said. "I could barely remember my own name for most of it."

"Ah, I love that," Katie said. "That's how it ought to be."

"This is so exciting!" Julia opened take-out containers to reveal freshly baked muffins and a side of Rebecca's delicious breakfast potatoes.

"Thank you so much," Cindy said, diving into a corn muffin. "I'm famished."

"Sexual marathons burn a lot of calories," Julia said.

"You ought to know," Katie said. "She went 'missing' for days when she and Deacon first got together."

Julia stuck out her tongue at her twin. "We were getting to know each other."

"Is that what it's called?" Katie asked.

"It hasn't been that long since you first got together with Shane," Julia said. "You remember what that's like."

"It's still like that, even after we got married," Katie said. "When we're together, I don't need anything or anyone else."

"I love that for you," Cindy said.

"Now you have it, too," Julia said.

"I wouldn't go that far. We had one crazy night. That doesn't mean it's forever."

"But it could be?" Katie asked hopefully.

Cindy was almost afraid to let herself go there, like if she gave it too much importance, she might be setting herself up for disappointment. "I just don't know."

"Where is he?" Julia asked.

"At a meeting."

"Is it the eight a.m. meeting at the church that Jeff goes to by any chance?" Katie asked.

"Yes."

"It's good that he still went, even after being up all night," Katie said.

"He never misses a day."

"That's important."

"You guys... I really like him. Like, really, *really* like him, but it's all so..."

"Big?" Julia asked.

"It could be."

Julia nodded as she released a wistful sigh. "I remember what that was like when Deacon came swooping into my life and became the most important thing over the course of a few days and how *terrifying* that was."

"That's a good word for it," Cindy said. "Terrifying."

"We all have good reason to be terrified of making a bad decision in the partner department," Katie said.

"Yeah," Cindy said. "Exactly."

"Don't you think you'd know in your gut if he was someone you needed to be worried about?" Julia asked. "You with all your intuition and all that."

"I'd like to think so," Cindy said, "but Mom didn't know what she was getting until it was far too late. That's what is so scary about taking this kind of risk with someone. You just never really know."

"We're not Mom," Julia said. "We know what to look for in a way that she didn't, since she had never been exposed to what we were."

"That's true," Katie said. "We do know more. It never would've occurred to her that the nice young officer she met at a dance was a monster. We're wired to expect the worst while hoping for the best."

"How do you ever really know, though?" Cindy asked.

"With Shane, it wasn't just how he treated me, it was how other people responded to him," Katie said. "He was obviously well loved and respected by his family and friends."

"Jace doesn't really have much in the way of family, and he hasn't been here long enough to make a lot of close friends," Cindy said. "Although everyone at the bar loves him."

"For me, it was how Deacon treated Pupwell and then seeing him with his nieces. He was so sweet and cute with them."

"You just have to put in the time and be vigilant," Katie said. "No one is perfect, but we can't go into every new relationship thinking that all men are monsters. We know that's not true."

"No," Cindy said, "but enough of them are that I'm never sure who I can trust."

"But look at Mom," Julia said. "If she can take a second chance on love, then surely the rest of us can take a chance, too."

"I think about that a lot," Katie said. "The way she is with Charlie is like meeting her for the first time, the person she was always meant to be rather than the person she became to survive being married to Dad."

"That's a good way to put it," Julia said. "I love who she is with Charlie. Watching her take that chance with him inspired me to give Deacon a shot. And I'm so glad I did. He's the best thing ever."

"I love seeing you guys and Mom and Owen so happy," Cindy said.

"We want it for you, too, Goose," Katie said, evoking Cindy's childhood nickname, given to her because she was supposedly a silly goose.

"Haven't heard that in a while," Cindy said, grimacing.

"Because you're not silly like you used to be," Katie said gently. "You don't laugh and joke and tease, and before you say anything, we know why."

In front of a crowd of family and friends, her father had told her to *stop acting like such a goddamned fool.* The memory of shame and humiliation brought tears to Cindy's eyes all these years later.

"Don't do that," Julia said. "Don't give him even one more minute of your time."

"I wish it was that simple," Cindy said, dabbing at her eyes with a paper napkin.

"I know," Julia said. "Believe me. I get it."

"We all do," Katie added, "but how about some good news?"

Cindy nodded. "Yes, please."

"Shane and I are trying for a baby again, but I'm only telling you guys. Just in case."

"Aw, Katie." Cindy hugged her sister. "I'm so glad you're doing that."

"Part of me wants to skip the whole thing after the miscarriage, but Shane convinced me that would be silly. We need to keep trying until we get it right."

"And the trying isn't awful, right?" Julia asked with a grin.

"Not at all. It's wonderful. I just wish I could shake the anxiety. I had myself convinced I was done with having babies when we'd only just started. Thankfully, Shane was super patient and helped me come around to trying again. He said at least we know now that we can. We just have to keep trying until we get the baby we were meant to have."

"He's so sweet," Cindy said.

"I love him so much," Katie said.

"I hope you guys know that you've inspired me, too," Cindy said. "It's not just Mom. It's you two and Owen and even Charlie. You were all able to get past stuff that should've ruined you forever to have your happily ever after."

"You're going to get yours, too, Cin," Julia said, squeezing Cindy's hand. "I just know it."

"I agree," Katie said. "It's been a long time since you were moony over a guy like you are over Jace."

"I'm not moony over him," Cindy said. "What does that even mean?"

Her sisters made faces that had Cindy convulsing with laughter.

"If I ever look that stupid, take me out and shoot me, will you please?"

Before her sisters could reply, the front door opened, and Jace strolled in, stealing the breath from her lungs as she watched him come toward her.

"Morning, ladies," he said.

"You remember my sisters Julia and Katie, right?"

"Of course. Nice to see you again."

"You, too."

"Anyone need a coffee refill?" he asked, going to the pot.

"I was getting ready to go to work for a couple of hours to catch up," Julia said, giving Cindy a look, "but why would I leave right when things are getting interesting?"

"I wish I could stay," Katie said, "but I'm meeting Shane for brunch in twenty minutes, so you'll have to tell me everything that happens, Jule."

"Oh, I will. Call me later."

"Can you two at least pretend not to be talking about him right in front of him?" Cindy asked.

Jace grinned as he leaned back against the counter and took a sip from his mug. "I was wondering if I was the topic of conversation."

"Your name might've come up," Julia said.

"Once or twice," Katie added.

"They were just leaving," Cindy said, giving them a "get the hell out of my house" look that made her sisters laugh.

"Why, do you have something—or some*one*—you need to do, Cin?"

Jace choked on his coffee.

"Get. Out. *Now.*"

"You bring a girl a muffin, and this is the thanks you get," Julia said. "Jace, it was great to see you. I hope we'll be seeing lots of you, and if you're anything other than sweet and kind to our baby sister, we will kill you."

"Julia!" Cindy glanced at Jace. "Don't listen to her."

"Yes, listen to her," Katie said. "She means it, and she's speaking for both of us. Well, all of us."

Jace extended a hand to Cindy. "You ladies—and your sister—have nothing to worry about where I'm concerned."

With knees gone weak from the way he looked at her, she took his hand.

"I want only the best of everything for her," Jace added, his gaze set on her face, which instantly heated.

"Well, I'd say we're not needed here, Jules," Katie said, taking Julia by the arm to lead her out as Pupwell trotted along behind them.

"If this love shack's a-rockin'," Julia said over her shoulder, "don't come a-knockin'."

"Oh my God," Cindy said, mortified as Jace shook with silent laughter. "I'm sorry about them. They're incorrigible, especially Julia. Every thought she's ever had comes out of her mouth."

"They're awesome, and you love them."

"I love them, but sometimes I also want to kill them." As soon as those words left her mouth, Cindy wanted to take them back. "I'm sorry. I shouldn't have said that."

"Don't do that. You were joking, and I knew it."

"Still, that's not something I should joke about with you."

"It's fine. I swear. I'm glad you had a nice visit with them, but was someone sharing our secrets by any chance?"

Cindy did her best to act like she didn't know what he meant. "I would never do that."

"Haha, right. Did they get all the dirty details or just a few?"

"They only got the gist, no details."

He put his hands on her hips and rested his forehead against hers. "What grade was I given in this gist you gave your sisters?"

"Stop! I didn't grade you."

"But if you had, how would I have done?"

"You know full well that you're an A plus. You don't need me to tell you that."

"Yes, I do, and an A plus, huh? That's impressive. I think that's my first-ever A plus."

"If you were any more of an A plus, I wouldn't be able to move today."

"It was pretty fun, huh?" he asked, kissing her neck and firing her up all over again, as if she hadn't had more orgasms than she could count in the last eight hours.

"Yes, it was." More fun than she'd ever had with any man, that was for certain.

"You still want to go to the beach, or might you be interested in a nap?"

"Like a sleeping nap or some other kind of nap?"

"I had no idea your mind was so dirty."

"It's not!"

Jace cracked up. "It's a little dirty."

"You're a bad influence on me."

He pulled back to look at her, seeming stricken. "Am I?"

"In the best possible way." She drew him into a kiss. "I needed you to shake things up for me, and you did that. And then some."

"Does that mean that what went down between us isn't a regular occurrence for you?"

"Ah, no. I haven't been with anyone in ages, and when I have done… well, *that*… it wasn't like… well, *that*."

"I think I followed *that*, and there was a compliment in there somewhere."

Cindy was so tired, she could barely see straight, let alone engage in a verbal sparring match that she was certain to lose.

When Jace's phone rang, he groaned and pulled back from her to withdraw it from his pocket. "It's Seamus. I need to take this."

"Go ahead."

Jace kept his arm around her when he took the call. "Hey, what's up?"

Only because she was standing so close to him did she hear what Seamus said. "I need to see you. Can you come by the office? Like, now?"

His entire body went rigid with tension. "Yeah, sure. Is everything okay? The boys…"

"They're fine, but we need to talk."

"I'll be right there."

"Thanks."

Jace put the phone back in his pocket. "What the hell is this now?"

"He said the boys are all right, and that's what matters."

"Yeah, true."

Cindy hugged him. "Do you want me to go with you?"

"No, you don't have to. I'm sure you've got your own stuff to do."

"I need to get to the Surf for some haircuts while I can still string together a sentence coherently."

He kissed her forehead and then her lips. "I see a nap in our future before work. Meet you back here in a bit?"

"I'll see you then. Call me if, you know, you need anything after seeing Seamus."

"I will." He stole one more kiss before he headed for the door.

Cindy hoped that whatever was going on with Seamus wouldn't cause new grief for Jace. He'd had more than enough already.

CHAPTER 20

hat the hell is this? Jace wondered as he walked toward Seamus's office at the ferry landing. Everything had been going so well between him and the O'Gradys. Was Seamus going to tell him he couldn't see the boys anymore? The thought of that sent a shaft of panic through him. What would he do then?

God, he hoped that wasn't it. The last freaking thing in the world he wanted was some sort of legal battle to see his kids. Because that's what he'd do if Seamus tried to cut him off from them. He'd fight for them—and for himself.

Please don't let it be that.

By the time Jace reached the offices of the Gansett Island Ferry Company, he was thoroughly worked up, especially when he noticed Carolina's car parked next to the company truck Seamus drove.

Jace stepped into the building and went to Seamus's office, knocking on the closed door.

"Come in," Seamus called.

When he walked through the door, Jace noted that Seamus and Carolina were seated together on the small sofa, and he couldn't miss that they seemed troubled.

"Thanks for coming," Seamus said.

"Sure. What's up?"

"Have a seat."

Jace sat even though he didn't want to.

"Yesterday, we were in the barn going through some of the things that came from Lisa's," Carolina said somewhat haltingly. "The boys were playing in the yard with the dog. You know how they are—they're so loud, we can always hear them."

"Right," Jace said, feeling more tense by the second.

"We were going through some of Lisa's photos when Jackson surprised us. We didn't hear him coming, and he saw... Well, he saw photos of you with Lisa, and now he's full of questions about who you are and how his mom knew you."

"Oh," Jace said on a long exhale. "What'd you tell him?"

"That his mom knew you, too, but he didn't seem to buy that."

"What did he say?"

"Just that his mom never mentioned you."

Carolina took hold of Seamus's hand. "We need to tell them the truth about who you are."

"It was one thing to pass you off as my friend when they had no clue," Seamus said, "but when he asks us directly who you are, we don't feel right about lying to him."

"We think he might suspect," Carolina added, "which is why the truth becomes important."

Jace tried to keep up with what they were saying as he processed his own emotional reaction to the news.

"We didn't want to say or do anything until we spoke to you," Seamus said.

"I... um... I appreciate that."

"What do you think we ought to do?" Carolina asked.

"I agree that we need to tell them the truth," Jace said, screaming on the inside at the possibility the boys would want nothing more to do with him after they knew how his mistakes had led to their mother being a struggling single parent.

"How much of the truth?" Seamus asked.

"All of it," Jace said. "Go big or go home, right?"

"You're sure about that, mate?"

"No, I'm not sure of anything except I love them and want the best of everything for them."

MARIE FORCE

"You need to start with that," Carolina said.

"Wait, so you want *me* to tell them?" Jace asked.

"We thought you might want to be the one to fill in the gaps for them," Seamus said. "Are we wrong about that?"

"No, you're not, it's just… God, what do I say to them?"

"You tell them the truth, Jace," Carolina said gently. "What will matter to them is that you love them and want to be in their lives but have no plans to upset their arrangement with us. At least I hope that's how you feel."

"It is. I'd never do that to them—or you." He ran his fingers through his hair as he tried to contemplate coming clean with his young sons. "I just wonder if they'll hate me after they hear my story."

"They won't hate you," Seamus said.

"You're sure about that? They're old enough to remember that their mother had to struggle and work multiple jobs to keep a roof over their heads because I was nowhere to be found. They know that when she was sick and dying, I wasn't here."

"I understand your concerns, Jace," Carolina said, "but one thing I know about the boys is they don't hate anyone or anything. They don't have that in them. They're all love and sunshine and happiness. Do they have their sad moments when they think of Lisa? Yes, they do, and they probably always will. But they won't hate you. They may have hard questions, and they may be upset by what you tell them, but I'd bet my life they won't hate you for mistakes you made years ago that you're sorry about now."

Carolina's assurances helped to calm the storm brewing in him when he thought about the reality of telling his sons the truth about where he'd been the past six years. "When do you want to do this?"

"Today," Seamus said. "As soon as possible."

"Oh damn. That soon, huh?"

"It's important to us that they trust us to be straight with them," Carolina said. "Jackson knows there's more to the story, and we don't want to let it fester."

It was the right thing to do. Jace knew that. But when he tried to picture himself telling the boys his story, he wanted to run and hide. At stressful times like these, addicts needed to be extra careful and protective of their sobriety, and he was no different that way.

162

"Where are they now?"

"At Ethan's. They slept over there last night, but Hope says they were out of sorts."

"Do you think we might pick them up and talk to them soon?" Jace asked. "I have to work at three today, so I want to be sure we have enough time."

Seamus glanced at Carolina, who nodded.

"Let's go get them now," she said. "We'll meet you at the house in thirty minutes?"

"I'll be there." Even if it would be among the most painful things he ever did, he would tell his sons the truth and then hope they still wanted him in their lives. He felt like he was going to be sick as he left the office and stepped outside into a glorious September day, for all he cared about the weather.

Throughout years of recovery, he'd learned to reach out for help when he needed it. As much as he wanted to talk to Cindy about this latest development, he needed someone who understood the sobriety issues that came with a situation like this. He texted Mallory. *Do you have a minute?*

She responded right away. *I'll call you in five.*

Thanks.

He walked to a bench that overlooked the ferry landing, which was all but deserted nearly a week after Labor Day.

True to her word, Mallory called five minutes later. "What's up?"

"Potential crisis."

"Oh damn. What's going on?"

He filled her in on what'd happened with Seamus, Carolina and Jackson, as well as their plans to talk to the boys. "I'm trying not to freak out over this."

"And how's that going?"

"Not so great."

"You're not feeling any urge to use, are you?"

"I wouldn't even know where to get it here."

"It's never hard to find if you're looking, but you're not looking, and that's what matters. You're doing the right thing by reaching out for support."

"I'm afraid they're going to hate me for the many ways I failed them

163

and their mother. Carolina says they don't have it in them to hate anyone, but there's a first time for everything."

"They won't hate you, Jace. If you tell them the story the same way you told us, they may have questions, but they won't hate you."

"I've just gotten them back in my life. If I lose that connection now..."

"You won't. If you tell them how you never stopped loving them or their mom and that you're sorry for everything that happened, that'll mean a lot to them."

Jace had tears in his eyes as he listened to her. "Yeah, that's true."

"Just keep it simple with them. They're still quite young, so the deeper meaning might be lost on them."

"That's true. Thank you for the words of wisdom. I was spinning a bit when I found out this was going to happen today. I thought I had years before I'd have to deal with this."

"In a way, it might be a blessing in disguise. If they found out when they were older and wiser, they might react differently—and not in your favor. This way, they learn the truth when they're young enough to still be forgiving."

"I hadn't thought of it that way, but you're right."

"I usually am," she said with a laugh. "Just ask Quinn."

Jace laughed as he wiped tears from his eyes.

"Are you going to be all right?"

"I hope so."

"Will you call or text me later if you need to?"

"I will."

"I know you're programmed to believe otherwise, but you're a good man, Jace. Your sons will see the work you've done to turn your life around, and one day, they'll respect you for it."

"I hope so."

"They will. I promise."

"Thank you, Mallory. I appreciate this more than you'll ever know."

"I'm glad you reached out. I'm always here."

"I'll see you in the morning."

"We'll be there."

After they said their goodbyes, Jace sat for a long time on the bench, staring out at the endless ocean and trying to find the words he would need to tell his sons the truth. He thought of Cindy and sent her a quick text. *Something came up. Might not make it home before work. Will see you later.*

He needed to fill her in on what was happening, but he'd rather tell her in person. As he got up to catch a cab to Seamus and Carolina's, he could only hope that the next time he saw her, he wouldn't be completely shattered.

CINDY RECEIVED Jace's text as she walked to the Sand & Surf Hotel to see Laura and Owen. She hoped whatever had come up wasn't bad news for Jace, right when things seemed to be moving in an interesting direction for them. She hated the niggling feeling of distrust that came rushing to the surface after she received that text.

Something had come up.

Could he be any vaguer? Was it about his sons, or was it something else? Or *someone* else?

"Ugh, don't go there," she said out loud as she crossed the street between the Beachcomber and the Surf. "He doesn't have anyone else." *Do you know that for certain?* Why did her inner voice have to sound so much like her father? She would give anything to never think of him again or to have him sowing doubts in her mind about the first man to genuinely interest her in longer than she could remember.

She refused to let Mark Lawry have a say in anything she did or who she liked.

"Why are you looking so stormy, Cin?" Owen asked as he came down the stairs from the hotel to the sidewalk.

"I'm thinking about things—and people—who are best forgotten."

"Yeah, don't do that." Owen hugged her. "Too many better things to think about these days, for all of us."

"That's right."

"Did you bring your scissors? Laura says I'm so shaggy, I'm borderline feral."

"I did, and you are looking kinda ragged."

"That's why I need you. I'm just running across the street for a minute. I'll be right back. Go on in. Laura is at the desk with the twins."

"Hey, O?"

Owen turned back to her.

"I just want you to know... I'm so glad I can see you any time I want these days."

"Likewise," he said, grinning. "I love that the whole family has followed me back to Gansett. We just gotta get Josh here to make it perfect."

"Let's work on that."

He gave her a thumbs-up as he crossed the street.

Cindy went up the stairs and into the hotel that had been a place of childhood magic for the Lawry kids. The smell of the place always took her back to the most idyllic days of her life, filling her with feelings of love and nostalgia. The memories tied to those summer days would stay with her forever.

Her sister-in-law, Laura, came around the desk to hug Cindy. "Thank goodness you're here. My whole crew needs you so badly."

"Auntie Cindy to the rescue."

"Sorry to do this to you on your day off."

"No worries. You know I love any excuse to see the kids."

"They're very excited for haircuts with Auntie Cindy."

The next forty-five minutes were sheer chaos as Laura, Owen, Sarah and Cindy corralled three toddlers into submission so Cindy could cut their hair. By the time they were finished, the adults were exhausted, and the kids were seemingly energized, bouncing off the walls of Laura and Owen's small apartment on the third floor.

"Why is it that we're wrecked, and they're shot full of jet fuel?" Laura asked as she flopped on the sofa.

"They're insane," Owen said. "We've known this for quite some time."

"Are you ready for your haircut?" Cindy asked him.

"I guess so. Some kinda day off this turned out to be for you."

"This is the most fun I've had in ages." Not counting the fun she'd had with Jace during the night, she thought, trying not to giggle. "Step into my office."

Owen sat in the kitchen chair they'd placed in the living room.

Cindy put a towel around his shoulders, and while the kids ran circles around them, she gave him a good trim.

"Take more," Laura said from the sofa. "So it lasts longer."

"No more," Owen said. "She's trying to fully domesticate me, and it's not going to work."

"I hate to tell you, brother, but you're already fully domesticated."

"I'm hanging on to my shaggy hair with everything I've got," Owen replied.

"But you're so hot and sexy when it's short," Laura said suggestively.

"Maybe a little more wouldn't hurt anything," Owen said with a dopey grin for his wife.

Cindy laughed. "You two are so cute. What's the secret to keeping it going after being together awhile?" That was where things usually fell apart for her. She tended to lose interest after the initial glow wore off and reality set in.

"We laugh every day," Laura said.

"Mostly it's her laughing *at* me, but it's still laughter," Owen said.

"And sex," Laura said. "We have a lot of sex."

"Children!" Sarah placed her hands over her ears. "There're parents present!"

Laura laughed at the face Sarah made. "Oh please, like you're not getting busy on the regular over there in your love shack."

"Do something about your wife, son," Sarah said, her face bright red.

"She's incorrigible," Owen said, "and I wouldn't have her any other way."

"That's right," Laura said. "He loves my mouth."

"Aren't you glad you asked, Cin?" Sarah asked, smiling.

"I'm getting more information than I need," Cindy replied.

"To summarize, the secret is laughter and sex," Laura said.

"Thank you for your wisdom," Cindy said.

"Speaking of laughter and sex, how are things with Jace?" Sarah asked.

"Wait, what?" Laura sat up straighter. "There's a Jace?"

"Maybe," Cindy said, keeping her focus on Owen's hair as her entire body heated with memories from the night before.

"Has our girl been keeping secrets?" Laura asked Owen.

"Looks that way. I'm going to have to pay a visit to the bar across the street one of these nights to really check this guy out."

"Don't do that," Cindy said. "I've already checked him out—"

Laura howled with laughter. "I'll just bet you have."

"That's not what I meant," Cindy said, mortified. "He's a good guy, and I like him. So don't go over there and do what you do with him, Owen." He'd intimidated every boyfriend she'd ever had until she moved to Dallas.

"Why should I stop now?"

"Because I'm telling you there's nothing to worry about."

"Leave your sister alone, Owen," Sarah said. "She's a grown woman who can make up her own mind about people."

"Since when do I leave my sisters alone when it comes to men?" Owen asked.

"There's nothing to see here," Cindy said.

"Nothing at all?"

"A few things, but nothing to be concerned about."

"You may as well tell him the rest, Cin," Sarah said, "because you know he'll go digging if you don't."

"Stop the screaming," Laura said to her children. "Let's watch *Encanto* for the nine hundredth time."

While Laura put the movie on for the kids, Cindy finished Owen's haircut, finding a happy medium between his wishes on the length and Laura's. As she moved to inspect him from the front, she found him looking up at her.

"What's the story with this guy?"

"Do you promise to keep an open mind?"

"When is my mind ever not open?"

Cindy groaned. "Do I need to remind you of all the times you judged guys we dated before you even got to know them?"

"And was I ever wrong?"

"No, but… I don't want you to do what you do with Jace. I really like him."

"What is it you don't want me to know?"

"It's not that I don't want you to know. It's that I don't want you to overreact."

"To what?"

Cindy looked into the eyes of the brother who'd been her childhood hero for taking the brunt of their father's rage to protect the rest of them. "He's a recovering addict who did time for armed robbery."

Owen's expression went flat, but his eyes conveyed the emotional response he had to hearing that.

"Before you leap to judgment," Sarah said to her son, "I want you to remember that Charlie was an ex-con when we met him. The story isn't always what it seems. If we had judged him only on his record at the time and hadn't taken the time to learn more about him, we would've missed out on one of the finest men any of us has ever known."

Sarah's words of wisdom took some of the tension out of Owen's posture. "I know, and I promise to keep an open mind."

"Thank you."

"Tell me more about him."

Cindy conveyed the highlights—or lowlights, such as they were—of Jace's story to Owen and Laura. "He's worked hard to turn his life around, and I like who he is now. He devotes time every day to maintaining his sobriety and is concerned about his sons." She hoped that whatever Seamus had wanted to meet with him about wasn't going to be a setback for Jace.

"He sounds like a very interesting person," Laura said. "And he's hot."

"Like fire," Cindy said with a grin for her sister-in-law.

"Easy, Mrs. Lawry," Owen said.

"What? Am I so married I can't appreciate a hot-as-fire man?"

Owen scowled at her. "Yes, you're that married."

"I'm really sorry Jace lost his brother that way," Laura said, deliberately changing the subject.

"It was extremely traumatizing for him, and then to be ripped away from his wife and kids... He's deeply regretful of the mistakes he made and the price his family paid for them."

"That counts for something," Owen said.

"It counts for a lot," Cindy said.

"Why don't you bring Jace to dinner some night soon?" Sarah suggested. "That'd be a good way for us to get to know him. We'll have the whole family."

"Because that wouldn't be at all overwhelming for him," Cindy said.

"We come with the package," Owen said. "May as well get him used to us from the beginning."

Cindy wasn't sure that was a good idea. "I'll ask him and see what he says."

CHAPTER 21

*N*ed Saunders gave Jace a ride to Seamus and Carolina's place shortly after one. They'd texted to say they needed more time because the boys and Ethan were having lunch. At some point, Jace needed to find a used car or truck to get around. Thinking about that was far better than worrying about what he needed to say to his sons and how they might take it.

"Gorgeous day," Ned said.

"Sure is."

"September is the crown jewel, if ya ask me. Best part o' the year. Tourists are gone, and things get back ta normal round here."

"I can see why you love it."

"Are ya enjoying livin' on our fair isle?"

"Yeah, it's great. Nothing not to love."

"The winters ain't so great, but we get by."

"I guess I'll find out."

"Want ya to know… I admire whatcha doing for them boys of yers."

Jace glanced up to find Ned looking at him in the mirror. He knew he shouldn't be surprised that people had heard who he was and why he was there, but Ned's comment caught him off guard just the same.

"A lot of fellas woulda come bombin' in, flexin' their muscles, whether that was good fer the kids or not."

"I've already done enough damage where they're concerned. I'm not looking to do more."

"Seamus and Carolina are good folks. Yer kids couldn't ask for better."

"I know." Jace debated for a second about whether to tell the older man the reason he was going there now and quickly decided he could use all the advice he could get ahead of this meeting. "We've been passing me off as a friend of Seamus's, but they saw a picture of me with their mother and had questions about how she knew me."

"Ah, damn. What'd ya do about that?"

"We've decided to tell the truth, much sooner than we'd planned to."

"And yer goin' there now fer that?"

"Yeah."

"Fer what it's worth, I'm a big fan o' the truth. Ya can never go wrong with that."

"I hope you're right."

"I usually am. Ask around. People'll tell ya."

For the first time in an hour, Jace grinned. "Is that right?"

"A man gathers a lot of wisdom drivin' people round. Ya hear a lot."

"I'll bet you do, and you're right. The truth is always the best plan. I just wish they were a little older and able to understand what I need to tell them."

"I consider Seamus a friend, and I've gotten to know them boys a little bit. I think they're gonna be just fine. Kids care about who loves them. The more people who love 'em, the better off they are."

"That's true."

As he pulled into Seamus and Carolina's driveway, Ned made eye contact in the mirror. "Just make sure they know how loved they are, and it'll be fine. I promise."

He pulled a ten-dollar bill from his pocket. "I'll do that. Thanks, Ned—for the ride and the advice."

"Both are free of charge. If you need a ride back ta town, gimme a call." He handed Jace his business card.

"Thanks again," Jace said, touched by the other man's kindness.

"Good luck to ya."

Jace sent Ned off with a wave and walked toward the house on legs that felt wooden. His entire body was riddled with tension as he approached the door to the home where his children lived. At times like this, the enormity of what he'd lost that night in the convenience store swept over him like an emotional tsunami. While Jess had died, so, too, had Jace's marriage and any chance he'd had to raise his sons.

He took full responsibility for the series of choices that had led him to being an outsider in his own children's lives and could only hope that the conversation he was about to have with them wouldn't ruin everything.

What if they never wanted to see him again?

Jace's heart broke at that possibility, but he pressed on nonetheless, knocking on the door and holding his breath until Seamus opened it.

"Come in."

The boys who usually greeted him with the unbridled excitement afforded to someone who gave them a lot of attention were subdued as they sat at the table with an untouched snack of cookies and milk. There wasn't a carrot stick or block of cheese in sight.

Every part of him ached as he realized Kyle had been told about the photo Jackson had seen, and both boys were upset about it.

Seamus nodded for Jace to take a seat at the table.

When he was seated, Seamus said, "We asked Jace to come by because there's something we want to talk to you about."

Jackson looked right at Jace, brown eyes full of emotion. "How did you know our mom?"

JOHN FOUND Big Mac McCarthy right where he'd been told to look—working on winterizing the family's marina in North Harbor. He was on a ladder doing something to one of the light poles on the long main pier when John walked up to him.

"Can I help ya?" Big Mac asked.

"I'm John Lawry."

"Oh, hey. Sorry. I didn't recognize you from up here."

"Heard you're looking for some security help at your place in town."

"You heard right. Would you mind holding the ladder for me so I can get this done before my son or Luke catches me up here and gives me a lecture?"

Smiling at the older man's commentary, John wrapped his arms around the ladder and held on tight while Big Mac changed the lightbulb. "I got you."

"All good. Coming down."

John stood by just in case he tripped, but he was agile like a cat as he descended the ladder and held out his hand.

"Good to see you again."

John made eye contact and shook the man's hand the way his father had taught him. "You as well, sir."

"Don't call me that. This is Gansett, and I'm Big Mac to you."

"Got it."

"Heard you were a cop in Tennessee."

"Yes, for eight years until recently."

"Made any plans?"

"Nothing beyond spending some time with my mom and the family. Beyond that, I don't know."

"We just finished our first full season at the Wayfarer, and one thing is crystal clear. We're in bad need of better security. We need someone who knows what they're doing. I'm not going to lie to you—in season, the job will be a gigantic pain in the ass. In the off-season, you'll be bored. We'd put you on an annual salary with bonuses for surviving the summer. We also provide full medical and dental insurance as well as long- and short-term disability." Big Mac named a salary number that piqued John's interest. It was more than he'd made in Tennessee. "What do you think?"

"I think it sounds great, but don't you want to check my references or anything?"

"You're Owen, Katie and Julia's brother. That's all I need to know."

John eyed him skeptically. "Is that how it works around here?"

"Yep. I think the world of them, your mom, Charlie, your grandparents, Cindy. Wonderful family."

"Thank you. They're pretty great."

"I assume you are, too?"

"I try to do the right thing in every situation."

"That's what we need, but I want you to know, the shit that goes on there in the summer would try the soul of the most patient of people. Nikki Stokes, our general manager, has some war stories you might want to hear before you accept."

"I assume there won't be anyone shooting at me."

"They're more apt to throw up on you than shoot at you."

"I'd take puke over a bullet any day. I'm not afraid of drunk and disorderly."

"We're concerned about it escalating from there. Had a couple of reports of unwelcome sexual advances this past season, which has me concerned about lawsuits and such."

"I have a lot of experience dealing with that, too. I'd do my best to keep things running smoothly for you."

"I promised Nikki I'd do something about the security situation in the off-season, so you're hired. If you want the job, that is."

Did he want to stay on Gansett indefinitely, including during the long, cold winter? He wouldn't have thought that would appeal to him until he'd come home and spent time with his family, not to mention the promising new friendship with Niall. "I think it sounds great," John said. "I accept."

JEFF LAWRY WAS IN LOVE. There could be no other way to describe the light-headed, carefree way he felt whenever Kelsey was anywhere nearby —and even when she wasn't. Just knowing she existed in this world made it a better place. The thought of leaving her in a couple of weeks was so painful, it kept him awake at night, rethinking his life plan so it might include her.

He'd come early to the McCarthys to pick her up after work, hoping for a minute alone with Mr. McCarthy, who was at home recovering from a vasectomy. The only reason Jeff knew about that was because Mr. McCarthy had told him to *enjoy your swimmers while you can.* That had cracked him up, especially as he tried to imagine his own father saying such a thing. Jeff hoped the McCarthy kids knew how lucky they were to have a dad like him.

He often wondered what his life might've been like if he'd been born into a normal family. Not that he'd trade his mom and siblings for anything, but what he would've given to have had a childhood free of violence and fear. The fear had been debilitating and had driven him to drugs and a suicide attempt. He gave thanks every day for the second chance he'd been given by the EMTs who'd saved his life that day as well as the grandparents who'd threatened legal action to get him out of his father's home. He'd been determined ever since not to squander his second chance, which was why he wanted to talk to Mr. McCarthy.

Jeff knocked on the sliding glass door.

From his post on the sofa, Mr. McCarthy waved him in. He had a stack of papers and a laptop on the table next to him. Was that a bag of frozen peas on his lap? Interesting.

"How's it going, Jeff?"

"Good, sir. How are you?"

"I'm better, and I told you before not to call me sir."

"Sorry, sir." After being raised by a career military officer with a mean left hook, the habit was so deeply ingrained in Jeff that he'd never be able to undo it.

"Kelsey is at the beach with the kids, but they're due back in a few."

"I know. She texted me. I wondered if I might speak to you for a moment?"

Mac looked up at him. "Sure. What's on your mind?"

Jeff sat in the chair across from him. "I was wondering if you have any job openings in your company. I did several summers of construction when I was in college and have experience in roofing, framing, drywall and finish carpentry."

"I thought you just graduated from college and had a job lined up in Tampa?"

"I did. I mean, I do. Sir."

"Why the change of plan?"

"I, um, well…"

"Does it have anything to do with my nanny?"

Jeff never blinked when he replied. "Yes, sir. It does."

"I see."

Jeff nearly stopped breathing while he waited to hear what Mac would say.

"How old are you, Jeff?"

"Twenty-three. Sir."

"You're young to be changing plans for a woman."

"I know, sir."

Mac frowned at the word.

"I'm sorry. It's just how I was raised. Sir."

"It's okay. What did you major in?"

"Computer science."

"Isn't there a lot of money in that?"

"Yes, sir. There is."

"There's not a lot of money in Gansett Island construction jobs."

"I'm aware, but I could live at home with my mom and Charlie. There'd be time later for me to pursue other opportunities because, as you said, I'm young. Kelsey is going to be here this year, so I'd like to be here, too. If possible."

"Have you spoken with Kelsey about this change of plan?"

"Not yet, sir. I need to land a job before I can seriously consider staying here."

"You may be in luck, my friend."

"How so, sir?"

"My family recently purchased a property on the west side. Do you remember the old alpaca farm that used to be out there?"

"I do," Jeff said. "My grandparents would take us out there to see the animals."

"It's fallen into serious disrepair. We're going to renovate it for a wedding venue."

"Oh wow. That sounds cool."

"We hope it will be. As a result of taking on that project, I plan to add a few people to my team this off-season. In fact, I was just working on the ad I'm going to post when you came in. If you're sure about this, I'd be happy to have you."

"You don't want to check my references or anything?"

"I know your people, especially Owen, Julia and Katie. We're good."

Jeff was caught off guard by the swell of emotion that hit him when Mac said that about his brother and sisters. "They're..." He cleared his throat. "They're the best."

"Yes, they are."

"You... You should know... I'm in recovery from a drug issue I had when I was younger. I've been clean for nine years and work the program religiously."

"Thank you for letting me know. I don't foresee that being any kind of problem."

"It won't be."

"Then we ought to be fine. Stop by my office in town tomorrow to see Julia about the paperwork. I'll text her to let her know you'll be in."

"I, ah, probably ought to tell my family there's been a change in plans before you do that."

"Let me give you my number. Text me when the word is out, and I'll follow up with Julia."

Jeff punched in the numbers Mac recited and added him to his contacts. "Thank you again for this. You won't be sorry you gave me a chance."

Mac held out his hand. "Looking forward to working with you."

Jeff shook his hand. "Likewise, sir."

"Knock that shit off."

"I'll try, sir."

"Try harder. My brother Adam runs a computer business on the island. You might want to check in with him, too, so you can keep your hand in your chosen field during your stay on the island."

"I'll do that. Thank you for everything."

"Sure thing. Make yourself at home until Kelsey gets back."

Jeff took advantage of the time to compose a text to his family. *Slight change of plan, y'all. I've decided to spend the year here on Gansett and will be working for Mac McCarthy's construction company. Having you all nearby has been amazing. Looking forward to some good times this winter. Josh—get your ass to Gansett. We're having all the fun without you!*

His mother responded first. *Didn't I just cosign on an apartment for you in Tampa?*

Working on getting out of that as we speak and hoping I can rent a room from you and Charlie for a while longer.

Our home is your home but figure out that lease situation!

Will do.

Is this about a girl named Kelsey by any chance? Cindy asked.

In part. It's also about you guys and Gansett and how fun it is to be here together.

But mostly about Kelsey, John said with laughing emojis. *While we're talking about plans, meet the new director of security at the Wayfarer. Year-round gig that's mostly four months of hard work.*

Julia responded with, *Congrats, Johnny! That's awesome!*

Your old Granny and Gramps are so happy to have you all here in our favorite place, Adele said. *Best news ever. Josh, honey, we need you here to make it perfect.*

No pressure, right? Josh responded. *I'll come visit soon. I promise. Congrats, Jeff and John. Happy for you guys!*

His phone was still buzzing with texts from his family when the slider opened to admit Kelsey, carrying little Mac as Thomas and Hailey trailed behind her. When she smiled at him, he was one hundred percent sure he was doing the right thing spending this year on Gansett.

"Am I late?" she asked.

"No, I got here a little early." He walked over to her and took baby Mac from her. "Can I help?"

"I just need to get these guys cleaned up and ready for dinner before I go."

"I can do that, Kels." Mac got up from the sofa, moving slowly. "Go ahead with Jeff and have a nice evening."

"Are you sure, Mr. McCarthy? Aren't you supposed to be taking it easy?"

"I'm sure. I've been taking it easy all day. Thomas will help, won't you, son?"

Thomas nodded. "I'll help."

"If you're sure…"

"All good." Mac took baby Mac's hand and headed for the stairs. "It's tubby time, buddy."

"Want Mama."

"She's napping with the babies, so you're stuck with me."

"Mama."

Mac laughed as he herded the kids up the stairs.

"You got some sun," Jeff said to Kelsey when they were alone.

"No matter how much sunscreen I slather on, the sun still finds me."

"Looks good on you." After she'd gathered her belongings, he followed her out the slider and down the stairs. "Can we go somewhere to talk?"

"I need to run home to shower. We can talk there if you'd like."

Jeff held the passenger door of his mother's car for Kelsey. He'd need to figure out getting his car to the island now that he was planning to stay. "That would be great."

CHAPTER 22

"What did I miss?" Maddie asked when the babies ended her nap with hungry cries.

Mac had helped her change them and was watching over her as she fed them. Breastfeeding twins was a feat, and Maddie excelled at the balancing act. "Well, Jeff Lawry asked me for a job because he wants to stay on the island this year."

"Is that right? Any particular reason?"

"As you well know, it's because of Kelsey."

"That's so sweet. I hope you hired him."

"I did, but I worry that he's giving up a much better job in Tampa to work with me."

"Some things are more important than money, and besides, he's got plenty of time to make money. They're so cute together. I hope they can make it work."

"I guess we'll see."

"How are you feeling?" she asked.

"Like I'm going to survive this nightmare, but just barely."

Maddie snorted out a laugh. "Oh, the *drama*."

"I'm glad I can only have one vasectomy in a lifetime. One was more than enough."

"And yet, I had six children. Hmmm…"

"You win. Hands down, no contest."

"I'm glad you realize that. Where are my other children?"

"Watching a movie while having ice cream for dessert. Thomas is in charge of making sure Mac doesn't get it all over the sofa."

"Let me know how that goes."

"Are you hungry?"

"Starving."

"I'll bring you dinner in bed."

"That's okay. These girls are done. We can come downstairs."

Mac took Emma from her and gave her a hand up as she balanced Evie. "How's your soreness?"

"A little better than it was, but still got a way to go."

He put an arm around her and, mindful of the babies, leaned in to kiss her. "In case I forget to tell you, you're the undisputed hero of this story."

"Oh, I already knew that, but thank you for confirming it."

Mac laughed as he escorted her downstairs, hoping his young friend Jeff might one day have what he did with Maddie.

JACE MET his son's earnest gaze and tried to find the words he needed to explain himself to the child. "Before I tell you how I knew your mom, I want you both to know that I love you so much and want nothing but the best for you."

The boys looked at each other and then at him, their gazes expectant, so he took a deep breath and forced himself to say the words. "I knew your mother because I was married to her. I'm your father."

Kyle let out a sound that defied description before he jumped up and ran out the front door.

When Jace started to get up, Seamus stopped him. "I'll go."

Jackson continued to stare at Jace without blinking. "Where have you *been*?"

"I was in prison."

Jackson blinked, his eyes going wide with shock. "Why?"

"I got involved in some bad stuff and was there when someone else robbed a store with a gun. I got caught and was sent to jail." He didn't think the child needed to hear he'd also lost an uncle in that robbery.

"Why did you do that?"

"Because I was hooked on drugs then and needed money for more. I made the biggest mistake of my life. I lost your mom and you boys, which absolutely broke my heart."

"Are you... Are you going to take us away from here?"

"No, I'm not. Seamus and Carolina are your family now, and this is where you belong."

"Why did you lie when we first met you?"

"We thought it was too soon after you lost your mom to tell you the truth about me. We were going to wait until you were a little older."

Jackson looked at Carolina. "Can I go outside now?"

"Sure."

Without looking at Jace again, he got up and went out the door.

Jace dropped his head into his hands, gutted by the exchange with his son.

"I know it might seem awful right now, but it won't always be," Carolina said. "This is new information that they need time to process. We just need to be patient with them."

"What if they don't want to see me again after this?"

"I don't think that'll happen."

"What if it does?"

"My son, Joe, was very young when we lost his father in an accident."

Surprised by the change in direction, Jace said, "I'm sorry."

"Thank you. It was a very difficult time for both of us. We had a lot of bad days and a few good days, but over time, the good days started to outnumber the bad as we both recovered from our loss. This isn't the same thing, but they're around the age Joe was then. It'll take time for them to process and decide how they want to go forward from here."

"What am I supposed to do in the meantime?"

"Keep showing up for them and prove to them that you're someone they can count on."

"I love them so much."

"Tell them that every chance you get. Kids can never have too many people who love them."

He recalled Ned saying the same thing. "Thank you for this and all you've done for my family."

"We love them very much, too. It's a pleasure to have them in our lives."

Seamus came in a minute later, carrying Kyle, who'd obviously been crying.

Jace held his breath as he waited to hear what his son might have to say.

Seamus sat at the table with Kyle on his lap.

"I'm mad that you weren't there," Kyle said, his lip quivering. "Mommy was sick."

"I know, buddy." Jace's eyes filling with tears. "I'm very sorry I wasn't there when you guys needed me. I would've given anything to be there. I loved your mom very much, and I love you and your brother, too. I always have."

"Why didn't you come when she was sick?"

"I was still in prison."

The child's light blond brows furrowed with confusion. "Do we hafta live with you now?"

"No, you're going to stay here with Seamus and Carolina, who also love you very much. I promise I'm not going to mess up your lives. I just want to be a friend to you and Jackson, if you'll have me."

"What do you think, Kyle?" Seamus asked. "Would you like to be friends with Jace?"

After an impossibly long pause, Kyle gave a slight nod that greatly bolstered Jace's spirits.

"Thank you," he said. "I'd love to be your friend and Jackson's, too."

"I don't want you to be my friend!" Jackson said, sobbing in the doorway. "We needed you, and you weren't there!"

Jace got up and went to him, kneeling before the child. "I know I wasn't, and I'll be sorry about that for the rest of my life. I'll do whatever it takes to try to make it up to you in any way that I can. It's a lot for guys your age to understand, that people can make terrible mistakes that cost them everything. That's what happened to me, and the worst part of it was that I hurt you guys and your mom. She didn't deserve that. She was a wonderful person and a great mom."

Jackson's chin quivered the same way Kyle's had.

Jace reached out a hand to him. "Man to man. I'm very, very sorry, Jackson." He held his breath, waiting to see what the child would do.

When Jackson took hold of his hand and let Jace fold him into a hug, he went weak with relief. "I love you and Kyle very much, and I always will. If you ever need anything, anything at all, you can come to me, even if Seamus and Carolina will be your parents."

"You can never have too many people who love you," Carolina said.

"Aye," Seamus said, sounding emotional, "that's very true."

Kyle came over to where Jace was holding Jackson.

Jace extended his arm to include Kyle and hugged his sons for the first time since they were babies. "I missed you guys so much when I was away. I thought about you all the time and wished I could be with you. And I'm so, so sorry you lost your mom."

He held the two boys for a full minute before they started to squirm. When he released them, they burst out the door with Burpy hot on their heels.

"Was that it?" Jace asked Seamus and Carolina. "Was that the worst of it?"

"It's hard to say for certain," Carolina said. "They're apt to have more questions and feelings about it all, but you handled it as well as could be expected."

"I agree, mate," Seamus said. "Well done."

Again, he was strangely honored to have Seamus call him that, knowing the other man well enough by then to know he didn't give away such things. "Thank you both for everything. I'll never have the words..."

"It's the honor of our lifetime to help raise your sons," Seamus said gruffly.

As Jeff drove Kelsey to her apartment in a building the McCarthys owned near the marina, his mind raced with things he needed to do now that he'd landed an off-season job. First, he needed to tell the company in Tampa that he wasn't going to accept their offer after all, and then he needed to get out of the lease he'd recently signed there.

"Is everything all right?" she asked.

Jeff realized he hadn't said a word since they left Mac's house. "I think so."

"What does that mean?"

"It's what I want to talk to you about."

"You're making me nervous."

He reached over to put his hand on top of hers. "Nothing to be nervous about. It's good news, or at least I hope you'll think so." A few minutes later, he parked the car outside her place and followed her inside.

Her apartment was one big room that had walls around a bathroom, but everything else, including a bed that was always neatly made, was out in the open.

Kelsey put down the bag she took to work and turned to him, hands on hips. "Tell me what's going on."

"I asked Mr. McCarthy for a job with his construction company, and he hired me."

"Wait. What? You have a job in Tampa."

"That I'm going to quit."

"Before you even start?"

"Before I even start."

"Why are you doing this?"

He took a step closer to her, smiling as he took in the gorgeous face that was made more so by her confused expression. "You really have to ask that?"

"Jeff… You can't blow up your whole life because of me."

"Who says?"

"I say! That's crazy."

"What would be crazy, at least from my point of view, would be going back to Florida when you're here for at least the next year."

"But what about your job? You said it was a great opportunity."

"It is, but my priorities have changed."

She shook her head. "Your mother won't be happy with either of us if you do this."

"I already told her, and she's fine with it. She wants us all to be as happy as she is with Charlie." He took a step to close the remaining space between them and put his hands on her shoulders. "Once she gets to know you better, she'll totally understand why I wanted to stay here with you."

"You have a college degree that you worked hard for."

"My college degree will still be there when I'm ready to use it. For now, this is what I want. *You* are what I want."

Kelsey leaned her head on his chest.

"Are you glad I'm staying?"

She nodded. "I was dreading you leaving."

"Now you don't have to dread anything."

"What does this mean for us?"

With his finger under her chin, he tipped her face up so he could see her eyes. "It means we're going to make a go of this, if you want to, that is."

"I want to."

Smiling, he said, "Thank goodness, because I'm about to blow up my whole life to be with you."

"You're really sure about this?"

He kissed her. "I'm positive."

CINDY HADN'T HEARD from Jace all day and had begun to seriously worry by late afternoon with no sign of him at home before he was due at work. She debated whether to text him and decided against it. Whatever was going on with him, if he wanted her to know, he'd tell her.

She hated this feeling of uncertainty that had crept in as the hours had passed without a word from him after the night they'd spent together. The feeling was all too familiar, but it was worse this time because she'd hoped for better from him.

She'd no sooner had that thought than she felt guilty for judging him before she knew what had happened. Whatever it was, it had something to do with his boys, and they needed to be his top priority.

As she sat on the sofa, she tried to focus on the journal she'd kept from the time she was a young child. For the first time in a while, she had something interesting to write about. Whatever it took to keep her from racing over to the Beachcomber to see if he'd shown up for work. And if he hadn't?

This was exactly why she didn't date much anymore. She hated wondering where he was, what he was thinking, if something was wrong, if he'd changed his mind about her after the night they spent together.

It was so *exhausting*.

The tug-of-war over whether she should go to the Beachcomber had her paralyzed with indecision, to the point that she couldn't write a thing, which was rare for her. She texted her brother John. *Are you going to the bar tonight?*

He replied right away. *I'm there now. You coming?*

185

Can I ask you something without you making ANYTHING of it?

Um, sure...

Is Jace there?

He's not. They said he called out sick.

What the hell was going on?

He's not at home? John asked.

No, he said something came up hours ago, and I haven't heard from him since.

And now you're spinning, am I right?

A little. It's weird for him to go off the grid for hours.

And you know him well enough to be able to say that's weird?

I hate when you make too much sense. I'm going to stand down now, and I'll see him when I see him.

Sorry to ask the obvious, but did you text him?

No...

Maybe you oughta?

I hate this.

I know. But he's a good dude. Don't automatically think the worst.

I'm preprogrammed to do that.

I know, but maybe don't this time.

What about you? Is Niall there tonight?

Yeah, he's playing.

Any progress?

Going to dinner sometime in the next few days.

Oh fun! Keep me posted?

I will.

I'm so crazy proud of you for telling the family. Do you feel better?

It's a relief that people know. Just got to tell the grandparents. That's kinda scary.

Nah, they love you no matter what. It won't be any big deal.

Thanks for encouraging me to come out. It helped.

Love u.

U 2.

CHAPTER 23

Cindy made a salad for dinner and forced herself to page through some of her old journals as an idea had taken root in recent months. She wanted to write about their family's ordeal and had begun some tentative steps in that direction. But tonight, her mind continued to wander—and wonder—making any kind of concentration nonexistent. She was asleep on the sofa when the front door opened, startling her awake. The clock on her phone read ten twenty. She sat up and pushed the hair back from her face.

Jace dropped into the chair across from the sofa. He looked exhausted. "Hey."

"Hey." She hoped he might say more, but when he didn't, she asked, "Everything all right?"

"I think it will be, but today was just… a lot."

"What happened?"

His deep sigh conveyed a world of exhaustion. "Seamus and Carolina have been going through the stuff that came with the boys from Lisa's, and there were photos of us that Jackson saw, which had him asking about me and how I knew their mom."

"Oh," Cindy said on a long exhale. "Oh God."

"Yeah… We told them the truth."

"How did that go?"

"It was rough, but we got through it. They had questions. I answered them truthfully." He shrugged. "It was…" Shaking his head, he seemed to sag into the chair.

Cindy didn't take even one second to think about what she was doing or how upset she'd been earlier over the hours of silence when she got up and went to him, sitting on his lap and wrapping her arms around him.

He responded in kind, his arms closing around her in a tight hug. "I'm sorry I went missing. I hope you weren't worried."

"I was a little worried."

"It was one hell of a day. I stayed to have dinner with them and helped put the boys to bed. After that, the three of us had a badly needed drink before I walked home."

"You walked all that way in the dark?"

"I needed the air to clear my head."

"I'm sorry you had such a tough day."

"I'm glad they know the truth now, as hard as it was to tell them. They were primarily concerned about whether they were going to have to live with me now. I told them they would be staying with Seamus and Carolina, but I hoped to be a friend to them, if they'd let me."

"For what it's worth, I'm proud of you for telling them the truth while knowing it might change how they feel about you."

"That was my greatest fear, but they deserved the truth, so that's what I gave them." He tucked a strand of her hair behind her ear. "And PS, it's worth a lot that you're proud of me."

"Can I say something else?"

"Anything you want."

"Even though I know why now, it was upsetting to me when you went dark for most of the day, especially after last night. That triggered some… insecurities for me."

"I should've texted you, and I'm sorry I didn't. It was just an insane day."

"I understand. Now."

He ran his hand over her face. "I never want you to feel insecure."

"And yet, I do. About many things."

"I hate that I made you feel that way. You have no reason to be insecure about anything with me. I couldn't wait to get home and talk to you about everything that happened."

Hearing him say that made her feel so much better than she had earlier. "I'm glad I was here for you."

"So am I. But I want you to talk to me about these insecurities so I can try not to do anything to make them worse."

"That's a complicated topic, and you've already had a complicated day."

"I've got room for more. Talk to me. I want to understand."

Cindy tried to gather her thoughts. "Like everything in the Lawry kids' lives, it goes back to our father, who never minced words in telling us the things he didn't like about us. He'd tell my sisters and me that men were going to take advantage of us because we were pretty and good for only one thing."

Jace's face went flat with shock. "He did not say that."

"Yes, he did, and so many other horrible things, such as 'no man is ever going to be interested in your brain, so I'm not paying to send you to college.'"

"I'd like to kick him in the balls for saying such a thing to you guys. That's horrible—and not true. You want to know the first thing I liked about you?"

"Um, sure."

"It was how you're always smiling and happy and in a good mood. I very quickly started to look forward to you coming in because you're like a ray of sunshine, lighting up my world. And that was before I got to know you and found so many other things to like."

"That's very sweet of you to say."

"It's true, and soon, I couldn't get enough of talking to you about everything and nothing. The fact that you're gorgeous didn't hurt anything, but it wasn't the first thing I noticed."

"You want to hear a confession?"

"Absolutely."

"I've never spent that much time in a bar in my life."

Jace laughed as he tipped her chin up for a kiss. "I sort of guessed that by the way you guzzle water."

"With lemon. Don't forget that."

"Fanciest cocktail I've ever made for anyone."

"Sure it is."

"I hope you know how much your friendship has meant to me since I came here, knowing no one, but wanting to live closer to my boys."

"Your friendship has meant just as much to me. I came for a visit and ended up staying indefinitely. And now I have this whole new life here that I'm really enjoying."

"Any part in particular?" he asked as he kissed her neck.

"Well, there's this sexy bartender I've taken a liking to. He makes a mean ice water, but he's not very good at checkers."

"Hey! That's because you cheat when I'm not looking."

"I do not!"

"I'm going to look at the security footage."

"You go right ahead. You won't see anything but raw skill on the video."

Smiling, he kissed her again. "Thanks for this. I needed it after today."

"I know it might seem hard to believe right now, but soon this will be a distant memory to the boys. If you keep showing up for them, they'll accept you as their father and allow you to play a role in their lives."

"I plan to keep showing up for them."

"That's all you have to do. It'll matter to them that you told them the truth when they asked. Take it from someone whose father never showed up for her. That will mean everything to them."

"I'm sorry he hurt you the way he did."

She shrugged. "I survived it. We all did, and that's what matters. Your sons are lucky to have you in their lives—and they know that. That's why they didn't tell you to get lost when you told them the truth."

"I was so afraid they would."

"Kids just want to feel safe and loved. I'm sure you gave them both those things today."

"Thanks for letting me come home and drop this on you."

"I'm glad you dropped it on me."

"Do you forgive me for making you feel insecure?"

"That's my issue, not yours."

"It's *our* issue if I'm the cause of it." He trailed his fingertip over the outline of her jaw. "I never want to be the cause of that."

"It matters to me that you care."

"You matter to me, and I do care. A lot." He lifted her chin and kissed her softly and sweetly, but the minute their lips connected, the fire from the night before ignited between them.

Her lips—and other important parts—were still sore, but that didn't stop her from clinging to him as one kiss became two and then three.

"You make me crazy," he whispered as he kissed her neck.

"Right back at you."

"Should we take this somewhere more comfortable?"

"Why not?" She was falling hard and fast for him, but for once, she couldn't find a single reason to hold back or slow things down. She could always find a reason to hold back, but not with Jace.

He helped her up and then followed her toward the bedrooms. In the hallway, he kissed her cheek. "Go get comfortable. I'm going to grab a quick shower."

"Okay."

Cindy changed into a T-shirt, got into bed and tried to calm her racing heart and hyperactive libido. She nearly giggled at the thought of having a hyperactive libido. That was so not like her. She was usually so busy trying to protect herself from being hurt that she didn't allow herself to let go with a man.

Jace was an exception to all her usual rules.

As she waited for him, she tried to find some semblance of control, but she felt nothing but a desperate need for more of the way he made her feel.

He appeared in the doorway a few minutes later, wearing only a pair of formfitting boxer briefs. And holy God, the man was indeed hot as fire.

Cindy held out her arms to him, and he came down on top of her, picking right up where they'd left off in the living room. If this was insanity, it was the best thing she'd ever experienced.

JACE COULDN'T GET ENOUGH of her. He'd come home wound up after a rough day, but she'd provided him with a warm, soft place to land that made him thankful to have her in his life. All he wanted, especially after hearing how he'd made her feel insecure by going dark all day, was to show her how much he appreciated her.

He tugged on her T-shirt. "You're overdressed for this party."

"Take it off."

As he helped her out of her shirt, he loved how free she was with him, how giving and open, and yet, he understood, somehow, that was unusual for her. They'd shared a connection from the first night she came into his bar that had only grown with every subsequent meeting. He trusted her, which was something that didn't come easily to him, especially after years in prison.

It was amazing to realize he'd trusted her immediately. That was truly a first for him, and it was why he was here, in her bed, kissing her senseless and loving every second he spent with her, because he felt safe with her.

"I thought about this all day today, even when I had other things I needed to deal with," he whispered as he kissed the tip of one perfect breast. "I was still thinking about you and this and how sexy you are and how much I couldn't wait to be with you again."

She grasped his head to keep him anchored to her chest as she lifted her torso to press her heated core against his erection.

"Did you think about me, too?"

"Just a little," she said on a laugh. "I could still feel you inside me all day."

Jace groaned at hearing that. He kissed her belly and then moved down until he was poised between her legs with only a thin scrap of fabric separating them. He pushed her panties out of the way and pressed his tongue into her sweetness, pulling back when she winced. "Are you sore, love?"

"A little."

"Then we'll do this nice and easy."

True to his word, he kept the strokes of his tongue and fingers as soft and gentle as he could manage, taking her on a slow, sensual ride that had her nearly pulling the hair out of his head as she urged him on.

He drew back a little, making her groan, before starting over and finishing the job this time.

She cried out as she came, her muscles tightening around the finger he had inside her and making his cock want in on this in the worst possible way, but not when she was sore. He moved up, kissing a path between her breasts, to her neck and then her lips as his erection pressed against her warmth.

He shivered from the effort to hold back.

"It's okay," she said. "We can."

"No, you're sore."

"I want to."

"Are you sure?"

She looked up at him with big eyes and nodded, her hands coasting down over his back to pull him to her. "Just go slow."

"I can do slow." Jace removed her panties and entered her in tiny increments, waiting for her to tell him to stop. "Are you okay?"

"Mmm, yeah."

He gave her a little more even as he heard his phone ringing in the other room. Ignoring that, he focused all his attention on Cindy, wanting her to feel as good as she made him feel. As he moved in her, he had the strangest feeling of homecoming, as if all the hell he'd been through had somehow been leading him to her, to this, to them.

God, she was sexy and sweet and so, so perfect in every way.

As he kissed her and made love to her, he vowed to do whatever was necessary to keep her close to him for as long as he possibly could. In just two nights with her, he could no longer imagine life without her.

His phone rang again.

He ignored it.

"Should you get that?" Cindy asked.

"I will. After."

Pressing his fingers to her clit, he coaxed her into another orgasm that sent him straight to heaven. Coming down off the highest of highs, he'd nearly forgotten about his phone until it rang again. He withdrew from her reluctantly and got up to see who the hell was blowing up his phone.

Seeing three missed calls from Seamus, he nearly had a heart attack. He put through a call to him.

"Oh, thank you, Jesus. I didn't know who else to call this late."

"What's wrong?"

"Right after you left, Carolina fell getting out of the shower and broke her leg—badly. They're going to medevac her to the mainland, and I need someone to stay with the boys. Joe and his family are in Ohio, and my cousin is off-island wedding shopping. We were going to call Mac and Linda, but it's so late and—"

"Seamus, I'll do it. Of course I will."

"Are you sure, mate? It's a lot to ask."

"I'm positive. Where are the boys?"

"At the clinic with me."

"I'll be right there." He put down the phone and went to the bathroom to clean up. "I have to go get the boys," he said to Cindy. "Carolina fell and broke her leg. They're taking her to the mainland."

"Oh my God." She put on her T-shirt and joined him in the bathroom. "Do you need help?"

"I don't know what I need."

"Can I come with you? Between the two of us, we can figure it out, right?"

He caressed her face and kissed her. "I'd love if you came with me. Thank you."

They cleaned up, got dressed, packed a quick overnight bag and were on the way to the clinic in minutes, hoofing it across town as a chilly early-September breeze blew in from the waterfront.

Jace held her hand as they walked. "I'm really sorry this happened when we were, you know, *busy*."

"Don't be. They're your kids. They come first."

"They never have before, you know? Like, I've never had to stop what I was doing to be there for them. Not once in their entire lives have I done that."

"You're doing it now, and that's what's important."

"Thanks for coming with me. That means a lot. I have no idea what I'm doing with two little boys."

"You'll figure it out, and the good news is, they're old enough to tell you what they need."

"True. Thank God for that."

Cindy laughed. "You've got this. Just take it one minute to the next."

"It's a big deal that he called me to help with them. I don't want to let him down."

"You won't."

"Means a lot to me that you have so much faith, even with what you know about me."

"All I see is a man determined to put his life back together and do the right thing by the people he cares about."

"I like how that man looks to you."

Cindy squeezed his hand. "I like how he looks, too."

CHAPTER 24

Thanks to Cindy, the tension Jace had felt since Seamus called let up a bit. He could handle two boys for a couple of days. But what about when he had to work? Shit, he'd have to figure something out, because he couldn't afford to miss another night of work.

At the clinic, the automatic double doors opened to admit them.

Seamus paced the waiting area, cell phone pressed to his ear. "Aye, it's a bad break and will need surgery. They didn't say how long she'll be in the hospital. You don't have to come, Joe. She's going to be fine. Yes, of course I'll tell her, and I'll call you when she's out of surgery."

After Seamus ended the call, he turned to Jace. "Thanks for coming, mate."

"This is Cindy. My girlfriend."

"I know Cindy," Seamus said with a small smile. "She cuts our hair. Didn't know you two were an item."

Jace put his arm around her. "It's a new development. Hope you don't mind."

"Of course not," Seamus said, running his hands through his hair. He looked completely undone, which was a side of him Jace hadn't seen before.

"What happened?" Jace asked.

"Craziest thing. She was getting out of the shower and talking to me and then there was this god-awful crash. I went running to her, and her leg was at this angle…" He sighed. "It was horrible. I had to get the boys up to follow the ambulance here. They're in with her now. I'd better go check on them."

"We'll be right here and can take them home whenever they're ready to go," Jace said.

"Thanks again for coming."

"No problem."

While Jace and Cindy sat to wait, he took her hand again. "I hope it was okay to introduce you as my girlfriend."

"It was okay, although it's been so long since I had a boyfriend that I'm not sure what the protocol is these days."

"How is it possible that you haven't had *all* the boyfriends?"

Cindy shrugged. "Didn't want them."

"How come?"

"Always more trouble than they're worth."

"Are you going to make an exception for me?"

"Seems like I already have." She gave him a saucy smile. "I let you call me your girlfriend, didn't I?"

"I'm honored to be an exception."

"You're an exception to all my rules."

"I promise not to be more trouble than I'm worth."

"I'm going to hold you to that."

THEY WAITED for thirty minutes before Seamus brought the pajama-clad boys out to them in the waiting room. They looked as if they'd been crying.

"Everything all right?" Jace asked as he stood to receive them.

"The poor blokes are terribly worried about Caro. We assured them she's going to be fine, but after what they've been through…" Seamus shrugged.

Jace squatted so he was at eye level with the boys. "Seamus and Carolina are right. She's going to be fine. The doctors just need to fix her leg at the hospital, and then they'll send her back home to get better. And when she gets home, you guys will help her with everything, right?"

Jackson and Kyle nodded even as their little chins quivered. They'd had a tough, emotional day and needed to get some rest before school in the morning.

"What do you say we get you guys home?" Jace asked.

"There's ice cream in the freezer for good lads who do what they're told and behave for Jace and his friend Cindy," Seamus said.

"We already had ice cream," Kyle said.

Jackson nudged his brother, as if to say, *Shut up, will you?*

"I don't think there's ever been a better night for a second scoop of ice cream," Seamus said. "Don't you agree, Jace?"

"Absolutely. What do you say, guys?"

Jackson looked up at Seamus. "You promise you'll be back?"

Seamus hugged the little guy and then his brother. "Wild horses couldn't keep us away from you two monkeys. Caro and I will FaceTime you after school tomorrow so you can see for yourselves that she's fine, okay?"

"Okay," Kyle said, still seeming reluctant to leave Seamus.

Who could blame him? Seamus and Carolina had provided stability since their mother's tragic death.

"They have to be to school by eight ten," Seamus said. "We get them up around seven fifteen because they're slow in the morning. They know where their school clothes are kept and how to get dressed on their own. They like cereal and juice for breakfast, and their lunches are already packed in the fridge. Look at what Caro packed for them so you know what to do for the next day. I'll call the school and let them know what happened so you can pick them up at three. If you have any problems at all, call our friends Big Mac and Linda McCarthy." He handed Jace a slip of paper. "That's their number. They've raised a bunch of kids and will know what to do in any situation." Seamus took a deep breath. "I can't think of anything else you should know off the top of my head, but if I do, I'll text you."

"We got it," Jace said. "Try not to worry."

"My nerves are shot seeing my Caro hurt so bad."

"I'm sure, but she's going to be okay, and the boys will be, too. Guys, this is my friend Cindy. Cindy, this is Jackson and Kyle."

She shook hands with them. "It's so nice to meet you. I've heard so much about you guys."

"You're pretty," Jackson said, giving her a goofy smile.

"Thank you," Cindy said, amused by the comment.

"Isn't she?" Jace smiled at Cindy as Seamus handed him the keys to his truck. "We'll take good care of them while you take care of Carolina."

"Thanks for this, mate. I owe you."

"No, you don't. It's my pleasure."

"There are sheets for our bed in the hall closet. Make yourselves at home."

"Don't worry about a thing." Jace herded the boys out of the clinic and unlocked the truck as they ran ahead to jump into the back seat. "Should I let them do that? Run into a parking lot that way?"

"At this time of day, it's not a problem. There's no one else around."

"I have no freaking clue what I'm doing."

"You'll figure it out like everyone else does when they're tossed into it."

When they got in the truck, Jace glanced at the boys in the mirror. "Everyone buckled in?"

"Yep," Kyle said.

As he drove them home on dark island roads, he was glad he'd taken the time to renew his driver's license when he got out of prison. He hoped he could handle the enormous responsibility he'd been entrusted with. Cindy was right—at least they were older and could help him fumble through. Although the magnitude of what Lisa had taken on when he'd suddenly disappeared from their lives occurred to him once again. He felt guiltier than ever, now that the boys were under his care for the first time ever.

As daunting as this was for him, it would be a hell of a lot easier than caring for and supporting two toddlers—alone—like she'd had to.

After getting to know the boys, it was obvious she'd done a brilliant job with them. They were bright, funny, polite, smart. Everything a man would want his sons to be, and it was no thanks to him.

Perhaps he might have the chance to change that going forward. They knew who he was to them now and had accepted him as their temporary caregiver. While he hated that Carolina had to be so badly injured to make it happen, these next few days would give him the opportunity to further bond with the boys, and for that, he'd be forever grateful.

"Are you okay over there?" Cindy asked.

"Yeah, just thinking. I'll tell you later."

"Okay."

When they arrived at the house, the boys burst out of the truck and went to find Burpy.

"Jeez, I forgot there's a dog to be kept alive, too," Jace said as Burpy ran out the door to pee in the yard.

Cindy laughed at the face he made and followed him inside, the dog pushing past them to get back to his boys.

"Let's do this ice cream thing and get to bed." He opened cabinets to find bowls and drawers looking for spoons. Thankfully, the ice cream was easier to find. He scooped some for each boy as well as himself and Cindy and placed the bowls on the table.

"You forgot the whipped cream," Kyle said.

"And the cherry," Jackson added. "Carolina always gives us a cherry."

"Whipped cream and a cherry coming up."

As he returned to the table with the additional items, he heard the distinctive sound of a helicopter flying overhead and glanced at Cindy.

The boys didn't seem to register that the chopper had come for Carolina, which was probably for the best.

After ice cream, the boys were sent to get ready for bed.

"What happens next?" Jace asked when he appeared in their bedroom door to find them wrestling over a toy.

"We gotta brush our teeth again 'cause we had more sugar," Jackson said. "Seamus says sugar is like a gremlin that eats your teeth while you sleep if you don't brush them before bed."

Jace choked back a laugh. Seamus had a way with words. "Then let's get rid of those gremlins."

Jace supervised them through using the bathroom, brushing teeth and washing hands before marching them back to their bedroom. "Into bed with you. No shenanigans."

"What's sh… nanigans?" Jackson asked.

Jace chuckled. "It means no fooling around. Straight to sleep."

"Are you sleeping here?" Kyle asked.

"I am. We're staying in Seamus and Carolina's room if you need us."

"Is your *girlfriend* sleeping over, too?" Jackson asked, giggling.

Jace couldn't help but laugh along with his son, thankful to be teased by him after the day they'd had. "Yes, she is. We'll both be here if you need us." Jace went to each boy and pulled the covers up over their shoulders the way his mother had done to him and Jess once upon a time when they slept in twin beds like Jackson and Kyle did. He hadn't thought about that in years. He ruffled their hair. "Sleep tight and don't let the bedbugs bite."

"There's no bedbugs!" Kyle said as Jackson giggled.

"Go to sleep."

Burpy jumped into bed with Jackson, who slipped an arm around the dog like it was something they did every night, so Jace didn't question it.

On the way out of the room, he shut off the overhead light.

"Leave the door open," Kyle said.

"I will." Jace also left the hallway light on and returned to the kitchen, where Cindy had washed the ice cream bowls and spoons and set the table for breakfast. He went to her, put his arm around her and kissed her forehead. "Thank you for the help."

"No problem. Let's go make the bed so we can get some sleep."

They worked together to change the sheets on the bed in the main bedroom and then put on the pajama pants and T-shirts they'd brought from home.

"I guess this means sleeping naked is out of the question for the time being," he said.

"You guess correctly."

"You're no fun at all," he said, affecting a pout that made her laugh.

"You know I'm lots of fun, but not with two kids sleeping nearby."

"Is this why people refer to their kids as cockblockers?"

"I believe it is."

"Not that I would ever say that about my sons."

Cindy laughed. "Of course you wouldn't."

"I'm just going to check on them one more time. Be right back." Jace tiptoed to the doorway to the boys' room, which Seamus had told him had been part of the addition they put on to make room for the kids in their home. They'd also added a deluxe playroom and the bathroom the boys shared. He'd expected to hear whispering, but they were quiet, so he returned to the main bedroom.

"Are they out?"

"Seems like they might be."

"See? That wasn't so bad, right?"

"Not bad at all. They made it easy—and you did, too."

She held out her arms to him, and he snuggled up to her like he'd been doing that for much longer than a day. He was so comfortable with her that he felt like he'd known her forever.

As he relaxed into her warm embrace, he released a deep breath for the first time in hours. "They're seven and eight years old, and that was the first time I've ever tucked them into bed that they'll remember. I'm so ashamed of that."

"They'll remember the times you were there, not the times you weren't."

"I know, but I still feel sick to think about what I missed, what they missed, what Lisa went through on her own. So many regrets."

"Maybe you should see the regrets as a blessing of sorts."

"How do you figure?"

"If you didn't have regrets, then that would mean you didn't learn anything from everything that happened. You've learned so much and traveled a million miles from who you were when it all went wrong. The regret means you've grown."

"I'm not sure how you manage to spin it in a way that makes so much sense, but that's a nice way to look at it."

"Just a suggestion."

"It's a good one. Do you have regrets?"

"Only one."

He waited to see if she'd share it with him.

"It's the same one we all have. We wish we'd told the truth about what went on in our home back when it could've made a difference for us and our mom. We wish we hadn't been so frightened by his threats that we kept silent when we should've been telling everyone who'd listen."

"That doesn't really count as a regret, because you did what you thought was right to stay safe—and to keep your mother safe," Jace said.

"We know that, but we have the regrets just the same."

"You're a good person, Cindy. You shouldn't carry that any longer. Your mom is happily remarried, and she wouldn't want you to have regrets on her behalf."

"No, she wouldn't, and you're right. I spent a lot of years in therapy figuring out how to put down the baggage from my childhood and move forward without it."

"You're doing a great job of that from what I've seen."

"It takes daily effort. I've been thinking about maybe writing a memoir about my childhood."

"Really?"

Nodding, she said, "I've kept journals my entire life and have everything that happened documented. I went to enormous lengths to hide the journals where he'd never find them. In one house, I kept them in an AC duct. I've always been a writer, and now that he's locked up, I think I might want to do something with them."

"That would be amazing, but only if you feel strong enough to revisit that time."

"I revisit it every day in one way or another. I think I could handle it, but I'd need to talk to my family about whether they'd want me to do it."

"I'm so impressed that you're thinking of writing a book. I want to be the first to read it."

"We can make that happen," she said, seeming amused by his enthusiasm. "If I ever do it."

"I think you will, and it'll be incredible. You know what I would've regretted?"

"What's that?"

"Not coming here and meeting you. This is the sweetest thing I've had in longer than I can remember, and it's become very important to me."

"Likewise."

CHAPTER 25

"*I*'m so sorry about this," Carolina said as tears slid down her cheeks. The roar of the chopper engine made it hard to hear her. "I've made such a mess of everything."

"Stop that, love." Seamus brushed away her tears. "We'll fix you up, and you'll be back to bossing us all around in no time."

"The boys are so upset. This is the last thing they needed right when they seem to be doing much better."

"They'll be fine. They're resilient lads who've endured worse than a broken leg. We'll get them through it."

"What if they decide they like their young, cool, tattooed daddy better than us?"

Her comment struck at the heart of one of his greatest insecurities since Jace had appeared on the scene. "Aw, love, don't go there. They know how much we love them, and they love us, too. The four of us and that mangy dog are a family." He brushed the hair back from her forehead and kissed her there. "Nothing can change that."

"I keep thinking how your family is coming later this month for the wedding and how much we need to do. The house is a mess and—"

"Stop. We'll hire someone to clean and cook. We'll make it happen." His cousin Shannon was marrying Victoria Stevens in three weeks, and Caro was right. They did have a lot to do before hosting the wedding in their backyard, not to mention the influx of houseguests. But he'd get it done. Somehow. "Don't worry about anything. I'm right here with you, and I'll take care of everything."

She squeezed the hand he'd wrapped around hers. "Remember when I thought I didn't need a much younger crazy Irishman in my life?"

"Aye, love," he said with a grimace and a laugh. "I remember all too well the merry chase you led me on."

"I was so wrong. I need you more than anything."

No one in his life had ever been able to reduce him to a puddle of unguarded emotion the way his Carolina could. He blinked back tears as he kissed her. "I need you just as much. That's what I was trying to tell you all those months I chased you around like a pathetic fool."

"I'm glad every day that I let you catch me."

"I thank the Lord for that all the time. I love this life, this family, and most of all, I love my sexy wife."

She rolled her eyes, and he was relieved to see some of her feistiness reemerging after the shock of her injury. "I'm going to be *really* sexy for the next few months."

He flashed a grin. "Don't worry, love. We can work around a little plaster."

WHEN HE OPENED his eyes the next morning, he had no idea where he was for a full ten seconds before the events of the previous night came rushing back to remind him that he needed to get his sons up for school.

I'm getting my sons up for school.

Such a simple thing that meant so much to him because it was the first time he'd ever done it. He refused to allow himself to dwell in the place of shame he'd felt over everything he'd missed with them. Rather, he intended to take Cindy's advice and be the best friend and role model to them now.

She was right. The only control he had was over the present, and he planned to make that count.

He went to wake the boys and stopped short at the sight of them asleep with the early-morning light sneaking in through the closed blinds. Good God, they were so cute and innocent and perfect, everything he and his brother had once been before it all went so bad. If he ever saw them heading in the wrong direction, he'd throw himself in front of that with everything he had.

He went to Jackson first, giving his shoulder a gentle shake. "Hey, buddy, time to wake up."

The little guy groaned and buried his face in the pillow.

Kyle popped up in the other bed. "Is Carolina okay?"

"I haven't heard anything yet, but I'm going to text Seamus as soon as I get you guys up and moving." He tickled the back of Jackson's neck. "Anyone in there?"

"*No.*"

"Up and at 'em, boys. Seamus said you can get yourselves dressed. Whoever is dressed and ready first gets a surprise." He had vivid memories of his own mother making a contest out of everything, knowing how competitive he and Jess were with each other. These boys were the same, and the challenge sparked some movement from Jackson.

Jace left them to get dressed and tried to think of something he could use as a reward for the winner that would also benefit the winner's brother. An after-school treat of the winner's choice. That'd do it. He was quite pleased with his performance thus far as he located cereal boxes and put them on the table along with a jug of milk.

Then he dashed off a text to Seamus. *The boys are asking about Carolina. Any update?*

He replied a few minutes later, as Jace pressed start on the coffeemaker. *She came through the surgery well. They said it was a bad break that'll take eight to ten weeks to heal completely, but she should make a full recovery and have no lingering issues other than some occasional aches and pains from the break site, thank the Lord.*

That's good news. Happy to hear it, and the boys will be, too.

How are they?

They seem fine, rolling with everything.

Glad to hear it. They said she could be here four days. I can come home before then.

Four days with the boys sounded wonderful to Jace, even though he'd have to find someone to watch them when he worked. *No need. I've got things covered. Stay with Carolina and take care of her. Do you need me to send anything over on the boats?*

That's good of you, mate. We might need some more clothes and stuff. I'll let you know.

Anything you need.

Tell the boys we'll call them tonight and to have a good day at school. I called the school, and they have your number if anything comes up. You've been added to the approved pickup list.

Jace had never felt more honored by anything than to be on the approved pickup list at his sons' school. *I'm on it. No worries.*

We're very thankful to you for stepping up for us this way.

And I'm thankful that you asked me. We got this.

He had just put down the phone when Kyle came bursting into the kitchen, fully dressed, his hair combed into submission, his face washed and his backpack on his shoulders. "I win!"

"Wow, my man. Very good job."

"What's my prize?"

"I'll tell you when Jackson comes out."

Kyle turned around and went after his brother.

"Damn, I'm good at this," Jace said.

"Are you giving yourself a high five already?" Cindy asked when she came into the kitchen, looking sleepy and pretty.

"I'm killing it over here. I've got one completely ready to go and incentivized to get the other moving. Seamus reports that Carolina came through the surgery well, but they're going to be in the hospital at least four days."

Cindy came to him, put her hands on his hips and went up on tiptoes to kiss him. "Fatherhood looks good on you."

"I'm digging it. But, you know, it's only temporary. Can't get too carried away."

"Maybe you can offer to cover for them so they can get away every now and then."

The idea sent a thrill through him. "Yeah, I could do that."

Kyle returned with a much less enthusiastic Jackson in tow. He was dressed, but his hair was still standing on end, and he was clearly not the morning person of the duo.

Jace got them fed and sent them off to brush their teeth with orders for Jackson to do something about his hair, too. He got out their lunches, took an inventory of what was in them and wrote it down so he wouldn't forget.

"Jackson doesn't like mayo," Kyle said. "I love it."

"That's good to know. What else?"

In a scandalized whisper, Kyle added, "He never eats the carrots that Carolina packs for us."

Jace gave him a playful bop on the head. "Don't be a tattletale."

"It's true! He doesn't. But I do because Seamus says they're good for your eyes, and I mean, we need our eyes, right?"

"We sure do," Jace said, laughing as he glanced at the clock. Had forty-five minutes ever gone by so fast? "We need to get going."

"Jackson!" Kyle screamed. "Let's go!" Rolling his eyes, he said, "He's like this every day. Seamus says he's the weak link in the morning."

"Go let Burpy out before he pees himself."

"He's like Jackson—not a morning person," Kyle said. "We have to wake him up every day."

He reminded Jace so much of Lisa with his morning cheerfulness. Jace had been exactly like Jackson as a kid. School mornings had been torturous for him.

"Make sure you feed him and check his water," Jace said to Kyle.

"Already did. That's my job every day 'cause Jackson can't get himself together. Seamus says poor Burpy would starve if he was relying on Jackson."

Jace absolutely loved knowing these little details about the boys.

Kyle looked up at him. "Can I ask you something?"

"Anything."

"What are we supposed to call you?"

Jace knew he meant now that they were aware of his true identity. "What do you want to call me?"

Kyle shrugged.

"Mr. Jace was working pretty good before, but if you come up with something else, I'll answer to whatever you want to call me, except for Poopy Head. I won't answer to that."

Kyle cracked up laughing and took off, screaming for his brother to hurry up before they got in trouble for being late. "Mr. Jace says we should call him Poopy Head!"

Jace watched him go, amazed at how the boys could touch him so deeply. "I did not say that!"

Somehow, he got them all out the door with ten minutes to spare. As he drove to the school that housed grades K-12, the boys gave him directions because he had no idea where the school was located.

"How can you not know where the school is?" Jackson asked, laughing at him as if he was the silliest person the child had ever met. He probably was, but that was fine. After what they'd learned about him yesterday, he was thankful to have them teasing him.

"Because I didn't need to know until I had to bring you two monkeys," Jace retorted.

"Will you be able to find your way back for pickup?" Kyle asked with a tinge of concern in his voice.

"I'll be here. Don't you worry." They'd been relieved to hear the good news about Carolina's surgery and were looking forward to talking to them later.

Jace pulled the truck into the circular driveway in front of the school, where a line of cars inched forward. "Is this where we go?"

"Yep," Kyle said. "You stop up there where the teachers are, and we jump out."

"Got it. You guys are pretty handy to have around."

"You couldn't have found the school without us," Jackson said with a belly laugh.

"Are they making fun of me?" Jace asked Cindy while the boys giggled.

"I believe they are."

"So much for the after-school surprise I was planning."

"Wait! What surprise?"

"The one Kyle won by being dressed first. He gets to pick anything he wants for an after- school snack. What's it gonna be?"

"Duh, fudge," Jackson said. "That's what he always picks."

"Fudge it is."

Kyle raised both fists in a victory dance Jace watched in the rearview mirror. "I won! I won! I won!"

"Shut up."

"You shut up."

"Boys, knock it off and get ready to jump." Jace kept an eye on the back seat to make sure they had everything. "Have a great day."

"Later," Jackson said as he got out first, with Kyle right behind him.

As he edged the truck forward, Jace made sure they were inside before he pulled away. "Phew. Did it."

"You did great."

"They made it easy on me."

"They're awesome kids. Cute, funny, smart, respectful."

"Thanks to their wonderful mother. She did a great job with them."

"Yes, she did. Where did the name Poopy Head come from?"

"That was a self-inflicted wound," he said, conveying the story to Cindy.

"I love that, and if I were you, I'd be afraid it's going to stick."

"I'm so happy to be with them that they can call me whatever they want."

Jace drove them home to drop Cindy off before he went to join his meeting already in progress.

"My mom texted to invite us to family dinner tomorrow tonight."

"She invited me, too?"

"Yep, and when I told her you're taking care of the boys, she invited them as well."

"That would be fun. I switched shifts with one of the other bartenders who wanted tonight off, so I'm off then. Tell her thanks for including us."

"What's your plan for the boys when you're at work?"

"I don't have one yet."

"I'll stay with them."

"Are you sure? That's a lot to ask."

"You didn't ask. I offered, and I don't mind. They're so cute and funny. I'd love to do it."

"In case I forget to tell you, you're the absolute best."

"Happy to help."

He leaned over to kiss her. "I'm going to catch the last half of my meeting." Tomorrow, he was due to see Mac at the alpaca farm and still had to figure out where that was.

"I'll see you in a bit?"

"Yes, you will," he said, stealing one more kiss. When she was safely inside, he backed the truck out of the driveway and drove to the church where his AA group met. Having wheels to get around was nice. He needed to get something for the winter, especially if he was going to be working for Mac.

And he'd need tools.

Shit, he thought with a deep exhale. He didn't have that kind of money.

Slow down and take things as they come. AA meeting. Home to shower. Go to the gym. Pick up the boys later. Tomorrow, he would see Mac and figure out what he needed and go from there. He was continuously thankful for the many lessons he'd learned in recovery. Taking things one day and one minute at a time was among the most valuable of those lessons. Letting his mind race and his stress level flare wasn't going to solve anything. Rather, it could lead to the kind of trouble he didn't need.

Not when everything was going as well as it ever had for him. He had this beautiful new relationship with a woman he truly cared about, and his sons were back in his life. They'd gotten over the hump of them finding out who he really was without too much angst, and he was on his way to a meaningful bond with them. Seamus, who'd once treated him with suspicion, was now calling on him to help with the kids, which was no small thing. Jace could envision a time when the two of them might become close friends as they worked to raise the boys into men they could both be proud of.

These were some of the things he shared with the group toward the end of the meeting.

"Everything is so good," he said in conclusion, "that I worry about what's going to happen to mess it up. Because in my world, something always messes it up."

"That's how it *used to be,*" Quinn said, "when you were using and making stupid decisions in the quest for more drugs. You're not going to mess this up because you know how much is at stake with Cindy and the boys."

Hearing someone as accomplished as Dr. Quinn James say those things about him made Jace feel ten feet tall. "Thanks for that. Means a lot."

"It's the truth, Jace," Mallory added. "You're a totally different person from who you were the night you lost your brother. You've got this amazing second chance to be in the lives of your sons. I can't see how anything could get in the way of that."

"I hear you guys, and I appreciate what you're saying, but I'm precon-ditioned to expect it all to go to shit."

"It's not easy to change that kind of wiring," Jeff said. "I'm sort of the same way, starting a new relationship with a woman I could really love, but still feeling like I'm not worthy of her because of mistakes I've made in the past. I'm trying to get past that and to focus on who I am now, but that other guy... He's still in there, you know?"

"God, do I know," Jace said. "I've been a loser in my own mind for so long that I have no clue how to be a winner."

"Yes," Jeff said. "Exactly that. You said it so perfectly."

"Neither one of you guys is a loser," Mason said emphatically. "You've been through and survived shit that would've killed lesser people. You're here every day, doing the hard work to make sure you never go back to the old ways. That makes you winners in my book."

"Mine, too," Mallory said as the others nodded in agreement. "And can I just say how much I love being part of this group and the support we give each other? I feel a little sorry for people who don't have this in their daily lives."

"I agree, Mallory," Nina said. "This group is one of the best I've ever belonged to, and I love the way you all support each other. I want to go back to what Jace said about his view of himself and how hard it is to reframe that. We've all been there, the lowest of the lows, with people telling us we needed to get our shit together, whether we were in trouble with drugs or alcohol or both. We know what it's like to feel like a loser, but you must know that every time you come to one of these meetings or step up for someone else in recovery, you're *winning*. Every day that you don't drink or use, you're *winning*. Every time you embark on a new relationship, whether romantic or family or friend, and put your whole heart into making that relationship work, you're *winning*. Please don't take any of these major accomplishments for granted. They're the prize for surviving this very long journey we've all been on for years."

Mallory started a round of applause that quickly took off.

Nina smiled even as her face flushed with embarrassment.

"So very well said, Nina," Mallory said when the applause died down. "And hopefully just what our friend Jace needed to hear."

"It was," Jace said, smiling. "Thank you all."

He left the meeting feeling pumped and uplifted by the words his friends had shared. He might've been a loser once upon a time, but not anymore.

Those days were over.

CHAPTER 26

On Tuesday, Cindy's day at the shop began with one of her favorite customers—Tiffany Taylor. The irreverent Tiffany was always good for a laugh, especially since she was pregnant with her third child. "Are you sure I'm going to fit in the chair?" Tiffany asked, eyeing it.

"Don't be silly," Cindy said, laughing. "Abby was saying the same thing when she was in, and she fit fine, too."

"And she's expecting quads, that overachiever. I feel like an absolute whale with one. I'm bigger than Maddie was at the end with twins."

"No, you're not."

"Even she says so!"

Cindy covered Tiffany with the cape and ran her fingers through the other woman's auburn hair. "She's your sister. She's paid to be mean."

"That's true."

"When are you due?"

"Not until February."

"Oh. Wow."

"*See what I'm saying?* I'm already huge."

"Was it like that with your girls?"

"No! That's why Blaine thinks he's finally getting some testosterone around the house. He's convinced it's a boy and says it has to be, because he can't handle any more ladies. The poor guy is our bitch."

Cindy sputtered with laughter at the description of Tiffany's brawny police chief husband. "What're we doing today?"

"Anything you want. I'm just gonna sit here, close my eyes and enjoy every second."

"How about we start with a scalp massage?"

"I might have an orgasm."

That was why Tiffany was one of her favorites, Cindy thought as she laughed again. She never knew what might come out of Tiffany's mouth.

"You're looking particularly perky today." Tiffany groaned with pleasure as Cindy massaged her scalp. "You've got a glow about you."

"Do I?"

"Uh-huh. In fact, it kind of reminds me of the way I looked after I first met Blaine—and well, just about every day since we finally got together. What's his name?"

"Jace."

"*Oh*, sexy Jace-the-Beachcomber-bartender Jace?"

"The one and only."

"Damn, girl. He's hot, and I know hot. Look at who I'm married to."

"He's pretty hot and sweet and all the important stuff."

"That's wonderful, Cindy. I'm so happy for you."

"Thanks. I'm rather happy for me, too."

"Tell me everything and then come by the store to pick out something sexy to wear tonight in exchange for this incredible massage."

Cindy went warm all over when she thought about wearing something sexy for Jace. "I might just do that."

"You should! You deserve it. You deserve all good things."

There it was again, the subtle nod to what her family had been through. As always, it struck at the little girl in her who was programmed not to acknowledge it, even though it was out in the open now.

"I almost want this for him more than I do myself," Cindy said, forcing herself to move past the disturbing thoughts about things that didn't matter any longer.

"That's how you know he's the one for you. When you want more for him than you do for yourself."

Was Jace the one for her? She couldn't say for certain. Not yet, but she was starting to believe Tiffany might be right. After only a few days officially together, she already couldn't imagine going back to who she'd been before everything changed between them. She'd had the best time watching the boys last night and could already picture them in her life going forward.

"Could I ask you something?" Cindy said.

"Anything. You know me. I'm an open book."

"How soon did you know—for sure—that Blaine was the one?"

"Honestly? The minute I first saw him. I was in my sister's room at the clinic. It'd been an awful day. Mr. McCarthy had been badly hurt in an accident at the marina. Mac was in the clinic with hypothermia after going in the water after his father, and Maddie was having early contractions. I was with her when Blaine came to her room looking for Mac. You know those stories you hear about explosions and how they suck the air out of the room?"

Cindy nodded, transfixed by what Tiffany was saying.

"That's how I felt when I saw him. Breathless. But I was still married to Jim, the douchebag, so there wasn't much I could do about it. We saw each other a few times over the next couple of months, and it was the same every time—incendiary. By the time I was free for us to act on our feelings, we were thermonuclear. We still are."

"I need a cigarette," Cindy said, fanning her face.

Tiffany cracked up laughing. "When you know, you know."

"I suppose that's true. I like that Jace and I started out as friends before anything else happened. There was always this aura of flirtation to it, but when I talked to him, he really listened to what I had to say. Even though he had other customers at the bar, he always ended up back with me."

"That's very sweet, Cindy, and friendship is a really good place to start something lasting."

"It feels good."

After she sent Tiffany on her way with her hair two inches shorter and new layers framing her gorgeous face, Cindy swept up the hair, refilled her water bottle and ate a granola bar. The bell on the door signaled her next client had arrived.

She stepped out of the back room to greet Lizzie James and her new baby daughter, Violet. Lizzie had called to ask if Cindy minded if Violet came. "Let me see!"

Lizzie put down the baby car seat and pushed back the top so Cindy could see the baby.

"Oh my goodness. Look at her."

"She's rather perfect, isn't she?" Lizzie looked elated and exhausted. "I still can't believe we get to keep her. It's like a dream."

The last time she'd come in, Lizzie had shared the struggles she and her husband, Jared, had been having with infertility.

They positioned Violet's seat so she could see her mother.

"Let's hope she'll take a little snooze," Lizzie said. "She usually does around now." Lizzie released a deep breath as she tried to relax in Cindy's chair.

"You look so happy," Cindy said.

"I've never been happier or more exhausted, but I wouldn't trade it for anything."

"I couldn't believe what I heard about the baby's mother leaving her with you at Quinn and Mallory's wedding and taking off."

"I was so torn between elation and fear. My first thought was, 'Good, go. You don't want her, and I do. I want her more than I've ever wanted anything.' But Jared… He was out of his mind, telling me we couldn't do it this way, that we had to find her."

"Ugh, I can't imagine how stressful that must've been."

"It was the worst thing I've ever been through, even worse than when Jared and I broke up for a time. Not knowing if her mother was going to come back for her and say it had been a terrible mistake… Jared put an investigator on trying to find her. It was so nuts."

"In the meantime, you were taking care of her."

"And falling deeper in love with her by the second. I'm not sure what I would've done if I'd had to give her up. I would've come apart."

"I'm so glad that didn't happen, Lizzie."

"God, me, too. Jessie, the baby's mother, signed over permanent custody to us, and we're in the process of adopting her. Jessie can still change her mind until it's final, but she's promised us she's not going to. I've decided to believe her, so I won't worry myself to death over that."

"Congratulations. I'm so, so happy for you and Jared."

"Thank you. We're happy for us, too. Now that we have signed paperwork that says she's ours to keep, it's like we've both allowed ourselves to fall completely in love with her. Jared is just over the moon for her. He gets up with her every night and stays up for hours with her sometimes so I can sleep. He can't get enough of her."

"That's lovely," Cindy said, moved nearly to tears by Lizzie's joy.

"I always knew he'd be the most wonderful father." She dabbed at her eyes with a tissue that Cindy handed her. "I'm sorry to go on and on. How are you?"

"You're not doing that. You're overflowing with joy, and it's wonderful to see."

"Thank you. I promise I'll stop gushing in a year or maybe eighteen of them."

Cindy laughed. "Gush all you want. You waited a long time for this moment. You need to fully enjoy it."

"Oh, I am when I'm not craving more sleep."

"From what I hear, they figure out the sleep situation sooner rather than later."

"God, I hope so."

"How are Cooper and Gigi doing?" Jared's younger brother Cooper had recently fallen for reality TV star Gigi Gibson.

"They're great, back in LA for now, getting ready to premiere the season of the show that she and Jordan filmed here on Gansett. They invited us to come out for the festivities, but we're staying at home with Miss Violet for now. Mason and Jordan and Riley and Nikki are going out for it, though."

"That's very exciting."

"I guess. To me, hanging with a newborn is far more exciting than the red carpet. But Cooper is so in love with Gigi—and vice versa. Jared and Quinn can't believe their wild baby brother has been domesticated, but Gigi is perfect for him. She doesn't put up with any of his nonsense."

"They were in for haircuts before they left. They're cute together."

"They really are. We're so thrilled for them. Anyway, tell me something fun that's going on with you."

"I seem to have gotten myself a boyfriend," Cindy said, smiling at the way Lizzie's eyes lit up with that news.

"Do tell!"

They were fully caught up by the time Cindy sent Lizzie and Violet on their way with hugs and a haircut that Lizzie said made her feel like a whole new woman. That was Cindy's goal with every client, to make them feel special and pampered during the hour they spent in her chair.

She was about to step out to find something to eat when Jace came through the door, carrying a bag.

"I figured that even the island's only stylist gets a lunch break, right?"

Smiling and thrilled to see him, she said, "She does, and you timed it perfectly."

"Oh, I love when I have perfect timing."

Cindy raised a brow. "Are we still talking about lunch?"

He stopped in front of her and kissed her. "We're talking about *all the things*. I wanted to do something to thank you for watching the boys last night."

"I loved every second with them." She placed a hand on his chest, once again appreciating the finely honed muscles under yet another of the sexy Henleys he seemed to own in every color. This one was a heathered sage that brought out the green in his eyes. "Did you have your meeting with Mac?"

"He pushed it to one thirty, which gave me time to bring lunch to my new girlfriend."

"She's very glad you did. What are we having?"

"I got salad and a sub from the grocery store. What's your pleasure?"

"Other than you?" She had no idea where that came from, but he seemed to like it.

Grinning, he said, "For lunch, Cindy. Focus."

"Oh, I'm focused. And how about we split them?"

"That works."

They set up their lunch in the reception area. He'd also brought her lemon-flavored water, which she opened and drank half of, and an iced tea for a midafternoon boost.

"You're only allowed to drink a tiny bit of that." Jace pointed to the tea. "We don't need any migraines around here."

"No, we don't, and I only have a sip or two late in the afternoon."

"I know. You told me that."

"And you remembered. Big boyfriend points for that."

His smile lit up his sinfully handsome face.

As Cindy stared at him, she wanted to pinch herself to believe this man was hers, that she was allowed to feel all the things for him and that he seemed to feel the same way about her. In her world, things like this happened to other people. Not her.

"What's with the wrinkle between the brows?" he asked, smoothing a finger over the spot in question.

"I'm amazed by this, by us."

"So am I. I'm amazed and thrilled and every other word I can think of. When I came here, earlier in the summer, I had one goal in mind—get to know my sons. It's been so much more than that." He took her hand and linked their fingers. "Not only do I have a beautiful, sweet, sexy new girl-friend, but I've made some of the best friends I've ever had in my life through my AA group, at the gym and the bar. I've made an unlikely friend of the man who's raising my sons and his wife. And there's this job opportunity with Mac." He shook his head. "It's just incredible. All of it."

"You're incredible, and people see that. They respond to your genuine desire to start over and live a productive life. And for what it's worth, you're amazing with the boys. I was already falling hard for you but seeing you with them really sealed the deal."

"That means a lot to me. I want to be good with them and to them."

"They see that, and they like you, or they wouldn't tease you the way they do."

"They are pretty ruthless," he said with a laugh. "I hate that Carolina got hurt, but to have this chance to step up for them… It means so much to me."

"I know, and you're doing a great job."

He put his arm around her and kissed her right there in the window, where anyone walking by might see them.

Cindy couldn't find the wherewithal to care if someone saw them.

"In case you were wondering," he said, leaning his forehead against hers, "you're not the only one who's falling pretty hard."

"No?"

"Not at all." He ran his fingers through her hair. "I haven't felt this good in, well, ever. I loved Lisa. I truly did, but my life was a mess the entire time we were together. I never got a chance to be this person with her."

"I'm sorry for her that she didn't get a chance to know this guy, because he's very special."

"I'm glad you think so."

"I do. For sure."

"I hate to say I have to go."

"I hate to let you go, but my next client is due in ten minutes."

He gave her one more lingering kiss. "That'll keep me until I see you later."

"Thank you for lunch and the visit." She walked him to the door, where he kissed her one more time.

"Thank you for everything."

She reached up to fix the hair that she'd disturbed during the kissing portion of their lunch date. "I still owe you a haircut."

"Something else to look forward to."

"Good luck with Mac."

"Thanks. Give me a call when you're ready for a pickup after work."

"We're due at my mom's at six thirty."

"Sounds good."

Cindy waved him off and disposed of their trash in the back room. Then she wiped off the coffee table and plumped up the pillows on the sofa. Chloe had made it such a warm, inviting space, and Cindy took pride in keeping it looking nice.

She took a seat while she waited for her next client and thought about what Jace had said about being on Gansett and the friends they'd made and the life they were making for themselves there. What she'd intended to be a brief stay had turned into so much more than she'd ever expected.

But she knew she shouldn't be surprised. Gansett had always been a magical place to her, and now was no different.

CHAPTER 27

*J*ace drove out to meet Mac, thinking about lunch with Cindy and how she'd confessed to falling hard for him. Thank goodness for that, because he was falling just as hard and just as fast for her. Although, when he thought about it, he'd been falling for her for weeks. Every time she came into the bar, his night shifted from ordinary to extraordinary.

He'd find himself watching for her around the time she normally came in, and on the rare night that she didn't show up, he'd been crushed.

At the time, he'd told himself he was silly for feeling that way, but he couldn't seem to help it. He loved being with her, and now he got to be with her all the time and couldn't be happier about that.

Despite the many good things in his life, he was still wary of the bottom falling out, because it always did. He shook off that unpleasant thought and parked next to Mac's truck. He'd had to ask around in town for directions to the alpaca farm, which was located at the end of a long dirt road he would've missed if he hadn't been told what to look for.

He was surprised to find an old farm in serious disrepair with rusty implements surrounded by overgrown grass, sagging roofs and a lingering stench that might've been urine.

"It's alpaca piss." Mac smiled as he walked over to shake hands with Jace. "How'd you end up with a ferry truck?"

"I'm watching the boys while Seamus and Carolina are on the mainland."

"Heard about her accident. That's horrible."

"I know, but she's on the mend after surgery. How're you doing?"

"Better, but anyone who tells you a vasectomy is no big deal doesn't have a penis."

Jace winced. "Ouch."

"Yeah, you said it. Let me show you around."

Mac walked him through the property, outlining the plans for a "shabby chic" wedding venue with a rustic vibe. "Our research has shown that brides and grooms love places like this where they can have a more casual sort of reception, but still have all the bells and whistles. They like to have photos taken with the rusty tractors and stuff." Mac shrugged. "I don't get it, but I hear there's money to be made in that sector, so that's our goal. Gansett is a huge wedding destination. We're sold out for the next two years at the Wayfarer, and the Chesterfield is booked for summer weekends three years out."

"Damn."

"I know, right? The island is ripe for another venue, and we're here for it."

"The location is spectacular." The property ended at the coast with a dazzling view of the ocean.

"It's ideal for what we want to do. Talk to me about your experience."

"I did three years of work release with a master plumber. He taught me everything he knew and even offered me a job when I got out."

"How come you didn't take it?"

"I wanted to live near my sons."

Mac eyed him warily. "You're not going to cause trouble for Seamus and Carolina, are you?"

"No, I'm not. The boys are happily settled with them. I'm thankful to play a peripheral role."

"I respect that you're willing to take a back seat because it's what's best for them."

"Their mother knew what she was doing when she asked Seamus and Carolina to be their guardians."

"Yes, she did. So, I need a plumber. Badly. Are you interested?"

Jace laughed. "Very much so, but I have an issue."

"What's that?"

"I don't have tools. I know what I need, but I can't afford the outlay. Not right now, anyway."

Mac rubbed his chin as he thought about that. "If I set you up with what you need, would you be willing to come on full-time?"

Jace's mouth fell open in shock. "Seriously?"

"Dead serious. Do you have any idea what it costs me to bring plumbers out from the mainland every time I need one?"

"Ah, no, but I have a feeling it's not cheap, knowing the usual hourly rate."

"Not cheap at all. It'll be cheaper to have you on the payroll than to bring people out when needed. My company is booming. We're booked two years out as well. Having my own plumber will be a lifesaver. If you're interested, that is."

"God, yes, I'm interested, but, um, you know I'm on parole, right?"

"I do."

"And that doesn't matter?"

"Not unless you plan to break the law. Then it would matter very much."

"I'll never go back to the life I was leading before I was locked up. You have my word on that."

Mac extended his hand to Jace. "That's all I need. Welcome to McCarthy Construction. You can stop by the office in town, and Julia will help with the paperwork."

Jace had a massive lump in his throat when he shook Mac's hand. "You'll never know what this means to me."

"I'm looking forward to working with you. I'd also be happy to support your efforts to get licensed. Just tell me what you need, and we'll make it happen."

"That would be…" Jace couldn't speak for a second. "Getting licensed would be incredible, and I want you to know you can ask me to do anything you need, not just plumbing. I'll do whatever."

"I appreciate that attitude. You'll fit right in with my close-knit group of cousins and longtime friends. We do what it takes to get the job done."

"That sounds great. When do you want me to start?"

"Would Monday be too soon?"

"Ah, no, but I need to give some notice to the Beachcomber. They've been good to me."

"You tell me when you're free and clear, and we'll make it work."

"Thank you again, Mac. You're changing my life with this opportunity."

"And you're saving mine. I've been needing a plumber for years."

They walked back to the trucks and parted company with another handshake.

Jace drove home feeling stunned by the turn of events. He'd landed a full-time job that would pay the kind of money he needed to really get his life together. He couldn't wait to text Darrell, his probation officer, with an update about the latest developments. Soon, he'd pick up his sons from school and spend the evening with them and Cindy and her family. If life had ever been better than this, he couldn't recall a time.

As he approached the island cemetery, he glanced at the clock, saw he had an hour until pickup and hung a left into the entrance, following the path to Lisa's grave he'd taken with Seamus. He put the truck in Park and shut off the engine, sitting for a minute before he got out to visit her resting place.

Since there was no one else in the cemetery, he felt comfortable taking a seat on the grass. He wrapped his arms around his knees. "Hey, Lisa, it's me Jace. I bet you're surprised to see me here on Gansett. I've got to admit... You didn't make it easy to find you or the boys when I got out, but I suppose that was intentional. You didn't want me to find you, and I don't blame you for that. I hate what I put you through... I never intended to leave you alone to raise the boys."

He brushed a hand across his face, stunned by the sudden flow of tears that talking to her unleashed. "I made such a mess of everything. When I got the divorce and custody papers in prison, I signed them without even reading them. I didn't blame you for wanting to be free of me and my never-ending drama. You tried to tell me so many times that Jess and I were heading for big trouble, but I didn't listen. I wish I'd listened to you. Jess would still be here, and none of this would've happened. You deserved so much better than what you got from me. When I heard about you getting sick and passing away... I was heartbroken for you and the boys. I'm so, so sorry you went through that alone. I should've been there for you, and I'm devastated that I wasn't."

Jace dropped his chin onto his folded arms, using his shirt sleeve to wipe away more tears. "The boys are doing great with Seamus and Carolina. They're wonderful kids. You did the best job with them. And don't worry, I'm not going to mess up the arrangement you made for them. We had to tell them who I am, and that went better than I expected. They had a lot of questions, but I was truthful with them about where I was and why I wasn't around. I wish I hadn't had to tell them those things, but I've learned to own my mistakes and to learn from them. I'm putting my life back together, Lisa, and I'm going to be there for our boys. Seamus and Carolina are their parents now, but I want to be a friend to them, and so far, that's going well."

He brushed some dirt off her stone and pulled a few weeds around the edges. "I'd give everything to be able to look you in the eyes and apologize for what I did. But since I can't do that, I really hope that wherever you are, you can hear me, and you know how truly sorry I am. I never stopped loving you or the boys, Lisa. I'll come by to see you once in a while and tell you how the boys are doing."

As he stood to leave, he looked down at her stone for a long time before he walked back to the truck, feeling strangely cleansed by the one-sided conversation. It'd felt good to share his remorse with her, even if it had tempered some of the elation that came from landing a new job.

Back in the truck, he put through a call to Dan Torrington, who answered on the second ring. "Hi, this is Jace Carson. I was, um, married to Lisa Chandler."

"Ah, okay. What can I do for you, Jace?"

"Seamus and Carolina O'Grady asked me to get in touch with you about Lisa's things. They've put aside what they think the boys would like to have, but they aren't sure what to do with the rest. They thought you might be in touch with her family."

"I've reached out to them," Dan said, "but haven't gotten anywhere. I was told they were estranged and preferred to stay that way."

"That's because of me," Jace said. "They told her not to marry me."

"They didn't say why, just that they were very sorry to hear she'd passed, but it was for the best to keep their distance. Wish I had better news."

It pained him that her parents had shown no interest in their grandsons, but then again, they never had, even before the shit hit the fan.

"Thanks for the info, Dan. Appreciate you doing what you could. I guess I'll ask Seamus and Carolina to put the boxes aside until the boys are old enough to deal with them."

"I'm sorry for your loss. Lisa was a wonderful person."

Jace felt guilty accepting condolences on Lisa's behalf, but that was his issue, not Dan's. "Yes, she was. Thank you for all you did to help her at a difficult time."

"It was my pleasure."

After they ended the call, Jace took a few minutes to get himself together before he picked up the boys. He couldn't wait to see them.

JACE DROVE into Seamus and Carolina's driveway around four thirty, bearing two dirty boys who'd enjoyed a trip to their favorite park. "You'd better get in there and let Burpy out," he told them as he noticed another car parked in the driveway.

The boys burst out of the truck, backpacks in hand, and headed for the house to get their best pal.

Jace got out to meet an older woman wearing a suit that seemed wildly out of place on the informal island. "Mr. O'Grady? I'm Justine Deavers from the Department of Children, Youth & Families. We spoke last week?"

"I'm not Mr. O'Grady. He's on the mainland with Mrs. O'Grady, who broke her leg in a fall two nights ago."

"Oh dear, I'm so sorry to hear that. We had an appointment this afternoon."

The boys came bursting out of the house with Burpy, who squatted to pee a river right outside the door.

"Seamus must've forgotten."

"And you are?"

"Jace Carson."

She shook his hand. "Pleased to meet you, Mr. Carson. You're helping with the boys while the O'Gradys are away?"

"I am."

"And you're a... friend?"

He wasn't sure what to tell this woman from the state who'd appeared out of nowhere. "I'm the boys' biological father."

"Oh. I see." Her expression changed from friendly to guarded, and he immediately feared he'd made a huge mistake telling her the truth. "Do you know when the O'Gradys will be returning?"

"Probably not until later in the week. She had surgery two nights ago, and they were told to expect about four days in the hospital. But I'll let him know you were here."

"Yes, please do. I'm sorry to have come all this way to not get to see them."

"Is there something wrong?"

"No, this is a routine part of them becoming the boys' legal guardians. We're required to do two home visits the first year. This was to be the second one."

"I see, well, knowing Seamus and Carolina, they'll be upset to realize they forgot about the appointment. They're doing a great job with the boys. They're very happy and well-adjusted after losing their mom."

"That's good to hear. I won't keep you any longer. If you'd ask Mr. O'Grady to get in touch to reschedule, I'd appreciate it."

"I'll do that."

The minute she drove off, Jace pulled his phone from his back pocket to text Seamus. *There was a lady here from the state department for children about an appointment you guys had...*

Seamus wrote back right away. *FUCK. Totally forgot. Was she pissed?*

I told her what happened, and she asked you to call to reschedule.

Damn it. I can't believe I forgot that.

You've had a few things on your mind. How's Carolina?

In a lot of pain this afternoon. They're working on trying to address that. We're both eager to talk to the boys.

Give us a call when you're ready. They're looking forward to it.

She's taking a rest now, but we'll call when she wakes up.

Sounds good.

Jace put his phone in his back pocket and went to check on the boys, who'd disappeared into the trees with the dog.

SEAMUS COULD NOT BELIEVE he'd forgotten that appointment. Ugh. With Carolina sleeping after a rough day, he stepped out of her room and into the hallway to call Ms. Deavers on the cell phone number he'd programmed into his phone after their first meeting. This would've been the last hurdle before their legal guardianship became final. As he waited for her to pick up, he hoped they hadn't screwed things up.

"Justine Deavers."

"This is Seamus O'Grady. I'm so sorry we missed the appointment today. Jace told me he filled you in on what's happened to my wife."

"He did, and I'm so sorry to hear that. Is she doing okay?"

"She's on the mend, but it's going to be a long road. Could we possibly reschedule for next week? And again, I apologize. I know it's a lot for you to come out to the island."

"Yes, next week should be fine, but, Mr. O'Grady, I have to express my concern about the fact that you've left the boys with Mr. Carson."

Seamus's stomach went into a free fall. "What? Why?"

"Our records indicate he's a convicted felon on parole."

"Yes, I know." Seamus tried to keep his voice calm when he was freaking out on the inside. "He's also the boys' biological father and has made a genuine effort to be part of their lives since he was released from prison."

"But to leave him in charge of them when you're off-island…"

"We left them with someone who loves them very much, who they're comfortable with and who was able to drop everything to be there when we needed him. We trust him implicitly, or he never would've gotten near them."

"I understand, but I'll need to discuss this with my supervisor."

"Discuss *what*?" He was no longer trying to remain calm.

"The situation."

"Ms. Deavers, I understand you have a job to do and that your job is to protect those kids, but when I tell you Jace Carson would take a bullet for them, I mean that. He made a mistake, paid for it with years of his life and lost his wife and children. He's a hardworking guy who's trying to put his life back together and be there for his sons. If you make something of this, you're going to cause more problems than you'll fix. Trust me on that."

"I hear what you're saying and appreciate your point of view, but I'm required to report this development to my supervisors."

"I'll be on the first boat or flight home if you're going to make an issue of it. I'll leave my ailing wife in the hospital and go home to our boys."

"I… I don't know what to say. I could lose my job if I don't report it."

"There is *nothing* to report. Do you honestly think that either of us would leave them with someone we don't trust?"

"No, but..."

"No buts. We trust Jace to take care of our children. End of story. Now, do I need to arrange to get home right away?"

"I, um, I'll give it a day and then check back on the status."

"What does that mean?"

"You need to get someone else to take care of your children, Mr. O'Grady. Someone who isn't on parole."

"I'll take care of it."

"Please notify me when you've made other arrangements."

"I will." He ended the call, feeling infuriated and unnerved. It had never occurred to him that asking Jace to watch the kids could lead to something like this. And how in the world would he tell Jace that he couldn't stay with them anymore? "What the hell do I do now?" He thought about that for a few minutes before he found Joe's number in his contacts and put through the call. "Hey, is that offer to come home still good?"

CHAPTER 28

"Holy crap," Jace said as they pulled into the driveway at Sarah and Charlie's. "*This* is your mother's house?"

"Yep. Charlie got a big payout from the state for wrongful imprisonment and told her to pick her dream house."

"Wow, I wish the state owed me that kind of money."

Cindy laughed. "You knew him, right?"

"I did. Everyone knew him and his story and how hard his stepdaughter was working to get him out. We all looked up to him. He was a bit of a father figure to us younger guys."

"He's a good man. My mom is so happy with him. It's lovely to see."

"I'm glad he's found a nice life for himself after everything that happened."

"I'm glad you have, too," she said, smiling.

He'd had just enough time to tell her about his job offer and to share a giddy moment of excitement with her before the boys had interrupted them. As much as he was loving every minute with the boys, he was looking forward to being alone with her later so they could talk about it more. He wanted to talk to her about everything.

"Looks like everyone else is already here," Cindy said as she took in all the cars.

Jace parked off to the side so he wouldn't block anyone in. "Remember your manners, boys," he said as they got out of the truck to follow Cindy inside.

Cindy had prepared him for a big crowd, and that was what they walked into as they took the stairs up to the main living area of the gorgeous house. It might be the nicest house he'd ever been in. No, it was. For sure.

She introduced him to her mother, Sarah, who hugged him. "I'm so delighted to meet you, Jace. Cindy has told me so much about you."

"And you're still delighted to meet me?" Jace asked, making her laugh.

She rested her hand on his arm as if they were old friends. "We don't hold the past against people in this house, especially not when we see them making a real effort to turn things around."

"Thank you, ma'am. That means a lot to me. These are my sons, Jackson and Kyle. Say hello to Mrs. Grandchamp, boys." He realized that was the first time he'd ever introduced them as his sons to anyone.

As they said hello to Sarah, they partially hid behind him. He hadn't seen their shy side before and found it endearing.

"I think you know my husband, Charlie."

"I do." Jace shook hands with Charlie Grandchamp, who looked like a totally different person from the hardened man Jace had known inside. "Good to see you again."

"You as well. The view is much better from here."

"You must have the best view on the entire island."

"It's not bad," Charlie said with his trademark gruffness. "How've you been making out since your release?"

"Pretty well, all things considered. Coming here was a good move."

"It was for me, too. I'm glad it's working out for you." He glanced at Cindy, who was talking to her sisters. "We love her very much."

"I think I might, too."

"Is that right?"

"Yeah. She's like this place of calmness in the storm." He glanced at the other man. "That's weird, right?"

"No, it's sweet, and I get what you mean. Her mother is the same for me. I'm sure you've heard about Cindy's father and his bullshit."

"I have."

"She has a new father now, and he won't be happy with anyone who messes with her, especially someone who's been inside. Do we understand each other?"

"We do, and you have nothing to worry about. I promise."

"I'll take that as your word and will sleep a little easier knowing she has a good man looking out for her, not that she needs that. She's independent and always has been, from what I've been told."

"She doesn't need me to look out for her, but I'm happy to do it just the same."

"That's the right answer."

"What are you saying to him, Charlie?" Cindy asked as she came over to them and wound her hands around Jace's arm in a possessive move that thrilled him.

"I'm saying dad things to him," Charlie said, giving her a pointed look.

"Oh. Well, I suppose that's okay, if you didn't threaten to beat him up or anything."

"Only if he hurts you, sweetheart, and then I absolutely *will* beat him up."

Cindy's smile lit up her pretty face as her eyes filled with tears. "That's very sweet of you, Charlie. Thank you."

Knowing what she'd endured at the hands of her own father, Jace was filled with emotion as he witnessed the touching moment between Cindy and her stepfather. "I won't give you reason for that, Charlie." He put his arm around Cindy. "I just want to make her happy."

"Are you going to introduce us to your new boyfriend, Cindy?" Katie's husband, Shane McCarthy, asked.

"You already know him," Cindy said, rolling her eyes at her brother-in-law.

Shane laughed and shook hands with Jace. "Good to see you."

"You, too," Jace said. "Give me the refresher course, Cindy."

"Jace, you know my oldest brother, Owen, and his wife, Laura. Shane is her brother, and he's married to Katie. That's Charlie's daughter, Stephanie, and her husband, Grant McCarthy, and you already know Katie's twin, Julia. That's her fiancé, Deacon. These are my magnificent grandparents, Adele and Russ. You know Jeff and John, and this is Frank McCarthy, father to Laura and Shane, and his fiancée, Betsy. Everyone, this is Jace Carson and his sons, Jackson and Kyle."

"Is there a map or diagram of who is married to who and who is related to who?" Jace asked.

"I'll draw you a picture," Shane said.

"How are you related to Mac?"

"First cousin and business partner."

"He hired me today."

"I heard, and we're excited. We need a plumber badly."

"Looking forward to it. So, remind me again how this works... You're married to Katie, and Owen is married to your sister?"

"That's right, and Frank over there is our dad. His brother Big Mac is Mac's father."

"The head spins."

"It will for a while, but then you'll figure us out."

"I'll take your word on that. How does Grant McCarthy fit into the picture?"

"Mac's younger brother."

"Ah, I see. And he's married to Charlie's daughter."

"Right. See, you're figuring it out."

"I still need that diagram."

"You know the movie *Indefatigable* about Charlie and his daughter, Stephanie?"

"Sure, everyone's talking about it."

"Grant wrote it. He also wrote *Song of Solomon* a few years ago and won an Oscar for that one. There's Oscar buzz about *Indefatigable*, too."

"Wow." Jace couldn't imagine having that kind of talent.

Sarah called them all to the table for a delicious roast beef dinner with mashed potatoes and gravy, green beans, salad and chocolate cake for dessert.

As he ate, Jace kept a careful eye on the boys to make sure they were remembering their manners. They were perfect, chatting with Sarah, who kept up a steady stream of conversation with them about school, baseball, their crazy dog and life with Seamus and Carolina.

"She broke her leg," Kyle said. "It was terrible. She was screaming."

"Oh my goodness," Sarah said. "That must've been so frightening."

"It was," Jackson said. "We didn't know what happened at first. And Seamus said we shouldn't look at how her leg was bent, but we did."

"It was *gnarly*," Kyle said.

"All right, fellas," Jace said, holding back a laugh. "No gory details at dinner."

"They're delightful," Sarah said to Jace when he helped clear the table after dinner. "You must be so proud of them."

"I am, but I can't take any credit. Their mother was the one who raised them. She did a great job."

"Yes, she did. I know the backstory. I'm glad you're able to spend time with them now."

"I am, too. Thank you for having us."

"It's my pleasure. I've never seen my Cindy smile the way she does around you. It does my heart good to see that. I've worried so much about my kids."

"It seems to me, as an outsider looking in, that you've also done a wonderful job raising your kids."

She smiled warmly at him. "I'm proud of who they turned out to be in spite of their chaotic childhood."

Adele linked her arm through Jace's. "Take a stroll with me to the deck so we can talk about Cindy behind her back."

Jace laughed at the older woman's brazen comment. "Lead the way, ma'am."

"Call me Adele. Ma'am makes me feel old."

"Where are you taking him, Gram?" Cindy called from the sofa, where she was seated with her sisters and Stephanie.

"None of your business," Adele said.

"You got the boys?" Jace asked Cindy.

She nodded as she eyed her grandmother curiously.

The boys had talked Charlie into a second piece of cake and were still at the table.

"Tell me all about you," Adele said. "And don't worry, I already know the bad stuff."

"That about sums me up," Jace said.

"That's not true! If my Cindy sees something in you, there's more than bad stuff."

"I care about her very much."

"I love to hear that. She's always been such a ray of sunshine from the time she was a little girl."

"That's how I describe her, too." He smiled, looking out over the ocean as the sunset lit up the western sky. "She speaks so highly of you and your husband and the summers they spent here."

"Yes," she said, her smile fading a bit. "We didn't know then what was happening at home. But we don't need to talk about that. Thankfully, it's all in the past now." She patted Jace's arm. "I won't keep you. I just wanted the chance to speak to you one-on-one, to tell you what our Cindy means to us."

"I've never known a big family like this one," he said. "It's quite something how you all look out for each other."

"You're welcome with us, Jace, and we'll look out for you and your boys, too."

Her words touched him deeply. "That's very kind of you, and I'm honored to be part of something like this. Although, you know, the boys don't really belong to me. Not anymore."

"They'll always be part of you, no matter where they live or who raises them."

"Yes, well, I suppose that's true."

"Do I need to rescue you, Jace?" Cindy asked when she came to the slider.

"Of course you don't." Adele laughed as she went up on tiptoes to kiss Jace's cheek. "I've had a lovely chat with your handsome young man, and now I'll leave you to go see if the boys ate all the cake." She hugged Cindy as she went inside.

"She's quite something," Jace said, smiling as Cindy stepped into his embrace.

"She sure is. I hope she didn't threaten to beat you up, too."

"Nah, she told me I was welcome here with your family, which was very sweet of her. It's been a long time since I was part of a family—and never one quite like this one."

"I'm very glad to have you here with mine."

He waggled his brows at her as he kissed her. "Today's been one of the best days of my life, and it's not over yet."

JOHN BIDED HIS TIME, waiting until his grandparents said their goodbyes and headed toward their cottage behind the main house. He slipped his arm through his grandmother's. "I'll walk you home."

She laughed. "It's right there, Johnny boy. I think we can find it."

"That doesn't mean I can't escort you, does it?"

"Happy to have you," Russ said.

"I was hoping I might talk to you guys about something," John said, his full stomach turning a bit. He'd been on edge all day, anticipating this moment.

"Are you all right?" Adele asked.

"I'm fine. It's nothing bad. At least I hope you won't think it's bad."

"Come in," Russ said when they reached the cottage. "And take a load off. You want a drink?"

"I won't say no to that." John sat on the comfortable sectional sofa Adele had wanted so there'd be plenty of room for visitors.

His grandfather made him a gin and tonic with a twist of lime and handed it to him.

"Thanks, Pop." John took a couple of sips of his drink while he waited for them to get what they wanted and join him in the living room.

"What's going on?" Adele asked.

"I shared some news with the rest of the family recently, and I wanted to tell you guys about it."

"Okay..."

"I came out to them." John forced himself to say the words quickly, to push past this last frontier on his way to living an authentic life. "As gay."

"Oh," Russ said. "We knew that."

Adele nodded. "Yep."

Astonished, John stared at them. "Since when?"

"Always," Adele said. "It was just something we understood about you. No biggie."

"I, uh, well... Needless to say, you guys continue to surprise me."

"We like to be unpredictable," Adele said, grinning. "Please tell me you weren't worried about talking to us about this."

"I was a little worried."

"We love you," Russ said. "We want all the best for you."

"Tell him the rest, honey," Adele said to her husband.

"The rest of what?" John asked, his gaze darting between them.

Russ gestured for her to do the talking.

"Pop had a younger brother named Andy. He, too, was gay, but in those days, he had to keep it to himself. Pop knew, but no one else did.

The sneaking around and the secrecy took a terrible toll on him. One day... Russ came home to find him hanging from the rafters in their garage."

"Oh God... Pop..." John blinked back tears. "I didn't know."

"Because I never talked about it with anyone," Russ said. "Even your mom doesn't know how or why Andy died. I made up my mind that I'd tell you the truth if this subject ever came up. I told your grandmother I wouldn't let history repeat itself."

"I'm so, so sorry you lost him."

"Thank you. You understand why I wanted you to know, right?"

"I do, and it means a lot to me that you shared it with me."

"Thankfully, things have changed since then," Russ said. "For the better."

"Yes, they have. Thank you for accepting me for who and what I am. I love you both so much."

"We love you, too, honey," Adele said. "Always."

JACE LED Cindy and the boys into the house and let Burpy out to pee. While the boys got ready for bed, he packed their lunches for the next day and got bowls and spoons out for breakfast. If you asked him, he was slaying this fatherhood gig and was enjoying every second he got to spend with the boys.

His phone rang with a FaceTime call from Seamus. "Hey. How's the patient doing?"

"Better, thankfully," Seamus said, looking exhausted. "How are the lads?"

"They're doing great. I'll get them so you can say hello." He went to the hallway. "Boys, Seamus and Carolina want to say good night."

They came running and took the phone from Jace. Their animated chatter and questions about Carolina's injury amused him. Would she have a scar? Would it be gnarly (their new favorite word)? Did the cast itch like Billy Jones's cast had itched? Was the hospital cool?

After about ten minutes, they began to get silly, so Jace took the phone from them. "Go brush your teeth—and I'm gonna smell your breath." His mother used to say that to him and Jess.

"You've already figured out all their tricks," Seamus said.

"I remember that one from when I was their age."

"So, um, Jace…"

Why did Seamus seem pained?

"What's up?"

"The thing with Ms. Deavers from the state has caused a bit of grief."

"How so?" Jace asked, genuinely confused.

"She has a file on the boys, and when you told her who you are, she recalled that you're on parole. She's questioning our judgment leaving the boys with you."

Jace was so shocked that for a full minute, he couldn't think of a thing to say.

"Look, we both know this is total bullshit, but we need her to sign off on the final paperwork for the legal guardianship. We can't take any chances with her making this into a federal case. Carolina's son, Joe, will be there tomorrow, and he's going to take over with the boys until we get home."

Cindy came out of the bedroom, changed into pajama pants and a T-shirt. She stopped short in front of him. "What's wrong?" she whispered.

"I, um, whatever you want," Jace said to Seamus. "I'll talk to you tomorrow."

"I'm sorry, Jace. Please tell me you know this is nothing personal. After everything is signed and legal, we won't have any hesitation asking you to stay with the boys if we have to be away."

"Yeah, I get it. I've, ah, got to check on the boys."

He ended the call and stuffed the phone into his back pocket, emotion threatening to overtake him.

"Jace? What is it?"

"A lady was here earlier," he said haltingly. "From the state. She's making an issue of them leaving the boys with me. Carolina's son is coming tomorrow to take over."

"Oh no. Jace… That's ridiculous!"

"Seamus said it's BS, but they can't take any chances on the guardianship getting messed up so close to the finish line."

Cindy put her hands on his chest.

Jace took a step back. "I can't. Sorry. I just… I'm going to go check on them."

CHAPTER 29

*A*s she watched him walk away, Cindy wanted to scream from the sheer injustice of the situation and this coming only a couple of hours after he'd referred to today as one of the best days of his life. Anyone could see how much he loved those boys. He'd do anything for either of them. That someone could suggest that he might be a danger to them was preposterous.

She ached for him as she listened to him talking to the boys, getting them settled in bed and laughing at something one of them said.

This would break him.

Because she didn't know what else to do, she got in bed and waited for him to join her. When he never showed up, she went looking for him and found him outside, sitting in a chair at the fire pit, looking up at a sky littered with stars.

"It's chilly," he said. "You should go in."

"Don't shut me out, Jace."

"I told you. Everything I touch eventually turns to shit. You should take this as a sign and keep your distance before I wreck things for you somehow, too."

For a second, Cindy debated what to do, and then she lowered herself to his lap and put her arms around him, kissing his neck and face. "I'm not going anywhere."

His body remained rigid under her.

"You can't push me away that easily, Jace. I care too much about you to let you go through this or anything else alone."

"Don't you see? This is my life as an ex-con on parole for the next five years. People are going to judge you the same way they judge me."

"No one who matters is judging you. Look at the way my family welcomed you tonight, and they know your story. We all see a man who's worked hard to turn his life around, who got a big new job today, who has two little boys who adore him—"

"And are being raised by other people because I was in prison when their mother died."

"I see a man who is doing everything he can to make up for the mistakes he's made in the past by trying to be the best person he can be for the people he cares about. And I feel very, very lucky to be one of those people."

"This is how it goes for me," he said, sounding almost desperate to get through to her. "You don't need to be dragged down with me when you've worked so hard to overcome your own shit."

"I do need you, and I want you, and I probably even love you."

"Don't do that."

"Sorry, too late." She put her hand on his face and compelled him to look at her. "Don't let this one thing derail all the progress you've made in building a new life for yourself. Who cares what one random person you'll never see again thinks of you?"

"It's what she thinks of Seamus and Carolina that matters."

"And they're dealing with her concerns. I'm sorry that hurts you, but if it's what's best for the boys in this moment, then that's what needs to happen. Seamus called *you* when Carolina got hurt, which means he trusts you. That's what matters here—the people in your life trust you. I trust you. Seamus and Carolina trust you. The boys trust you. None of us care if you're going to be on parole for the next five years."

"You say that now, but what if people stop coming into the shop because you're with me?"

"Who's going to do that?"

He shrugged. "People in town who don't want to associate with the girlfriend of an ex-con."

"I don't know anyone who falls into the category. Certainly none of my customers do."

"That you know of."

"I understand that this has stirred up some issues for you, but if I'm not worried about what people think of me, then you shouldn't be either. If people don't come into the shop because my boyfriend was in jail, then I can't do anything about that."

"It could hurt your business."

"Every appointment I have is booked two to three weeks in advance. You're looking for problems where there are none."

"I don't want to hurt you."

She rested her head on his shoulder and released a sigh of relief when his arms encircled her. "Then don't. If you push me away, you'll hurt me."

"I make a mess of everything, Cindy. You should look out for yourself."

"You don't make a mess of everything. You've had some tough hits to be certain, but does this, right here, feel like a mess to you?"

He held her close. "No, it feels like heaven."

"I rest my case."

JACE SLEPT LIKE SHIT, tossing and turning and reliving the horribly awkward conversation with Seamus a thousand times. He'd been given the boot with his own kids. That hurt worse than anything had in a long time, especially since he'd been doing such a great job with the boys.

He got up early and used his phone to look up how to make pancakes. If this was going to be his last morning with the boys, he was going to make it count.

By the time he woke them half an hour later, he had a stack of steaming pancakes waiting for them. As usual, Kyle popped right up, but Jackson took some cajoling. He loved knowing what they were like in the morning and how to work around their dueling personalities.

"I made pancakes."

"You know how to cook?" Jackson asked, sounding skeptical.

"Not really, but I figured it out."

"Smells good," Kyle said.

"Hey, guys, so later… Joe is getting here today, and he's going to pick you up at school and stay with you tonight, okay?"

"How come?" Kyle asked, blond brows furrowed.

"I have to go back to work tonight, and he was coming home to see Carolina, so we decided he should take over here."

"We want you," Jackson said.

Had three words ever meant more to him than those did? "I want to be here, too, but this is better since I have to work at the bar until late tonight. You guys like Joe, right?"

Please let them say yes.

"Joe's cool," Kyle said. "He lets us drive the ferries."

"Then you'll be in good hands for another day or two until Seamus and Carolina get home—and then you'll have to be a big help to her, because she'll need that for a while."

"Will you come visit?" Jackson asked.

"I sure will. I promise."

He wanted to weep from the agony of having to step aside, but he'd do whatever was needed to ensure the boys' lives didn't get any more chaotic than they'd already been. No matter what it cost him.

They devoured the pancakes and teased Cindy about not being a morning person when she appeared, looking sleepy, a few minutes before they had to leave for school. "I stripped the bed and remade it with clean sheets."

"Thank you."

He packed lunches into backpacks and made sure homework folders were in there, too, before sending Burpy out to pee one more time while the boys brushed their teeth.

"You're great with them," Cindy said.

"Thanks. They make it easy."

"You told them what's happening?"

"Yeah."

"How'd that go?"

"Fine. They don't get it, but then again, neither do I. They said they wanted me to stay, which was nice." He shrugged, trying to pretend his heart wasn't broken. "I guess it's just as well, because I have to work tonight."

"I would've stayed with them again."

He kissed her cheek. "Thank you for all the help and support."

"I hardly did anything. You didn't need any help."

MARIE FORCE

"You helped a lot."

They piled into the truck for the ride to town, and as Jace pulled into the drop-off line at school, he was crushed. In just a couple of days, he'd fallen in love with fatherhood, and now he had to give it up. "You guys be good for Joe, okay?"

"We will," Kyle said.

"I'll be by to see you tomorrow."

"Okay," Jackson said.

"Hey, guys?"

"Yeah?" Kyle asked.

"I just want you to know... I love you. I really do, and I'm so proud of what great boys you are."

"Thanks," Jackson said.

"Yeah," Kyle said. "Thanks."

Then the door opened, and they were gone, rushing into school with their friends, pushing and shoving as they went.

Jace watched them for as long as he could before he had no choice but to move along to let others drop off.

"You did good," Cindy said.

If that was true, then why did he feel like absolute shit?

"JACE TEXTED to say he dropped the boys at school and left the truck at the ferry landing," Seamus told Carolina. "They remade the bed and washed the towels."

"I feel awful about this," Caro said. "The poor guy. He must be devastated."

"I'm sure he is, but he wouldn't want to be responsible for causing any problems for us or the boys."

"No, but it's not fair that he's being treated this way when he's done nothing but be there for all of us."

Seamus took a seat next to her hospital bed, as exhausted as he'd been in his entire life after the last couple of days. The trauma of seeing her seriously injured would stay with him for a long time. "He's a good bloke."

"You haven't said much about how you feel after telling the boys the truth about who he is."

Seamus shrugged. "What's there to say? He's their da, and they have a right to know that."

"No, Seamus. *You're* their da, and he's the man who fathered them. If you think those boys are suddenly going to forget everything you've done for them and been to them, think again. They know who's been there for them—and who hasn't."

"It wasn't because he didn't want to be."

"I know that, and they will, too, but you're the one who's been there every day and will continue to be. This doesn't have to change anything."

"It does, though," he said wearily. "They know he's their real father. I'm going to have to cede some ground to him."

"I remember when we first moved here after Joe's father died and how worried I was about him growing up without a father. Part of me wanted to keep him all to myself, but I quickly realized that the more people who loved my son, the luckier he was. The same is true for Jackson and Kyle. Jace is one more person who loves them, but you'll be their everyday father."

"You're right, love, as usual. The boys are lucky to have him in their lives, and we are, too. I was all set to hate his guts when he first came around."

"I remember," Carolina said with a huff of laughter.

"That didn't go so well, because he turned out to be a decent sort of guy."

"Who's had some tough breaks in life."

"Yeah." Seamus glanced at her. "I guess he's part of the family now."

"Which is what's best for the boys." Carolina gasped when the faces of her grandchildren, PJ and Vivienne, appeared in the doorway, followed by their dad. "Get in here and see me, you guys!"

Joe came in, carrying the children, who giggled at her reaction to seeing them. "Remember what I said about being gentle with Grammy. She hurt her leg."

Both children gave her sweet kisses and hugs while their daddy held them over her bed.

"I'm so glad to see you guys!"

"Grammy broke her leg," PJ said solemnly.

"Grammy is a clumsy girl," Carolina told him.

"How're you feeling, Mom?" Joe asked as he handed the kids to Seamus so he could hug and kiss his mother.

"Hanging in there."

"How's the pain?"

"Better than it was."

"Thank the Lord for that," Seamus said as he bounced little ones on his knees.

"When are they letting you out of here?"

"They said tomorrow."

"And what's the plan for getting home?"

"We're going to have the chopper take her back to the island, and the ambulance will take her home," Seamus said. "It's all arranged. Just waiting for the docs to give us the green light."

"I'm so sorry to drag you guys home in the middle of your semester," Carolina said to Joe.

"It's no problem. I got one of the grad students to cover my painting class, and Janey will have some quiet time to study. We're where we need to be."

DARA WATKINS EYED the pregnancy test with trepidation. She was almost certain it would be positive, as the familiar signs of pregnancy were hard to ignore—sore breasts, a ravenous appetite even when she was nauseated and an overall feeling of things changing the way they had when she was expecting Lewis.

Her eyes filled with tears, which was another thing that'd been happening more often lately—emotions run amok and thoughts such as what right did she have to be expecting another child when Lewis was dead?

She shook her head and reached for the wand, determined to find out for certain one way or the other.

Like with Lewis, the second the pee hit the stick, it seemed to pop positive.

She laughed as she cried, torn between competing emotions—elation and grief and the staggering realization that this baby would never know his or her big brother. After wiping her tears, she disposed of the box and paperwork in the brown paper bag from the pharmacy but tucked the wand itself into her medicine cabinet.

Emerging from the bathroom into the bedroom, she found Oliver sitting on the bed, looking as anxious as she felt.

Dara nodded as she smiled, and he launched off the bed to wrap his arms around her.

"*Yes,*" he whispered, twirling her around.

She didn't have the heart to tell him that might not be a good idea with her stomach in the usual morning uproar.

"How do you feel, babe?"

"Conflicted, but mostly happy. And scared. And excited. And nauseated."

"Anything else?"

"I think that's about it."

Oliver put her down, buried his face in her hair and held her tightly. "I'm so excited, Dar. I want you to be, too."

"I am, even if part of me feels I have no right to this."

"You have every right to this," Oliver said fiercely. "What happened to Lewis was a freak accident. Neither of us did anything wrong."

They'd been trying to convince themselves of that since the day their three-year-old son let himself out of their house and was hit by a car, while she was working and Oliver was napping.

"We were good parents, and we will be again," Oliver said.

"I just worry that I'll never be able to relax."

"We'll find a groove. I know we will."

"What's going on up there?" Monique called from downstairs.

"Let's go share the happy news," Oliver said.

Dara let him lead her to the spiral staircase that went down to the lighthouse's living room and kitchen. Coming to Gansett Island to spend a year as the lighthouse keepers had been the best thing they'd done for themselves since they lost Lewis. Somehow, someway, they'd managed to heal there.

"Y'all are looking mysterious," Monique said from her post on the sofa. "What's up?"

"Well, it seems we're pregnant," Dara said.

Monique jumped up so fast, she nearly spilled the mug of coffee she'd been sipping from. She put down the mug and rushed over to hug them both. "That's the best news I've ever heard."

"You really think so?" Dara asked.

Her big sister pulled back to look at her. "Hell yes, I really think so. Why wouldn't I?"

"I just wonder if people will question whether we should be trusted with another child."

"*What?* No one will do that, Dar. Not one single person who knew you guys as parents has ever thought that. You were *wonderful* parents, and you will be again."

Dara blinked back tears and hugged her sister as it all became real to her. They were going to have another baby and a second chance at parenthood. A year ago, that would've seemed preposterous to her. But now… She felt stronger than she had since that awful day, and against all odds, their marriage had also recovered from the terrible trauma.

They would never again be who they'd been before they lost Lewis, but she was incredibly thankful for the second chance they'd been given.

CHAPTER 30

Over the next few days, Jace went through the motions. He attended daily meetings, went to the gym, worked at the bar and visited the boys every afternoon after school. For them, nothing had really changed, but for him, everything had. The incident with the woman from the state had hurt him deeply, and there was no denying that it had been a setback for him, right when things had been going better than ever.

Even things with Cindy had changed, despite her best efforts. He just couldn't seem to get past the emotional storm raging inside him.

"Are you going to tell us what's going on?" Mallory asked over coffee three days after the morning he'd dropped the boys at school for the last time.

Seamus and Carolina had gotten home two days ago and had settled in with the boys with Joe and his kids spending a few more days with them. Things were back to normal for everyone but Jace.

It took Jace a second to realize Mallory was talking to him. "Huh?"

"What's with you the last few days? You're here, but you're a thousand miles away. You sit in the meetings and brood, but never say a word. What's going on, Jace? And don't say it's nothing."

"I don't want to talk about it."

"Obviously, but what you're doing isn't working. You're getting more remote by the day. You were so excited about your new job, things with Cindy and being with your boys. What happened?"

"It's easier just to tell her," Quinn said. "Otherwise, she's like a dog with a bone, beating you over the head with it until you spill your guts."

"You be quiet," Mallory replied. "You're the one who asked me what's wrong with Jace."

"You're not yourself," Mason said bluntly. "If something's wrong, you know by now that stewing over it only leads to trouble, and we've all had enough trouble."

They were right, and Jace knew it, but it was upsetting to talk about what'd happened and how he felt about it. But since Quinn was right about Mallory not letting it go, he decided to fill them in. "While I was taking care of the boys, a woman from the state department of children and family services showed up at the house as part of finalizing the legal guardianship for Seamus and Carolina."

"Okay…" Mallory said.

"Seamus forgot about the meeting in all the craziness with Carolina breaking her leg. The woman asked who I was, and I told her. She had the lowdown on me and questioned their judgment, leaving the boys with a parolee, even if he's their biological father."

"Stop it," Mallory said, her expression conveying shock. "She did not say that."

"Yes, she did. She told Seamus he needed to make other arrangements, or she'd have to notify her bosses about the situation. That's when Joe was called home to take over with them."

"Oh my God, Jace." Mallory looked as stricken as he felt, even days later. "I'm so sorry that happened."

"It's true, though, right? It doesn't look good for them that they left the boys with a convicted felon on parole."

"They left the boys with someone who loves them and wants nothing but the best for them," Mason said in his typical blunt way.

"Who also happens to be an ex-con on parole for the next five years." Bitterness poured out of him like acid, threatening to devour all the progress he'd made since coming to Gansett. "From her perspective, I'm the last person in the world who should be taking care of them. But I was really enjoying the time with them."

"I'm sorry." Mallory reached across the table to put her hand on top of his. "That totally sucks, but you can't let it undo all the good stuff."

"Cindy said the same thing, but I've just been in this spiral since Seamus called to tell me I was being fired as their caregiver—in the nicest possible way, of course. He felt terrible about it."

"It's an unfortunate development no matter how you look at it," Quinn said, "but it happened, you punted and now you move on with the boys still in your life and all the other good things still there, too. Like a new job you're excited about and a girlfriend who makes you happy. The only one who can let a setback ruin everything is you."

"I hate to say it, but he's right," Mallory said with a saucy grin for her husband. "This bad thing happened, but you must move on from it. It doesn't change anything that truly matters about your new life."

"It brought home all the ways I've fucked up and how that's going to haunt me for the rest of my life."

"No, it won't," Quinn said emphatically. "You're doing everything right. You can't let someone else's judgment—in a situation where the woman was only doing the job she's paid to do—derail you. You just can't let that happen. Who the fuck cares what she thinks?"

Jace grunted out a laugh at Quinn's unusual outburst.

"Let it go, Jace," Mallory added in a gentler tone. "It happened. It sucked. It's over, and you're still fine. You have a great new job and a wonderful new relationship with Cindy and your boys are back in your life. It's all good, so just let it go."

"I'm trying."

"Try harder," Mason said.

"You're a tough crowd," Jace said, feeling immeasurably better after airing it out with them. He should've known they would help. They always did.

"We're telling you the truth, and you know it," Mallory said.

"I do know it, and I appreciate it. I think more than anything, it was embarrassing to have my past possibly screwing things up for Seamus and Carolina, especially after they'd entrusted me with the boys."

"Understood," Mallory said. "But it didn't screw up anything. It's not like they didn't know you'd been in prison before this happened."

"Yeah, I guess."

"They knew that, and they *still* asked you to be the one to care for the boys during their emergency," Quinn said. "From what you said, they didn't hesitate to ask you."

"They didn't, and he said they'd ask me again if they ever need coverage."

"That ought to be what matters," Quinn said.

Jace nodded. Quinn was right. They all were, and he needed to let it go. "Thank you for listening and for the tough love. I needed it."

"We're here for that any time." Mallory smiled as if she was proud of herself for busting him out of his funk. "We did good work here, gentlemen."

"She's going to gloat about this all day," Quinn said. "In case you were wondering."

Jace laughed at the face Quinn made as he said that.

Mallory leaned into her husband. "You love me."

He put his arm around her. "Someone's gotta."

JOHN ASKED his brother Jeff to drop him off in town. "You need a ride home?" Jeff asked when he pulled over by the ferry landing.

"Nah, I'll get a ride."

"You look good. Where are you heading?"

"To meet a friend for dinner."

"A friend or a *friend*?"

"The former. For now, anyway."

"But you like him."

"Yeah, I do." John looked over at Jeff. "Are you seeing Kelsey?"

"Yep."

"I'm glad for you. She seems like a nice girl."

"She's one in a million, and I'd like to think I'm smart enough not to let her get away."

"I hope it works out for you guys."

"Likewise, with you and your friend. I'm glad you're sticking around. We just gotta get Josh here."

"He's got something going with a woman in Virginia. I don't think he's coming."

"We'll see," Jeff said. "Anyway, if you end up needing a ride, call me."

"Will do. Thanks for the lift."

John got out of the car and waved to his brother as he drove away. He was glad to see Jeff doing so well and settling into a healthy relationship. Jeff's suicide attempt had scared the hell out of them, and to see him thriving was such a relief. Like so many things in their lives, that, too, was thanks to the involvement of their amazing grandparents.

The story Russ and Adele had told him about Russ's brother had weighed heavily on John's heart and mind the last few days. He was so incredibly thankful for the unwavering support of his family and knew how lucky that made him.

He stepped into Stephanie's Bistro, where he was due to meet Niall, and looked around for him.

Already seated at a table, Niall waved him over.

John's heart beat a slow tempo as he crossed the crowded dining room and took a seat across from Niall. For once, he didn't care who saw them together or who might make something of it. All the people in his life who mattered had given him their unconditional love and support, freeing him to fully enjoy this evening with a new friend who might turn out to be more than that.

"How's it going?" Niall asked in the sexy Irish accent that had first caught John's attention at the Beachcomber weeks ago.

"It's going better than it ever has, actually."

"Is that right. How so?"

"Well, everyone who's anyone in my life knows the truth. I've landed a fabulous new job that'll have me working my ass off in the summer with a relaxed schedule the rest of the year. I've got ninety-five percent of my family living nearby, and I'm making some fun new friends."

"Wow, you're having a good week."

"Best week ever."

"Where's the new job?"

"Right here on Gansett." Was it his imagination, or did Niall perk up when he said that? "Managing security for the Wayfarer."

"Oh, that's cool. I heard they need that after a wild season."

"That's what I was told. But like I said to Mr. McCarthy, drunk and disorderly people aren't usually pointing guns, so it'll be a relief from what I'm used to on the job."

"Did you see a lot of guns pointed at you when you were a cop?"

"A lot more than I ever expected when I started out. The domestic situations were particularly hairy that way."

"I give you so much credit for doing that work. I wouldn't have the stomach for it."

"Your talents would be wasted in any other job but the one you have."

"Thank you. It's still fun, so that's something. I'd love to see it go beyond playing in bars on Gansett and recording at Evan's studio, but so far, that hasn't happened."

"It hasn't happened *yet*. Doesn't mean it won't."

"True."

The waiter came by to take John's drink order and to run down the specials. He asked for Maker's Mark bourbon on the rocks.

"Bourbon, huh?" Niall asked, smiling.

"You can't live in Tennessee for long and not develop a taste for such things."

"I'll take your word for that. I'm more of a Guinness kind of guy myself."

"So I've noticed."

When the waiter returned with John's drink, Niall held up his glass. "Here's to new friends."

John touched his glass to Niall's. "To new friends."

As CINDY SWEPT up after her last customer of the day, she felt the telltale signs of a headache forming and took the medication she always had with her for when that happened. Hopefully, it would kick in fast and nip the headache in the bud. Sometimes it worked, other times it didn't. Her stress level had been high the last few days as she'd navigated around a broody, quiet, withdrawn Jace.

Following his shift at the bar last night, he'd fallen asleep on the sofa and spent the night there.

After only a few nights sleeping together, she'd missed having his body wrapped around hers and had slept fitfully as she wondered if he was going to bounce back from the crushing disappointment. She totally felt for him in this situation and understood how hurtful it had been for him to be kicked off the gig with the boys because of his past. It was easy to see how he must be wondering what more he had to do to get past all that.

But she was also sad for herself. The few days before the incident had been among the best of her life, and since then, she'd been left feeling adrift inside her own relationship. He'd promised not to cut her out of what he was thinking and feeling, but he'd done it anyway, and she had no idea how to bridge the chasm that had formed between them.

The ache of their situation had hung over her all day as she'd made small talk with clients and gone through the motions at work, and it was probably why she had a headache forming. Stress had always been one of the worst triggers for her.

As she leaned on the broom, she closed her eyes, took a deep breath and released it slowly, determined to reset her heart and mind so she might stave off the headache and get herself back on track, whether that was with Jace or without him.

When she opened her eyes, movement outside the glass doors to the salon caught her attention. A huge bouquet of flowers appeared in the window.

Intrigued, Cindy went to unlock the door.

The flowers were lifted toward her.

"Who goes there?" she asked, amused.

Jace put the flowers aside to reveal his face. "'Tis I, asking the fair maiden for a chance to apologize for being a moody jerk for days."

Smiling and filled with relief at the gesture, she said, "Come in." After Jace stepped into the salon, she closed and locked the door again.

He held out the bunch of colorful blooms. "Peace offering?"

She took them from him and breathed in the fragrant scents of lilies and roses. "They're gorgeous. Thank you."

"I'm sorry about the last couple of days."

"You seem better. Are you?"

"I guess so. Something shitty happened. There's nothing I can do about it, so there's no point in letting it infect the rest of my life, or so I've been told by people wiser than me."

"I was worried about you."

"I'm sorry for that, too."

"And I was worried about us. It's all so... new. I wasn't sure how to handle distant, withdrawn Jace or whether I was welcome to try."

He stepped closer to her, gazing down at her with the warmth and affection she'd missed so much. "You're welcome in every corner of my life."

"That's good to know."

Caressing her face, he said, "I'm sorry if I made you wonder about that."

"I understand that what happened was a kick in the teeth for you."

"It was just a reminder that you can't escape the past entirely, no matter how hard you try."

"No, you can't, but you also have to remember that the past made you who you are today, and I like who you are today."

"That makes me feel incredibly lucky." He took the flowers from her, set them on the reception desk and then put his arms around her. "I'm sorry for checking out on you. That's the last thing I wanted to do."

"I'd say it was okay, but it was stressful, and stress isn't good for me."

"Do you have a headache?" he asked, brow furrowed with concern.

"The start of one."

"Are you done here? Let's go home, and I'll pamper you."

"You're not working tonight?"

"Nope. I'm down to just Saturday nights at the Beachcomber now that I have a day job."

"How's that going? You haven't said much about that, or anything, for that matter."

"It's been good. I like working with Mac and his cousins. Did you know your brother is working for him, too?"

"Yes, that's what he's doing instead of going to Tampa."

"Yep, and he's very good at construction."

"He did that for a lot of years in high school and college. I never imagined he'd go back to it after getting his degree. He must really be into Kelsey."

"From what he says about her, it seems like he is."

Relieved to be back on a somewhat normal footing with Jace, Cindy gathered her things, picked up the flowers and followed Jace out the door, turning to lock up.

He put his arm around her for the walk home. "We need a car."

"Do we?"

"Shane has been picking me up the last few days, but I need to get my own wheels. I saw a truck for sale out on the east side, but I haven't had a chance to go look at it."

"We can do that on Sunday if you want."

"Sure."

"You don't want to?"

"I feel like I shouldn't make any big decisions."

"Why's that?"

"I don't know. It's just this feeling that it would be a mistake to get too comfortable in my new life here."

Cindy's heart sank when he said that. How could she help him to see that he was safe to get comfortable? She wanted him to be more comfortable with her than he'd ever been with anyone, but how could she help get him to that point?

She was no closer to an answer when they got home. Under the sink, she found a vase Kevin had left when he moved out, added water and arranged the flowers, placing them on the kitchen table. She was staring at them, still thinking about what he'd said, when he came into the kitchen and put his arms around her from behind, resting his chin on her shoulder.

"What're you thinking about?" he asked.

"What you said about not being comfortable here."

"I'm preconditioned to expect everything to go to shit. The thing with the boys was a reminder not to get complacent."

Cindy turned so she could see him. "What do you think is going to happen?"

He shrugged. "I don't know, but something always happens."

"That was before, when you were strung out on drugs and doing whatever it took to get more of them. That's not who you are anymore, so why do you still assume things won't work out?"

"Because it always goes to shit."

"Not anymore it doesn't. A well-respected business owner gave you a job, knowing your background. You're a hardworking guy who's been clean for years. You work hard on your sobriety every day. You show up to work on time, ready to give it your all. You care about your sons and your friends. You need to learn how to appreciate the good things."

"The bad has always outweighed the good for me."

255

"What if that isn't the case anymore? I mean, this, with us… It's pretty good, right?"

"It's way better than pretty good."

"I'm not going anywhere. I'm not going to suddenly wake up and decide I don't want this or you anymore."

The vulnerability she saw in his eyes touched her heart. "How do you know that?"

"I love you, Jace. Those aren't just words to me."

He closed his eyes and leaned his forehead against hers. "Those are the best words I've ever heard, and I love you, too."

"You're going to have to have some faith in me, in yourself, in this new life you're building."

"It might take me some time to stop anticipating doomsday."

"I've got plenty of time. Do you?"

"Yeah, I do."

"I want to spend as much of my time as I can with you. Is that what you want, too?"

"Absolutely."

"Then we shouldn't have any problem making this work, but you have to talk to me when you're feeling unsettled or worried. I can't help if you don't share it with me."

"I'm not used to having someone who wants to share the load."

"Well, now you do, and the only way this works is if you let me in, Jace. All the way in. Can you do that?"

He drew back to look down at her, and she was relieved to see the tension that had gripped him for days was gone. "I can try like hell."

EPILOGUE

Over the next few weeks, Jace and Cindy cheered on the boys at their fall baseball games, attended a recorder recital at school that had made their ears bleed and had dinner with her family members to celebrate new jobs for Jace, Jeff and John, who'd invited Niall Fitzgerald to join them.

The two had been spending lots of time together and seemed content.

Everywhere he looked, Jace saw happiness. It infected every moment of his life with the kind of peace and tranquility that had evaded him before now. And nowhere was that truer than in his relationship with Cindy.

She was the sun around which his life revolved.

Like she had from the moment they first met, she brightened every day with her sweetness, her positivity, her laughter and her light. She cut his hair. He took her to the gym. They laughed and loved and made plans.

He loved his new job, the great people he worked with and the salary that had enabled him to buy the truck he'd seen for sale on the island's east side.

He adored his groups of friends from AA, the gym and the bar, where he tended to a big crowd on Saturday nights.

He loved every second he got to spend with his boys. Last night, they'd cooked dinner for the O'Gradys, wanting to help while Carolina recovered from her injury. As he'd hoped, Seamus and Carolina were beginning to feel like close friends. The previous weekend, Jace had helped Seamus clean up the yard in anticipation of Shannon's upcoming wedding.

All of that was wonderful.

But Cindy… She was like the frosting on top of the best cake he'd ever tasted.

As they walked home from dinner with Owen's family at the Sand & Surf, Jace put his arm around her, wanting her as close to him as he could get her after missing her during the long hours at work.

"My ears are ringing from kids screaming," Cindy said, laughing. "I don't know how they manage three little ones and make it look so easy."

"They have a good groove with them, and I think they laugh a lot."

"I suppose you'd have to. Otherwise, you'd be crying all the time."

"How many ankle biters do you want to have?" he asked in a casual tone.

"Uh… Are you seriously asking me that?"

"I think I am. I'd love to have another chance at fatherhood and do it right this time, from the beginning."

"Oh, um, well… I haven't really thought about that."

"Like, *ever?*"

"It hasn't come up in past relationships, usually because I cut and run before we ever came close to that."

"Do I need to be worried about you cutting and running on me?"

"No," she said, laughing. "You know you don't."

"So then maybe we could talk about the possibility of kids, since you've convinced me to have faith in you and us and promised it's not going to go to shit."

"Have I convinced you?"

"I'm getting there, thus my question about kids. The more time I spend with Jackson and Kyle, the more I want a do-over, but only if that's what you want, too."

"If I said I don't want kids, that would be okay?"

"I'd be sad to not have the chance for more kids, but I'd be sadder if I didn't have you."

Cindy went up the stairs and used her key in their front door.

Jace followed her in, feeling more at home in this tiny house than he'd ever been anywhere else, and that, too, was thanks to her.

She turned to him, her expression unreadable. "That was a really good answer."

"What was?"

"That you'd be sadder without me."

He put his arms around her and breathed in the fragrance that had been imprinted upon his soul. "I couldn't live without you."

"Same. How'd that happen, anyway?"

"I'm not sure, but I'll be thankful that it did for the rest of my life."

"Can I tell you something I've never told anyone?"

He pulled back and tucked a strand of her hair behind her ear. "I wish you would."

"When I was nine, I made a vow to myself that I'd never have kids because I wouldn't want them to ever feel the way I did every day growing up with my father. I fully intended to honor that vow until I saw you with your boys. That changed the game for me. You're a wonderful father. You'd be nothing like my father was, and our kids would be so lucky to have you in their lives to guide them and teach them. So, yes, Jace. If you'd like to have more children, I'm down with that."

Nothing anyone had ever said meant more to him. "I don't know what I ever did to deserve you and the way you love me, but it's the greatest gift in a life suddenly full of amazing gifts."

"You're the best thing to ever happen to me, too. I hope you know that."

He'd felt guilty to realize that as much as he'd loved Lisa, what he had with Cindy was on a whole other level. He was overwhelmed every day with feelings he'd never experienced so intensely before, and now was no exception. "That means everything to me, sweetheart. I promise I'll never let you down."

For once, he felt comfortable making a promise like that. He knew for certain he would keep it or die trying.

"How soon can we start making some babies?" he asked.

Cindy laughed as she drew back from him and looked up at him with her heart in her eyes. "What're you doing right now?"

He bent at the knees to put her over his shoulder, chuckling at her shriek of surprised laughter as he carried her to bed.

. . .

THANK you so much for reading *Resilience After Dark*, the TWENTY-FIFTH Gansett Island book! How'd that happen?!?! As always, it's such a joy to spend time on the island with some of my favorite people. I hope you enjoyed your visit on the island and Jace and Cindy's emotionally charged story. I absolutely loved writing Jace as he worked to put his life back together and as he found the perfect soul mate in Cindy, who's known her own struggles.

People are asking me if there'll be more from Gansett, and the answer is YES. Why quit now when we're still having so much fun? If you're not already a member of the Gansett Island Reader Group, join here *www.facebook.com/groups/McCarthySeries* for updates and insight on upcoming books. Join the Resilience After Dark Reader Group *www.facebook.com/groups/resilienceafterdark/* to discuss Jace and Cindy's story with spoilers allowed.

A special thank-you to my author friend Carly Phillips for sharing her experiences living with migraines. I'm sorry she is so well versed in the matter. Thanks as always to my amazing team for all their great help behind the scenes: Julie Cupp, Lisa Cafferty, Jean Mello, Nikki Haley, Ashley Lopez and Gansett Island cover designer Diane Lugar. A huge thanks to my beta readers Anne Woodall, Kara Conrad and Tracey Suppo, as well as my editors, Linda Ingmanson and Joyce Lamb. A special shout-out to Gwen Neff, who's helping me keep the details straight in my various series, which becomes harder all the time. I'm very appreciative of her help.

Thanks to the Gansett Island beta readers: Judy, Amy, Katy, Mona, Kelly, Jaime, Jennifer, Juliane, Doreen, Andi, Michelle and Jennifer.

And finally, to all the readers who've been with me on the Gansett Island journey since 2011 and over twenty-five books, thank you SO MUCH. The McCarthy family and Gansett Island changed my life forever, and I couldn't be more thankful to everyone who made that happen. Much more to come!

xoxo

Marie

ALSO BY MARIE FORCE

Contemporary Romances Available from Marie Force

The Gansett Island Series

Book 1: Maid for Love (*Mac & Maddie*)

Book 2: Fool for Love (*Joe & Janey*)

Book 3: Ready for Love (*Luke & Sydney*)

Book 4: Falling for Love (*Grant & Stephanie*)

Book 5: Hoping for Love (*Evan & Grace*)

Book 6: Season for Love (*Owen & Laura*)

Book 7: Longing for Love (*Blaine & Tiffany*)

Book 8: Waiting for Love (*Adam & Abby*)

Book 9: Time for Love (*David & Daisy*)

Book 10: Meant for Love (*Jenny & Alex*)

Book 10.5: Chance for Love, A Gansett Island Novella (*Jared & Lizzie*)

Book 11: Gansett After Dark (*Owen & Laura*)

Book 12: Kisses After Dark (*Shane & Katie*)

Book 13: Love After Dark (*Paul & Hope*)

Book 14: Celebration After Dark (*Big Mac & Linda*)

Book 15: Desire After Dark (*Slim & Erin*)

Book 16: Light After Dark (*Mallory & Quinn*)

Book 17: Victoria & Shannon (Episode 1)

Book 18: Kevin & Chelsea (Episode 2)

A Gansett Island Christmas Novella

Book 19: Mine After Dark (*Riley & Nikki*)

Book 20: Yours After Dark (*Finn & Chloe*)

Book 21: Trouble After Dark (*Deacon & Julia*)

Book 22: Rescue After Dark (*Mason & Jordan*)

Book 23: Blackout After Dark (*Full Cast*)

Book 24: Temptation After Dark (*Gigi & Cooper*)

Book 25: Resilience After Dark (*Jace & Cindy*)

Book 26: Hurricane After Dark (*Full Cast, coming 2023*)

The Miami Nights Series

Book 1: How Much I Feel (*Carmen & Jason*)

Book 2: How Much I Care (*Maria & Austin*)

Book 3: How Much I Love (*Dee's story*)

Nochebuena, A Miami Nights Novella

Book 4: How Much I Want (*Nico & Sofia*)

Book 5: How Much I Need (*Milo and Gianna*)

The Wild Widows Series—a Fatal Series Spin-Off

Book 1: Someone Like You

Book 2: Someone to Hold

The Green Mountain Series

Book 1: All You Need Is Love (*Will & Cameron*)

Book 2: I Want to Hold Your Hand (*Nolan & Hannah*)

Book 3: I Saw Her Standing There (*Colton & Lucy*)

Book 4: And I Love Her (*Hunter & Megan*)

Novella: You'll Be Mine (*Will & Cam's Wedding*)

Book 5: It's Only Love (*Gavin & Ella*)

Book 6: Ain't She Sweet (*Tyler & Charlotte*)

The Butler, Vermont Series

(Continuation of Green Mountain)

Book 1: Every Little Thing (*Grayson & Emma*)

Book 2: Can't Buy Me Love (*Mary & Patrick*)

Book 3: Here Comes the Sun (*Wade & Mia*)

Book 4: Till There Was You (*Lucas & Dani*)

Book 5: All My Loving (*Landon & Amanda*)

Book 6: Let It Be (*Lincoln & Molly*)

Book 7: Come Together (*Noah & Brianna*)

Book 8: Here, There & Everywhere (*Izzy & Cabot*)

Book 9: The Long and Winding Road (*Max & Lexi*)

The Quantum Series

Book 1: Virtuous (*Flynn & Natalie*)

Book 2: Valorous (*Flynn & Natalie*)

Book 3: Victorious (*Flynn & Natalie*)

Book 4: Rapturous (*Addie & Hayden*)

Book 5: Ravenous (*Jasper & Ellie*)

Book 6: Delirious (*Kristian & Aileen*)

Book 7: Outrageous (*Emmett & Leah*)

Book 8: Famous (*Marlowe & Sebastian*)

The Treading Water Series

Book 1: Treading Water

Book 2: Marking Time

Book 3: Starting Over

Book 4: Coming Home

Book 5: Finding Forever

Single Titles

Five Years Gone

One Year Home

Sex Machine

Sex God

Georgia on My Mind

True North

The Fall

The Wreck

Love at First Flight

Everyone Loves a Hero

Line of Scrimmage

Romantic Suspense Novels Available from Marie Force

The Fatal Series

One Night With You, *A Fatal Series Prequel Novella*

Book 1: Fatal Affair

Book 2: Fatal Justice

Book 3: Fatal Consequences

Book 3.5: Fatal Destiny, *the Wedding Novella*

Book 4: Fatal Flaw

Book 5: Fatal Deception

Book 6: Fatal Mistake

Book 7: Fatal Jeopardy

Book 8: Fatal Scandal

Book 9: Fatal Frenzy

Book 10: Fatal Identity

Book 11: Fatal Threat

Book 12: Fatal Chaos

Book 13: Fatal Invasion

Book 14: Fatal Reckoning

Book 15: Fatal Accusation

Book 16: Fatal Fraud

Sam and Nick's Story Continues....

Book 1: State of Affairs

Book 2: State of Grace

Book 3: State of the Union

Historical Romance Available from Marie Force

The Gilded Series

Book 1: Duchess by Deception

Book 2: Deceived by Desire

ABOUT THE AUTHOR

Marie Force is the *New York Times* bestselling author of contemporary romance, romantic suspense and erotic romance. Her series include Fatal, First Family, Gansett Island, Butler Vermont, Quantum, Treading Water, Miami Nights and Wild Widows.

Her books have sold more than 10 million copies worldwide, have been translated into more than a dozen languages and have appeared on the *New York Times* bestseller more than 30 times. She is also a *USA Today* and #1 *Wall Street Journal* bestseller, as well as a Spiegel bestseller in Germany.

Her goals in life are simple—to finish raising two happy, healthy, productive young adults, to keep writing books for as long as she possibly can and to never be on a flight that makes the news.

Join Marie's mailing list on her website at *marieforce.com* for news about new books and upcoming appearances in your area. Follow her on Facebook at *www.Facebook.com/MarieForceAuthor*, Instagram at *www.instagram.com/marieforceauthor/* and TikTok at *https://www.tiktok.-com/@marieforceauthor?*. Contact Marie at *marie@marieforce.com*.

CPSIA information can be obtained
at www.ICGtesting.com
Printed in the USA
LVHW081113290622
722311LV00003B/36